RICHIE

LAD

CHRIS SPECK

Copyright © 2022 Chris Speck
Flat City Press 2022
All rights reserved.
ISBN-13: 978-1-8381273-9-8

FOREWARD

At the turn of the eighteenth century, there were growing concerns around the nation about criminality and public order. Towns and cities were seen as dens of disorderly behaviour, drunkenness, prostitution, and scandalous theatre, whereas in the country, robbers and highwaymen stalked the roads and terrorised rural communities. Some believed the only way to reverse this backslide was to return to godly standards of living. One such group of religiously inspired East Riding merchants, mariners, and tradesmen banded together to combat the 'abounding sin & wickedness of the present Age'. The Society of the Reformation of Manners in Hull was formed in 1698, and their main tactic was to initiate prosecutions of their neighbours by informing magistrates of their 'moral' crimes. People caught swearing were summarily fined, and habitual drunks were put in the stocks to sober up. One poor sod was even prosecuted for 'travelling with fish' on a Sunday. Needless to say, they weren't hugely popular. To the hundreds of ordinary folk subjected to their campaign, the reformers were busy-bodies, meddlers, and snitches. But to Church authorities, these societies represented something much more dangerous. Many of the reformers were dissenters from the Established Church – Congregationalists and Presbyterians – and their moral campaigns challenged Anglican control over the spiritual health of the nation. This was a threat to both the religious and political order. Some churchmen even believed that this moral crusade might rekindle the divisions that ultimately led to the English Civil War. So, they starved the reformers of support and – at least in Hull – the campaign eventually dwindled away to nothing.

These contemporary attitudes to criminality sharply contrast with those of nineteenth-century authors who reimagined offenders of the previous century as romantic rogues; it was the clergy who they thought were dissolute and ungodly. The reputation of the eighteenth-century Church was sufficiently tarnished by Victorian mudslingers that it was commonly believed that Dick Turpin served as a footman to

Archbishop Lancelot Blackburne of York. Well, what more could you expect of a prelate who was supposedly a pirate in his youth? Many historians today are guilty of repeating this tall tale despite evidence of his legitimate ministry in the Caribbean. That's not to say that clergymen of the eighteenth century were beyond reproach. The uncle of novelist Laurence Sterne was an Archdeacon and Justice of the Peace in Holderness (and on another day might have participated in Turpin's real-life arrest). He had a known propensity for violence, and in 1734 was charged for beating up a barber in York during the heated general election of that year. But sometimes there's little desire to shake off a good yarn. In 1924, Archbishop Cosmo Lang responded to a lecture disputing Turpin's time at Bishopthorpe by saying, 'I shall continue to tell the story of his residence there for what it is worth!'

Dr Daniel Reed
Coventry
June 2022

CHAPTER ONE

Dalton Estate. East Riding of Yorkshire. April 1722

The moon is out, and the silver of her light makes dark shadows through the branches of the forest. Richie is somewhere in the northern part of the Dalton Estate woods, and he should not be there. If he's caught, he'll certainly be in trouble, but it's unlikely he will hang.

He's poaching.

The tall lad squats down in the bushes and takes off his floppy hat to rub his face. Nana promised him it would rain and made him take it, now, in the heat of the forest, he wishes he hadn't. Tucked into his belt is the battered flintlock pistol that once belonged to a man he knew well, someone he called his father. Richie should not have brought it, it's of no use, for he has neither powder nor bullets and the action is rusty above a fouled barrel from misuse and age. Richie carries it because he fancies it gives him a swagger and a look of someone who may be dangerous and here, in the quiet of the Dalton Estate woods, a few miles from North Burton and his home, Richie can pretend that he may be in the great forests of New England with native Indians around each dark corner. As he moves among the bushes and undergrowth, he flits from fantasy to reality. Richie set traps a week or so back that may have snagged a rabbit, or if he is very lucky, a deer, because poor folk like Richie don't hunt with guns, that's for the rich and the good of the world, like Miss Charlotte and her ageing father Mr Pennyman up at the estate.

He tracks back through the forest after he has checked his empty traps but keeps out of the open spaces. The moonlight is strong and makes hunting easy, so, Richie might not be the only one in the great forest at this time of night. Lord Grantham's gamekeeper himself could be out for a wander and it would be awkward indeed if he were to catch Richie, a

North Burton lad, at work poaching. He stops to sit down against a great oak, brings his knees up to his chest with his back flat on the trunk so he's covered in darkness. You can use your eyes as much as you like in the forest, but sometimes, it's as good to use your ears, a rustle says a lot. Richie rubs the back of his hand across his sweaty forehead and closes his eyes. His shirt is open and shows the bird scar just above his nipple. When he was a very little lad, Richie tripped and nearly fell into the fire at the cottage in North Burton. He burned his chest on one of the fleur-de-lis style edges of the grate, and Nana caught him before he could go headfirst into the flames. The scar looks like a swallow and the old woman says when he sees it, he should remember her and what she did for him that night, and what she always does. Nana doesn't do a great deal of anything to be fair, except talk.

The rustle of the forest in the light breeze fades in and out of his senses, there's the noise of an owl far away in the distance and the creak of the big oak branches above, scratching somewhere nearby, nothing untoward. Richie takes a deep breath in through his nostrils and there's the scent of fox poo, sweet wild garlic that is going a little sour, the richness of the soil below his worn-out boots. Richie knows the sounds here. He opens his eyes as something comes on the wind from behind him, a voice, a whisper. His hand goes to the gun, not that there is any point, and he slinks off into the dark undergrowth beside the oak.

People approach. Two of them.

Richie watches through leaves as they pick their way along the forest path, they're too noisy to be poachers and they arrive at the great oak, that but a minute before, Richie had sat with his back against. One of them is fat with a big stomach and bum, his trousers are pulled up over his belly button and he wears braces atop his white shirt, on his feet are big, oversized boots. He rests a musket on the trunk as he fiddles at his trouser button. The other man is smaller, just five foot with a handkerchief around his neck and a hooked nose like an eagle. Richie does not move. They are too badly presented to be gamekeepers, and not sharp enough to be hunters, or they would have seen him there, squatting in the bushes. The fat one undoes the buttons on his trousers and fishes around for something inside. He's about to relieve himself.

"Twelve o'clock midnight," rasps this fat man as he walks a few steps over to Richie and pulls out his smalls. "The carriage will pass at twelve, the driver told me, you best check the time, Mr Woodhatch." The fat man begins to pee into the bushes and into Richie's general direction, but he does not look down, instead keeps his eyes on his associate who is holding up a pocket watch in the moonlight to read it. A few yards to the right and Richie would get wet, as it is, his hat is getting a light spray. Richie does not move. There is something a little foul in these two, the accent on the fat man is foreign to Richie's ears, English though, and the small one with a hooked nose has beady eyes that glint as he winces down at the time.

"We have ten minutes, Mr Rail," he answers. The fat one does up the buttons on his trousers and picks up his musket from the tree. He removes the ramrod and takes a packet of powder from a pocket and rips it open with his teeth.

"Shoot the driver first," he whispers as he loads the gun.

"I thought he was the one that gave you the tip off?"

"He was, that's why you'll shoot him first." Mr Rail uses the ramrod to jam the bullet and the powder down into the barrel of the gun. He hands the rifle over to the smaller man, who he calls Mr Woodhatch and takes a pistol out from his belt. He loads this one too.

"How much will we get out of this?" asks Mr Woodhatch.

"Depends what he's carrying but it'll be worth it just for the horses alone. If we get split up, head for Kingston upon Hull, due south of here on the river. There's a lad on Silver Street who'll buy anything we can give him. You got that?"

"Aye," whispers Mr Woodhatch. He pulls the handkerchief from around his neck, so it is over his nose. Mr Rail effects the same disguise with a piece of cloth from one of his trouser pockets, they turn and, much as they did a few moments earlier, make off through the woods.

Richie does not move for a second. A few minutes' walk behind him is the road that leads past the great forest and down towards Etton. The moon makes tonight perfect for travelling, you can at least see where you are going, and the air is warm enough and so it seems, these two men are to make the jump on some carriage coming up the road.

Richie's heart is beating in his thin chest. He feels the smooth handle of the pistol without bullets or powder in his right hand. Of course, Richie should not be there, not at all. He should learn to keep quiet, get comfy in a bush and wait for all this to pass and if there's a gunshot, Nana will tell anyone who asks that Richie was asleep at home. He swallows and his mouth is dry. He thinks about who might be on the carriage coming up the road and who the driver will be. It'll be someone he knows alright. Richie wipes the light sweat away from his brow. Who are these two anyway, to come tramping through Richie's forest with their guns and plans? He stands and makes his way to the tree trunk with the pistol held low, his nostrils flare and he grits his teeth. There's a little of Nana's anger in him, now he thinks about these two, threatening people he might know, in his forest on his hills. He creeps behind as the men in front follow a little path to the road. He can't just do nothing. Richie isn't all talk, he's not like Nana.

They set up well these two. The fat one who is Mr Rail, gets behind a wide tree to hide his girth, and the smaller one, Mr Woodhatch, goes on the other side of the road behind a bush. They do not whisper to each other now and the forest returns to the night sounds, a hedgehog digging away somewhere and moths flapping up at the moonlight. Richie has moved down wind of them and is on the same side of the road as Mr Rail and squatting in the undergrowth.

Richie has heard tales of highwaymen, more than most lads, for the man who lived under Nana's room eight years previous was of that kind as well. They called him the Pearlman in the circles he knew, but he'd given it all up to be with Meg and pretend he was Nana's son, John. He was good to Richie in the time that he was there, he taught him how to load and clean a pistol, and to shoot it too, showed him how to play cards and count the deck so you know what hands will come out. Richie was good with his fingers and the Pearlman showed him tricks also, sleight of hand with a coin, he taught him how to add up and read numbers with a stick in the dirt; but most of all the Pearlman told Richie stories about his days in the army and on the road with his band of lads – Dandy Jim and Carlos. The Pearlman left the pistol that Richie grips in his right hand, without bullets or powder, he left the hat that Richie wears too, a floppy affair and twenty years out of style, he left never to come back. So, Richie thinks of the Pearlman as he sits there in the bush with the moonlight still and the light spring breeze rustling the treetops. There are hidden armed men in front of him, waiting for a carriage to come up over the hill. He does not know why he's followed them, and he does not know what he is going to do.

Soon enough, an orange glow appears ahead, it's the lamp by the side of the driver, and it dulls the light of the moon as it bobs closer with the movement of the two horses that pull it. Richie's palm is wet on the pistol. There are a few plays the highwaymen can take, they can just shoot the driver and rob the carriage, or they can wave him down. The Pearlman told Richie about how his gang did it, they'd step out into the road and pass the time of day with a smile and a wink before they drew their pistols and robbed whatever the rich folk didn't need. Richie gets the feeling that it wasn't like that at all, and it won't be like that now with these two men who have birds for names. In the moonlight, Richie can hear the creak of the carriage wheels on the hard mud and the coach driver whistling to himself under his breath, Richie knows this carriage, he knows this driver, it's the coachman and constable, Peter Dawson from the village. Inside must be Mr Pennyman himself, or Miss Charlotte. Richie's nostrils flare. He's no great like for either of the two of them but the idea of them getting robbed doesn't sit well with him, like it wouldn't Nana, the folk of North Burton are the ones who get to rob the Pennymans, no one else. The whistling gets closer, somewhere far off there's the call of a fox, and scratching again from the undergrowth, over the fields an owl calls once more.

The carriage draws near and the little highwayman, who is Mr Woodhatch, moves his rifle into position. Richie's stomach grumbles as he hears the click of the hammer falling onto the flint, he sees the blaze of light and then, a dull boom and sparks illuminate the darkness, a horse rears up in the moonlight and Peter Dawson tumbles down from his sitting position off onto the mud road below. Richie thought he would do something, but his legs are frozen solid to the ground. Fat Mr Rail steps up and catches the rein of the horse that has reared and calms it with clicks in the back of his throat, Mr Woodhatch takes the other. The voice of Mr Rail calls out to the stopped carriage in his best queen's English.

"You're being robbed," he yells to the closed wooden door. "Open up and step out as calm as you like. We've no reason to hurt you, but we will if you don't do as we say." Mr Woodhatch has reloaded his rifle with none of the finesse and speed of his colleague.

What is Richie to do? His legs are rooted to the spot. His chest is tight and with his throat pinched closed so he can hardly breathe. It's fear that grips him.

The door to the carriage opens and a white-haired man steps out into the road and the warmth of the night. He is slight and well dressed with a frock coat and a grey necktie. It is Mr Pennyman himself. Behind is a smaller woman with dark hair and a wrinkled grimace, it's Miss Charlotte.

"Right then gent and lady," says Mr Rail. "Empty your pockets and toss whatever you have on the floor in front of you. Your wallet, watches, any rings you have."

"This is an outrage," whispers the old man. "Where's the coachman?"

"Most probably laid with a face full of lead, Sir. You'll be in the same position if you don't do as I ask. Be quick about it, too."

Mr Woodhatch has unhooked the orange lamp from where it sat on the carriage, and he holds this high so the faces of the two travellers are illuminated. Mr Pennyman is advanced in years, thin and gaunt, Miss Charlotte well past her best also with wrinkles across her face and the skin tight on her cheekbones. Nana says she was pretty once upon a time. She looks up at these two with cold eyes.

"You do know who we are?" she asks.

"I'm not too bothered, Miss, but I'd like you to begin tossing your effects in front of you."

"This is the East Riding of Yorkshire. Do you think there's a single rock around here that you can hide under? As soon as day breaks, the both of you men, and any of your associates with be swinging by the neck." Her voice is slate grey and real. Miss Charlotte has a temper on her, her tall husband left some five years since, and she's taken to the drink hard. It's made her cruel. Mr Rail raises his pistol.

"I can put you out of your misery, Miss," he whispers.

"That would suit me, highwayman," she answers and means it.

"I'd be happy to kill you both," says Mr Rail. "The dead don't talk. I was just giving you the chance to take off your rings so I didn't have to touch your body when the life is all gone out of it." Mr Rail is a robber and no doubt. There is no drama to him, and he will enjoy the barbarism.

"Get about your business then, boy," says Mis Charlotte. Mr Rail steps forward, she's made him angry, for even here, where he holds the gun, this toff still has the arrogance to treat him without respect. He raises the pistol to her head and the hammer is already pulled back.

A twig breaks. Mr Woodhatch gasps. There's someone else here.

It's Richie.

Without knowing why, he has stepped forward and the end of his pistol without bullets is pressed into the back of Mr Woodhatch's skull under his dirty hair. Richie is a good six foot four and so his figure with the dark floppy hat looks menacing in the darkness.

"I've followed you two for miles," calls Richie. "Drop that pistol or I'll take off your friend's head." The fat man smiles.

"Shoot him for all I care, it'll save me a job."

There's the rush of someone moving, Peter Dawson the coachman, appears behind Mr Rail with a savage look on his face and blood all over his chest. He clobbers the fat man with his right hand, the pistol fires off target and, Mr Woodhatch turns and elbows up and into Richie's jaw.

The world spins.

Richie is looking upwards at the tips of the tall trees in the moonlight, his eyes wide and his brain spinning. The next moment, the hook-nosed face of Mr Woodhatch is over him with his rough hands around Richie's neck. He can hear Miss Charlotte yelling and screaming into the night as the little man above him tightens his grip. Richie blinks and twists, remembers Nana's wrestling advice and pivots his body below. It's of no use, for Mr Woodhatch has done this kind of thing before and his whole weight bares down on Richie's neck as he grits his teeth. If Richie hadn't spent so much time at work on the Pennyman Estate then this robber may have already snapped his neck, but the tall lad has been trained to be strong, he's baled many a hayfield with Jonny Low, built fences, shovelled dirt and manure, chopped and carried logs, moved stone, clipped sheep, and every other horrible and hard job there is to do for a poor lad on a farm. He manages to free his left hand, forms it into a fist and wallops the hook-nosed robber across his face so he rolls off into the grass. Richie lays there for a moment as he catches his breath. He hears Peter Dawson shouting obscenities at the darkness as he discharges his musket into the woods after the two men as they run away.

"And don't be back round here again," he bellows. Mr Peter Dawson's voice does not sound quite right.

Somewhere in the distance Richie hears the call of the dog fox. His neck hurts.

It's dawn in the kitchen at the Pennyman estate.

The cook is making bread and Miss Charlotte sits on one of the farmhouse chairs. In front of her is a glass of brandy - her third one. Richie stands opposite with his floppy hat in his hands. He's a mess of blood and sweat, his shirt has been torn open and the swallow scar on his chest is visible. He's afraid. On the floor next to the fire, is the body of Peter Dawson, the coachman and constable for North Burton, the wound above his stomach blackened and his face ash grey, dead as stone. The cook, Mrs Heather, is busy with kneading as if this is a normal event and the new day fire crackles under a black pot of water. Mr Pennyman has retired upstairs shaken and afraid. Miss Charlotte on the other hand, takes a gulp of her brandy. The highwaymen from a few hours before are long gone to the forest of Dalton Park, one carrying a bruise across his face that Richie gave him, the other with a broken jaw delivered by Peter Dawson before he expired in the carriage on the way home. He did not go easy. Richie's face is grey with exhaustion and fear. Miss Charlotte finishes her brandy.

"Will you take a drink, Richie Jackson?" asks Miss Charlotte. The tall lad shakes his head. Nana has told him, several times, never to drink with a Pennyman.

"What was Richie Jackson doing in the Dalton Park Estate at twelve o'clock at night?" she asks.

"I was out for a walk, Miss." Her face does not change. She knows he was out poaching. Dalton Park is nothing to do with her estate, more is the pity, and so she doesn't care why he was there. She pours herself another drink from a clear decanter. Her blue eyes are cold.

"You saved our lives tonight, Richie," she says.

"I did what I thought was right, Miss." She looks at him. He's a fine lad, tall, sharp, brave and lonely somehow.

"You're to be careful of that in the future, Richie lad."

"Pardon me, Miss?"

"Doing what you think is right. It's not always the best option and it's dangerous. Sometimes, you have to do what is best for you and not for everyone else."

"Yes, Miss." Richie looks down at the stone floor. This is the worst kind of advice from someone rich enough not to know anything about the world at all.

"But, I'm glad you did the right thing, for I may not be sitting here if you hadn't. I'm going to reward you, Richie."

"There's no need, Miss Charlotte." She stands up.

"Nonsense, lad." Now she has spirit in her guts, Miss Charlotte is focused. She walks to the kitchen door and holds it open. "We'll go to the livery, Richie, and you'll pick whatever horse you want." The cook looks up from her kneading with surprise. Miss Charlotte gazes back at her and is slightly drunk. "You can tell them all," she barks, "Young Richie here saved my life and my father's too, he'll have the pick of the stables, any horse he likes, and I mean it."

Richie finds himself falling into step behind Miss Charlotte as they walk to the livery yard over the cobbles. The spring sun is beginning over the wide expanse of the fields and there's heat in the day already. Mr Farthing stands outside one of the stable doors with a barrow of hay and he sees Miss Charlotte walking towards him with her dress ripped and her face dirty.

He knows what has happened already. All of North Burton know, perhaps all the way to Beverley, folk will be whispering the story of the robbery to each other. That's how fast news travels.

"He's to have any horse he wants, Mr Farthing," she shouts as she approaches. "Any horse, and he can keep it here too, to ride whenever he feels the need. Any horse mind." Mr Farthing does not greet her, his brain races at the problems this could cause.

"Not the stallions, Miss Charlotte, the big one is worth fifty guineas."

"Any horse," she repeats. She turns back to Richie, and he looks down from his great height at them both. Confused. This is a turn of events. Richie is a brave lad, and a strong lad too but, he does not like horses. They have not been kind to him. One winter when he was mucking out, a big bay squashed him against the stable wall, they've head butted him, stood on his feet and, across his right arm there's the scar from a nasty bite through to the bone from a time a nag reached out and bit him as he walked by a stable door. It's been a blessing in many ways that Richie is too poor to have much to do with horses.

"You'll make your choice then, Richie-lad," says Miss Charlotte. He nods. Mr Farthing looks concerned. He's worked in this yard for the last twenty years or so and like Richie, he does not want any of the beasts to be given away. He has to play along with Miss Charlotte however, especially as she has had a shock and now a few drinks.

"How about a reliable gelding, Richie," he says. "Fun to ride and sturdy, and you could take the Arab, you'd be a sight for the ladies in Beverley town on a horse like that." Richie takes a deep breath. He looks into Mr Farthing's eyes. They both know the idea of a working lad like Richie riding with the well-dressed of Beverley on Sunday morning is as ridiculous as it is impossible.

"Perhaps you should let me think on it," replies Richie, "and I can come back tomorrow or in a week and tell you then." Mr Farthing nods at this. Without the aid of drink in her stomach, Miss Charlotte would not have made such a rash decision.

"I agree with the lad, Miss Charlotte. He's had a shock and been as brave as a lion, but choosing a horse, his first horse at that, why, that's something a man has to think about."

"It has to be today," says Miss Charlotte. "I might change my mind tomorrow and he deserves it." Mr Farthing nods. It's going to be a long morning.

The three of them pace around the yard from stable to stable. Miss Charlotte looking whiter and paler by the moment and Mr Farthing listing the qualities of the horses as they pass. First a bay, then a grey cob, "this one is fourteen hands, she's got a temper," and then, "good as gold he is, you have to watch him, she's a biter, he'll throw you if he gets chance." Richie is confused and at moments between Mr Farthings explanations, he sees the face of Mr Woodhatch who he fought the night previous. He hears the calls of Peter Dawson as he died in the dawn too. It makes him feel sick.

At the last stable, there is no horse and Mr Farthing pops his head inside to have a look. There's something he had forgotten about within. He undoes the latch, swings open the door and enters. Richie and Miss Charlotte follow, the smell is rich and warm. In the corner, looking back at them, is a thin and dark hunting dog. She has huge wide eyes and a long smooth face, she's young and just out of her puppy fat, perhaps nine or ten months old.

"I got her from the breeder up at Weighton," says Mr Farthing. "Her father was a greyhound. I thought we could use a dog in the yard."

Richie goes to his knees and the dog comes forward to him without fear. He smiles as she licks his face. Mr Farthing and Miss Charlotte stand at the doorway with the sun behind them.

"I'll have this dog here," says Richie. He stands to listen to her decision and Miss Charlotte looks into his eyes in the darkness of the stable. He's a bright lad. She was going to gift him a horse that she'd keep. She was going to elevate him to something more than just a flat, grey worker who breaks his back in the fields, she was going to use him, but Richie here is too quick to be used by her. She should have known. A slight smile reaches her lips. He wants a dog. He could have any horse in the yard, he could have the stallion that racehorse owners will pay ten guineas to put their mares too, and he chooses the dog; but it's not guile that causes Richie to make his decision, he just knows what feels right.

"You shall have your dog, Richie Jackson," says the woman.

Miss Charlotte stands beside Mr Farthing, and they watch young Richie walk off with the dog following him on a rope lead.

"He's a bright lad, that Richie," says Mr Farthing.

"How so?" she asks.

"Because," he explains, "if you gave him a horse, the moment you were sober, you'd take it back off him." She smiles. Nobody else talks to her so, and she allows Mr Farthing this little freedom, just this once.

"You're right, Mr Farthing, he is a bright lad."

CHAPTER TWO

It's August and full summer. Much has changed. Granddad Blackwell and his son Miles are both laid to rest. The Bay Horse pub across the way is open again with a new sign swinging from a pole and a landlord, Philipson, a big man from Driffield and his sister. The Rector up at St Michael's is a well-meaning but dullard Yorkshire lad, Reverend Page. Farmer Thorne is long gone too, and the farm sold off to a family from Bridlington way who have yet to move down. Adam Gamble is still the sexton but a family man now with the Farthing lass as his wife. Miss Charlotte's husband ran off some time ago and she is bitter with it. Mr Pennyman's hair is as white as snow and his wits dulled. Much has changed in North Burton.

Not Nana.

It's Sunday after church. She sits in front of the hearth in her chair like always, with a scarf wrapped round her grey hair and her fat, swollen legs together. She might be seventy-five or eighty-two but, by and large, Nana has looked the same for as long as anyone can remember. She considers Richie's thin greyhound dog. It took him a week to train it not to wee in the house and the thing eats a lot more than it should but, Richie can catch more rabbits than he can in any traps. He calls it Bess. She sleeps on him, follows him everywhere and looks at him when he talks. It feels like the dog has lived with them forever. Nana often refers back to the decision that Richie made in the stable some four months ago. It plays on her mind.

"You could have got something better than a dog, a bottle of brandy, or a few guineas, or a loaf of bread even? Richie? The dog eats more than you." Richie's eyes are red and weary because last night he was up late playing cards in the pub across the road. Playing cards is a cover story for drinking,

"I wasn't thinking," he replies as he settles down into the

long bench against the wall and stretches out.

"You could have got one of them mares and flogged it up at Beverley for a few quid and we'd be eating plum pudding now. I could be dressed in lace." Nana is open to flights of fancy now and them.

"I can't even ride, Nana," he answers.

"Anyone can bloody ride," she snaps, "all you have to do is sit there." This is a cruel simplification as anyone who knows horses will tell you. The dog approaches Nana with big dark eyes, she's not afraid of the old woman and as she ruffles the black fur, the dog begins a low groan of pleasure that comes from her chest. Nana smiles and shows her two missing front teeth. "Bess is a whore's name," she says.

"What would you know?" asks Richie. She looks down on the sleek fur of the hound and rubs her hands along the velvet soft skin. Nana does not mean the horrible things she says, most of the time.

"I'm not just a village lass," says the old woman. "I've been up to Driffield and York a plenty." Nana is a village lass. She's never been more north than Market Weighton and despite what she says, has never been to York or Lincoln or London. She hasn't left North Burton for the last thirty years or more. That doesn't make her stupid, however. "I just don't know why you did it, Richie."

"We've been through this," says the lad. Nana likes to go over arguments they have already had, to ring out all the talk she can. They have had this discussion several times.

"You're not to go protecting a Pennyman, Richie, not under any circumstance. And you shouldn't drink with them neither."

"It's Mr Pennyman who owns this house and pays my wages, Nana. If he were to be found dead, there'd be a load more trouble than that. You've heard how Lord Grantham treats his people, little better than slaves, at least with Pennyman there's a pint of ale at Christmas." Richie has heard

Nana say this sort of thing before, he's just reporting what he's listened to. Nana would argue with herself if Richie wasn't here.

"There's not a Pennyman or his sort, Richie, who would spit on you if you were on fire. They hate us and they hate our kind." This is the truth, in a round about kind of way, because, Nana is right about most things, even when she is wrong. She's got the tart sting of a wasp in her tongue and thorn prickles in her words but, as she has got older, parts of her have become softer, especially for the lad and now this dog. Years gone, Nana had a son who married a lass from a village a few miles away called Meg, he went away to war and came back, literally a new man. He wasn't Nana's son, but they called him John, like they did her boy, even though he was the Pearlman. Meg was in love with him, but he didn't stay long, not more than a handful of years before he was off again. The lass he married went back over to Etton and it left Richie and Nana together in the old house. Richie was born a long time before all that, on the stable floor of the Pennyman Estate and Mr Pennyman had wanted the young bastard to die as his mother had done, but Nana would not have it, and so he became her son and has been ever since. The old women talk about blood being thicker than water, but Nana's lived her life nearly right through to the end and knows that's a great lot of shite. Family is who you love and those that love you. That's all it's ever been.

The dog has a tendency to lean on people that she likes, so Bess leans on Nana and the pressure on the old woman makes her feel safe. Her fingers find the dog's ear.

"Shouldn't you be at that bible?" she nags.

"I'm not reading it."

"You don't have to believe it, but a lad that can't read won't get on, I've told you that."

"Where am I going to get on to?" Richie would go up the ladder and sleep on the straw mat upstairs, but Nana can shout at him if he's there just the same.

"You've to be good at reading, Richie, Pennyman might find a use for you, a brave tall lad like you."

"It's Sunday, Nana, for God's sake."

"Don't you bloody swear in my house," she starts. She'll tire in five minutes. The walk to the church at the top of the village has taken a lot out of her and she won't be able to keep up the complaining. She'll be asleep by one.

There's a sharp knock on the wooden door of Nana's cottage and Richie, with his eyes still full of sleep makes his way over to the door and opens up. Standing in the sunshine in the street is Mr Farthing.

"You could have got washed, Richie," he says. He wears a necktie and has combed his hair and had a shave. Mr Farthing is in charge at the Pennyman livery yard, an Essex man originally, and it's he who acts as farrier, vet and muck shifter. He and his wife came to North Burton some twenty years ago and have been here ever since. Now he runs the whole house for the Pennymans.

"What is it?"

"The magistrate is at the pub, Richie. He needs to see you. Did you not get word?"

"Not I," he replies.

"Get yourself sorted then, Richie lad, Mr Middleton's not the sort of man to be kept waiting."

"What does he want with me?"

"I don't know, lad. I told your Nana he was coming last night." She will have forgotten.

"It's not my bloody job to take your messages Richie Jackson, along with everything else I do in this house," she shouts from behind.

Richie wipes down his trousers, closes the door slightly and unhooks his black jacket then puts it on as he steps outside into the sunshine. Bess follows him through the door even though she looks like she doesn't want to. Richie's arms are too long for the sleeves and the collars are tatty. Mr Farthing flares his nostrils at the lad, he wouldn't dress a horse as badly as this, but, these will be the only clothes that Richie has. The two men make their way across the road to the step of the ale house and Mr Farthing holds the door open for Richie and Bess to step inside. Dogs are not normally allowed in through the front door, but Bess is.

There's the smell of ale and smoke from inside a big room and a long wooden bar at the far end. Philipson, the new landlord, had lads come and fix the roof before he moved in, and he's improved the place. There are tables and stools, no fighting allowed, cards can be played but not for money and there are dominoes he'll lend you. He brews bitter beer does Philipson and it takes a bit of getting used to, but it's passable. Richie has drunk quite a lot of it on weekends gone by. He dips his head to miss some of the low beams as he walks through the room. Philipson stands up from behind the bar. He has short black hair with a high-pitched voice. There are three lads sat in the corner around a table and a man with a bald head at the bar. It's quiet.

"The magistrate's in the back room, Richie," says Philipson. "I'll send Mary through with a tray of ale soon enough." Richie nods. He likes this Philipson, he pays a fair wage for those that help him, his sister is a backward lass of stunted growth, with big eyes and a fat tongue that makes her sound daft. Philipson looks after her and she's a good, strong and hardworking bar lass. Richie and Nana like family that look after each other. That's what they do.

"Thank you, Philipson," comments Mr Farthing. The two men pass the bar and go up some steps and into another chamber through a heavy red curtain. The back room is used by important people. That's why Richie has never been in.

At a large wooden table, sits a man with a thin, clever face, red cheeks and round glasses under straight blonde hair. He looks up as Richie and Mr Farthing enter. This is the magistrate, he is called Mr Stephen Middleton and years ago, was in the employ of Miss Charlotte and Mr Pennyman as the constable of North Burton as well as a coach man. He is a country lad, but not one such as Richie, he comes from the village of Middleton on the Wolds and his father owns a great deal of the land there. It's known also that Stephen Middleton has done things in his past as a young man, he has pilfered larders, got drunk on borrowed spirits, played cards for money, told a good many bawdy jokes and turned up late too many times. There are those also that will tell you of the young lasses he promised the world to and that they disappeared, for there are two sides to many coins. Now that he has reached middle age, he has swapped his wayward path for a respectable wife in Beverley and young children, but, he is a rare breed of judge and lawman who knows how the world works from the bottom up. He knows what people get up to round here, that's why he's such a good magistrate. He knows Richie too, and Nana. They have met before.

"Good day to you, Richie," he says. He holds out his hand for the lad to take a seat in front of him. Richie pulls out a stool and sits down. "I won't be needing you, Mr Farthing as you weren't there that night. I need only to talk to Richie here." Mr Farthing nods, turns and walks back through the heavy curtain leaving Stephen Middleton and Richie alone. Richie squints around the dim room, at the pictures hanging on the wall, the faded curtains on the little windows onto the mud street outside, the oil lamp next to Stephen Middleton and his big book on the table. The magistrate removes his eyeglasses.

"How are you and your Nana?" asks Stephen Middleton.

"Well, thank you, Sir."

"And Meg?" Mr Middleton refers to the lady who married Nana's son.

"She's returned to Etton, she's the cunning lass in the stead of her mam."

"I know this, Richie. I mean, how is she?"

"It's been a time since I saw her, Sir," Richie's face looks blank. Mr Middleton keeps an eye on North Burton because he knew it in his younger days.

"I heard she's quite the wise woman now," says Mr Middleton. He means that she heals cuts and wounds, cures ailments and mixes potions, makes compresses, sets bones, heals broken hearts too. Stephen Middleton knows that the wealthy women of Beverley and the great houses of the East Riding would rather see Meg of Etton than learned doctors who have only read books in darkened universities paid for by their rich families.

"She's a good lass to know," says Richie. Stephen Middleton looks at the lad sitting tall on the stool in front of him, he examines his open shirt, the tatty black jacket and his thin collar bones showing proud. The magistrate best get to business, that's why he's come to North Burton. He knows what Nana is like, and this boy will be no different, they will steal what they can get away with but they are not thieves.

"I'm here to talk about what happened with those highwaymen back in spring. I'm investigating Peter Dawson's death." Richie nods. He's fine to talk. "You were at North Dalton Park on that night?"

"Aye, Sir."

"What were you doing there?" Stephen Middleton knows he was poaching, and he will gauge the measure of this young man by his answer.

"I was trapping rabbits, Sir." Stephen Middleton nods. It's illegal to do so on land that is privately owned, and Richie could face charges for this. "I could lie to you, Sir, but you would see through it." Stephen Middleton cocks his head.

"You must learn to play the game, Richie. I know what you were doing but if you admit it as clear as day, the law will fall upon you. Let me ask again. What was your business up at North Dalton Park that night?"

"I was taking the night air, Sir, I've been advised that moonlight is good for my disposition."

"Much better," whispers Stephen Middleton. "Do you know what disposition means?"

"My health, Sir." The magistrate does a half smile.

"Not quite. Go through what happened for me, would you on the evening in question." Richie coughs, before he begins, Stephen Middleton cuts in. "This time you must tell the absolute truth, Richie." The lad nods.

"I was in the forest, and I heard the two men. The robbers. I heard them wait for the carriage and I waited too. When they pulled the coach up, I stepped up and pointed my pistol at one of them. There was a fight, he fell on me and, I clobbered him."

"Why did you not shoot him?"

"The pistol was not loaded, Sir." Stephen Middleton smiles. This is the spirit he expects from Jacksons.

"You took on two highwaymen with no lead in your weapon? Was that wise?"

"I don't know, Sir. I was angry."

"Why?"

Richie has a frown and a think.

"I didn't want them to rob Mr Pennyman or Miss Charlotte."

"Why not?"

"They own my house, Mr Middleton, without those two, who would pay for anything that I have? Who would I work for? They're not the best landowners, but… They own the land round here and I am their lad." Richie wishes this were not true. Stephen Middleton nods. He can smell the truth.

"Did you hear any of these men talk? Did you hear a name, or any mention of anything as to where they came from?" Richie cocks his head and looks back to himself sitting in the darkness under a bush on Dalton Park with the sounds of the wind in the trees and an owl hooting off in the distance.

"The fat one was Mr Rail. The other, the one I struck was Mr Woodhatch." Stephen Middleton considers this information and takes a deep breath in through his nose. This is not good news at all.

"Do you know those names?" asks Richie.

"In a way." Stephen Middleton does not want to say too much to Richie. He knows the lad is a good egg, but he must be careful. "There is an association, Richie, I believe new to this area who wish to capitalize on the wildness of our region."

Richie blinks back at the magistrate, he is confused. Stephen Middleton stands up and takes his handkerchief from his pocket to mop his brow. Despite the darkness of the room, it's still a hot day. He wanders to the window to look at the hard mud of the main street of North Burton, he sees a cart pass, led by a battered nag with its head down.

"The East Riding is wealthy, Richie. However poor you might be, there are houses up here with jewels and silver a plenty, but, unlike the rich houses in London, they do not have many men to protect it. There is an association, so I have heard, that sees opportunity in these wild lands. Did you catch the accent of these men?"

"It was not from round here, Sir," answers Richie. He would not know where they came from.

"I believe there will be more robberies, not necessarily here, but perhaps so. Did you hear of that young lass out at South Cave, the one kidnapped at Christmas?"

"I did," answers Richie. His blood runs a little cold at mention of this.

"They ransomed her and took a tidy sum of money to return her back to her rich father, but she was not the same woman when they brought her back." Stephen Middleton turns to look at Richie to add drama to the story. "It's not known what they did to her, but she never spoke of it, and within the week, she was dead." Richie has heard this story. It makes him angry.

"There are some foul people in the world, Sir." Richie's voice has a little fury in it.

"The coachman and constable, Peter Dawson, where was he shot?"

"Just above his stomach, he was dead on the Pennyman kitchen floor last time I saw him." Stephen Middleton knew this. "There's more, Sir. I heard the two men talk, I heard them say the driver tipped them off as to when he would be passing and where."

"Do you think the driver was in on it?"

"I don't think anything. I'm just telling you what I heard. It could be another coachman."

"It could be, but sadly, he can't answer any questions." Stephen Middleton returns and sits down. He picks up his thin eyeglasses and fits them around his ears. "It means North Burton will need a new constable."

"Aye," answers Richie.

"Do you know anyone?" Richie shakes his head. Stephen Middleton looks at this young man with a frown. "I know someone."

"Mr Farthing? There's Adam Gamble too?"

"You, Richie."

"I?"

"Yes."

"I'm seventeen years old, Mr Middleton. I'm one of Mr Pennyman's working lads." Richie's voice is shocked.

"Can you count?"

"Aye."

"And read."

"Some."

"Can you shoot?"

"Aye."

"You'll make a shilling every quarter." Richie raises his eyebrows. That could buy a lot of ale. Even so. Richie Jackson - a constable of the peace at North Burton? He's afraid.

"It won't stand, Mr Middleton. Mr Pennyman and Miss Charlotte won't allow it. The folks around here won't allow it neither."

"Not so. I also heard rumours about the coachman, Mr Dawson, so did others and yet he was the constable, was he not? It's my belief that we need someone who we can trust in a position of authority."

"Miss Charlotte will never let it stand," repeats Richie.

"It was her idea, lad."

"What if I say no?"

"She wouldn't be happy."

"I'm not right for it, Mr Middleton, you know that. I'm a drunk, sometimes a drunk here in this alehouse. I'm a poacher too, and I thieve eggs. I pinched a pair of knickers from the Pennyman washing line and sold them for a penny at Beverley Market, then spent the money on ale. I sell rabbits that I catch. I kissed the Abbot lass from Leconfield and told her I'd marry her if she did, and I didn't marry her at all." Richie's eyes are watering, his throat is dry, and his voice is strained. "I can't be the constable, Mr Middleton. I'm just a lad. I look after my Nana, I fall asleep in church, I never read the bible and at Christmas last year, I cheated that Greenwood lad out of a half penny at cards – and gambling isn't allowed." Richie's eyes cast up to the ceiling, searching for more of his wrong doings. "I don't know how many times I've poached in Dalton Park, Mr Middleton, maybe a hundred times, maybe more." Stephen Middleton holds his hand up to stop the boy from going on.

"You're an honest lad, Richie. Miss Charlotte holds you in high regard. You saved her life that night." Richie swallows. "I've written a note here," says Mr Middleton as he pushes a piece of paper across the table to Richie. "It's a note to Porter's the gunsmith on the marketplace in Beverley. You'll go there this afternoon and collect a box of bullets and powder for that pistol, Miss Charlotte's orders." The lad picks up the note in his long fingers.

"I'll have to tell Nana," says Richie. It's the first thing he thinks of. "I'll have to tell Meg too."

"Of course," says Stephen Middleton. "I know what she'll say. I know what both of them will say."

"What?"

"They'll say that you've been given the job because whoever is the constable in North Burton after what has gone on, will be in danger."

"Is that true?"

"I don't know. Maybe. But Miss Charlotte and I need someone who we can trust. There have been other highwayman sightings, Richie, from here to Bridlington.

"And you would trust me more than the servants up at the Pennyman Estate, more than the horsemen, more than the other workers in the village, more than the landlord here, or the farmers in the bigger houses?"

Stephen Middleton taps his fingers on the table as he speaks: "I know your family, Richie and I know what kind of lad you are. I know Meg. You'll report to me whatever you hear." Richie looks down at the note in his hands and then back up to the clever eyes of the magistrate, Stephen Middleton.

"Aye," he answers.

"You'll go to Porter's this afternoon."

"It's a good walk, Mr Middleton, could you spare a penny for a drink when I get there."

"You'll get a shilling a quarter, Richie Jackson, not a penny more, and nothing from me now."

CHAPTER THREE

It's a fine summer afternoon. Richie walks up the hill to St Michael's church, past the duck pond and towards the Pennyman House. He wears his big floppy hat and has a wide honest smile like he generally does. People in North Burton think he's always happy, so they will say things to Nana like 'He's got a great big smile that lad.' It's just the way Richie looks. Bess walks beside him with her ears down.

At the church, Adam Gamble is smoking a pipe on the steps. He has black hair and a thin face.

"I hear you're to be made the constable, Richie lad."

News travels fast in North Burton.

"Aye, a shilling a quarter," says Richie back.

"If you get to the end of this quarter."

"What's your meaning, Mr Gamble?"

"There's a gang come up here, from London, they say. I heard Miss Charlotte talking about it. They're here to rob every last estate house in the East Riding." Richie has just heard something similar.

"I've seen them off once, Mr Gamble. I can do it again."

"Now just wait on, Richie." Adam Gamble stands up and positions himself in front of the lad so he has to stop, he looks up into Richie's face. "You've to be careful. I know you can't refuse the job, anyone would be an idiot to turn down the money, but it doesn't mean you have to change who you are." If Richie does become the constable, it could be more difficult for Adam Gamble to continue with his card games on Friday night for money, he might have to pay the lad off.

"They'll put you in the line of fire first," he continues. "You just don't have to do the job as thoroughly as you might, do you understand me?" Richie is not nearly as sharp witted as Adam Gamble, and thinks the man is just concerned about his safety, which he is, to some degree.

"I'm not the constable yet, Mr. Gamble. I'm to go to the

Pennyman house tonight to make my mark on the papers."

"Where you off to now?"

"Beverley, to Porter's." Adam Gamble knows the gun shop on the market square with a great bay window.

"You just go careful then, Richie. He's not a nice fella, you know." It's the wrong time to mention card games, thinks Adam Gamble.

"I will," he answers, and his smile sweeps over his face.

Richie goes across Elier's Field, picks his way through the sheep who bleat at him and Bess, and down the rough wagon track. It's not a main road by any means. The thin dog keeps her head down and close to Richie. When he stops, so does she, and when he looks out across the fields and the swaying heads of corn, she gazes up at him with a sense of wonder somehow. Nana says it's because he feeds her that she loves him so, but Bess is not an overly greedy dog and Richie is more than just a benefactor, they are part of the same pack. Richie rolls up his sleeves in the sunshine and pins the side of his floppy hat up. His shirt is open to the chest and the swallow scar shows dark brown. It's a grand afternoon and Richie and Bess run at a jog, he ties his satchel tight over his shoulder and they set off at an agreeable pace. He likes the feeling of sweat on his brow and his heart beating in his chest. What does a man need a horse for if he can run, with his dog at his side and the sun in the blue sky? They angle down past Dog Kennel Lane and Muddy Farm where the guard dogs bark at them as they run across the entrance, then up and over Constitution Hill, and down towards Molescroft and Beverley. Bess has her tongue out as she lumbers on beside him.

There's the sound of hooves in front and Richie looks up to see two riders approaching at a mid-canter. Ahead, on a white horse is an older man with a wrinkled face and a serious demeanour under a powdered wig. He's dressed in a riding coat and has polished boots. People know people round here, especially if they are rich. This is Lieutenant Pike, a Beverley gentleman, altogether living a different life from Richie and Nana. Behind on a smaller brown horse, is a fine and tall lass with ginger hair to her shoulders and hazel eyes. At once, as he notices her, Richie's eyebrows raise and he steps from the path. This is Lieutenant Pike's daughter, she is Miss Elizabeth Pike and they live in a house as big as a whale on the main street of Beverley called Toll Gavel. They will not know Richie, but he knows them. He smiles up as they ride past, these two, clean, pale and resplendent with the smell of perfume coming from Elizabeth and her white riding dress with gold embroidery down the front. The Lieutenant snarls down at Richie is he passes,

"Mind that bloody dog," he bellows at Bess as she scuttles out the way. He's already ridden past by the time Richie's friendly smile drops. Elizabeth Pike looks down with her face full of freckles and gives a weak, almost apologetic smile, and they are gone. Richie stands back on the path and watches them ride on to North Burton. He is not jealous of these two out for a ride on a Sunday afternoon because he knows as little about their life as they do about his.

"If I had a lass like that, Bess," he whispers. "I'd give you up in a heartbeat." People round here say this sort of things though they don't mean it. Richie has seen Elizabeth before, on trips to the market in Beverley, with her high cheekbones and gloves and a different dress for everyday of the week and a big smile and those hazel eyes and a calm laugh. She's a tall one, perhaps six foot, Richie has heard that she is considered too gangly and freckly to be beautiful. He noticed her before, chatting to the barrow lad opposite the Minster as she bought chestnuts, with her father beside her dressed in his uniform and his medals down his chest. Too tall to be beautiful, he scoffs to himself, for Richie who is six foot four, she's about the right size. He thinks about her some days, sometimes as he drifts off to sleep. A lad can have dreams. "We were lucky to see her," he says to the dog.

She smiled at him.

It's been a good day so far.

Mr Porter is fat in the way that important rich men are. They are fat because they don't have to shovel coal or chop wood, work the fields, milk cows, cook or sweep up. Richie has had to leave Bess outside which he does not like doing, for poor lad's dogs are not allowed in. Porter's is a posh shop that deals with posh people, working folk like Richie don't have guns. Porter himself stands behind his shiny wooden counter, looks down at the note that Richie has given him, and reads the words that Richie has not. His head rises to consider the lad.

"I'm not meant to be open on a Sunday, you know?" Richie knocked on the window of the shop earlier, he told the owner he was on important business for the magistrate. This is all true. "Two boxes of musket balls and one of powder and…" he chooses his next words carefully. "Are you sure this is correct?"

"Yes, Sir," answers Richie. "In truth, Sir, I didn't read the note. I just handed it over to you."

"It says here you're to be given a gun also."

"A gun?" asks Richie.

"Aye. It's signed by the magistrate himself, Mr Middleton." Porter has a loud voice that sounds important. He examines Richie a little more. "Are you that Jackson lad who saw off those highwayman back in spring out at North Burton?"

"It is I," he says.

"I heard you had a knife fight with one." This is not correct. Richie just punched the man.

"I did." It's easy to lie when someone makes it easy. Mr Porter examines him more.

"How tall are you?"

"Six foot four."

"By God."

"Did you kill him?"

"Maybe – he gave it legs before I could finish him off." Richie will only stretch the truth so far.

"They say you're a bastard too." This is not a compliment, but Porter's face does not change. Richie is a bastard, and his mother did bear him on a stable floor out of wedlock before she died. People like Porter in Beverley are the sorts who think this is important, as if a person's birth gives them worth or title and the right to sit in a good position in church and have a warm house and a chest full of medals. Richie blinks back at Mr Porter and thinks about Bess who he has left out on the busy street. The gun seller has made him suddenly aware that this is an unfriendly place in an unfriendly town. These busy cobbled streets all speak of wealth, just like the huge St Mary's Church he and Bess walked past a few minutes earlier, with intricate stained-glass windows and a heavy oaken door.

Porter turns and fetches down two boxes of musket balls from a shelf, puts them on the counter in front of him and then does the same for the powder. They will be in slim packages that you rip open with your teeth. It makes Richie a little excited.

"I have my dog outside, Sir. Do you think he'll be pinched? And I have an errand back at the Pennyman House." Richie says this to make the gun seller move more quickly.

"I'll go at my own speed, boy. You're not talking to some bloody highwayman now, you pull your knife on me and I'll throttle you." Richie feels some of Nana's barbed words forming on his lips but keeps quiet. It won't help. Porter shuffles from behind one counter to behind another. On the wall there is a row of rifles and muskets side by side. The man reaches for one in the middle and takes it down. He sets it on the counter gently.

"This is a Long Land Pattern musket," he says. "Standard issue to the British army. At a hundred feet it will take a man's head clean off his shoulders." The fat man taps the barrel. "It's not a toy. It seems that the magistrate wants you to have this. I've heard all sorts happening out in the countryside, and I don't think the answer's arming some country bastard, but who am I to say. Do you know how to load it?"

"Aye," answers Richie. His face has turned sour.

"Good, because I'll not be showing you. Now, if you don't mind, grab your bullets and your musket and get out of my shop. I hope someone has made off with your dog." Richie opens his satchel, puts the three boxes inside and goes for the musket. Porter keeps his hand on the barrel.

"You know where some of these guns come from, boy?" he asks. Richie shakes his head.

"Some of them, they pull from the arms of dead men. I fix them up and sell them on again. So, a favour, keep this one as clean as you can, will you? It'll save me a job when it comes back." He releases his hand and Richie picks up the musket. He keeps his eyes fixed on Porter as he does so. This is some of Richie's temper getting the better of him, as it does sometimes. This is why Richie can get into fights when he ought not to and why he's not allowed in any of the pubs in Walkington.

"Get out of my shop," says Porter.

As soon as Richie is a mile or so out of Beverley, he sits down on a hillock and examines the musket. Any other gunsmith might have provided a strap with such a weapon, but not Porter, it was not specified in the note written by the magistrate and so he did not fit one. The flintlock is oiled, the stock smooth and clean, Richie looks down the barrel across the yellow fields with corn heads bobbing in the breeze. It's a fine weapon. He thinks about loading it, but it's been quite a while since he fired one, as long as he has been alone with Nana in the house, and since the man he called father left them. He thinks about him, about how tall he was, his dark hair and his blue eyes and a ready smile. They called him John, but Richie knew that was not his real name, in the dark places in London or Manchester, in the backstreets of Leeds or Sheffield or Lincoln, they called him the Pearlman for it was he who could sense what something was worth. It was he who taught Richie how to play cards, how to count well, how to box and, how to load and shoot a musket.

There's the sound of hooves again. This time coming the other way and going back to Beverley. It's the same couple, Lieutenant Pike and his daughter Elizabeth. Richie swallows. To see the tall lass twice in a day may be a little bit more than he can take. He sits atop the hillock with the path going a little below him, the musket he has just acquired across his legs and Bess sat upright next to him. His hat is pinned up at one side, and he has his sleeves rolled. The rider approaches, but not as quickly as previous. Lieutenant Pike is ahead, on his white horse and with his face looking a little less fresh than when Richie saw him before. Elizabeth behind seems tired after their ride, they must be returning home. Richie feels self-conscious somehow, suddenly, sitting on the little hill with his long legs out and his hat all wrong, his tanned face and huge thin dog with her tongue out. Lieutenant Pike pulls up twenty yards away, he has a look of concern across his face.

"You there," he yells.

"Aye," calls Richie.

"What's your business?" he looks nervously back at Elizabeth behind him who returns his glance with a worried look of her own.

"On my way back to North Burton with my dog here. Just taking a rest."

"We're not but a mile out of Beverley, mister," calls Lieutenant Pike. "You try anything out here and you'll be hunted down within an hour." Richie gets to his feet and holds the gun loosely in both hands, he does not mean to look threatening. From his position, he is higher up than both the riders and he sees Lieutenant Pike's frown and narrowed eyes.

"I'm not a robber, Sir," says Richie. "I've just been to the gunsmith in Beverley to pick up this musket." Lieutenant Pike examines Richie once more, he sees the ready smile and the battered hat, the hole in one of his trouser knees and the tatty boots. Lieutenant Pike has heard about highwaymen who hold up strangers and rob them on the roads between towns. Now he sees that his instincts about Richie were unfounded.

"What's a ragged lad like you doing with a gun like that?" asks Lieutenant Pike. These are not unkind words, they are simply a matter of fact as seen by a man who knows soldiers

"I'm to be the constable at North Burton, Sir," he answers. Lieutenant Pike looks back at Elizabeth with one of his eyebrows raised. He looks again at Richie.

"I don't think so," he says. Now Lieutenant Pike has appraised the situation he walks his horse on towards Richie without his previous fear. "Come down off that hill and let me look at you." Richie clambers down a few steps until he is standing facing Lieutenant Pike's horse. He tips his hat first at the gentleman and then at the lass.

"You're a tall one," says Lieutenant Pike.

"Six foot four, Sir."

"What's your name?"

"Richie Jackson of North Burton, Sir." Lieutenant Pike looks down upon him. They could not be more different, these two. Richie is tanned from working outside, his shirt is open to the chest and tatty, his collar bones strong and with a wide smile. Lieutenant Pike is well fed but not as out of shape as most of the well-to-do men of Beverley.

"I very much doubt that the Pennyman Estate would allow one of their farm workers to become constable of the peace, Richie Jackson of North Burton. They have a little more sense than that and there are things going on that need a steady hand. There are highwaymen on these roads – and an attack a few months ago over at Etton." Richie knows this. Lieutenant

Pike is the same as the Pennymans, you shouldn't take a drink with them and minimise any chatter, have as little to do with them as possible. He has already said too much. Elizabeth edges her horse forward so she is next to Lieutenant Pike, she smiles wide and Richie smiles back.

"I like your dog," she says. "What's the breed?"

"They say her father was a greyhound, Lady."

"I'm not a lady, Richie Jackson. Is she fast?"

"Aye, Miss, like the wind." Elizabeth nods and looks over the dog. Next, she examines Richie in the same way she inspected the hound, like an animal. Richie can see the simplicity in her eyes for him, and he wishes this were not so. He takes a deep breath.

"You want to be careful," says Lieutenant Pike down his nose, "carrying a big musket like that around and sitting by the side of the road, people might get the wrong idea. I must confess I rather did."

"Could you deal with a highwayman, father?" asks Elizabeth in a frivolous way. His face darkens but he does not take his eyes off Richie.

"Not without my pistol," he mutters.

"Could you deal with a highwayman, Richie Jackson of North Burton, if one was waiting for you by the side of the road?" Her tone is playful.

"Aye, Miss. I did so previous, in the forest behind North Burton many months back." The smile drops from her face. Richie does not like to boast. "I fought one of them and clobbered him. Miss Charlotte Pennyman believes I saved her and her father's life, and so, the magistrate from Beverley has seen fit to make me a constable of the peace." Elizabeth looks at this young man differently, he's no longer cute, more savage and unwashed. She glances nervously at Lieutenant Pike who does not seem impressed.

"Perhaps you'll be able to afford something appropriate to wear?" says Lieutenant Pike. Richie should listen to Nana, you don't pass the time of day with these people, but he cannot help himself, it's that temper again.

"I do hope I'm around to help, Sir, if there are any dangerous gentlemen in your way, I'd warrant you can neither shoot nor fight."

"I don't brawl in alehouses, Richie Jackson of North Burton, but I can give a man a hiding if he touches a nerve." The air is turning sour. There's not a chance that Richie will lift a finger against this man, it would cost him his job and the house they live in. He should really keep his mouth shut.

"Would you like me to accompany you back to Beverley, Sir, to make sure there's no danger? There may be another lad sat on a hill with his dog." This is not the right kind of thing to say to Lieutenant Pike. He is not as much entitled as other such wealthy men of Beverley, and the position he occupies was bought at least in some part by merit, although Richie does not know this.

"I believe the horses are tired, father," says Elizabeth.

"Quite. It is a pity you can't come along to watch over us, Richie Jackson, you could wash down the horses as well." Just let him have the last word. Richie is about to reply when Elizabeth cuts in.

"Thank you for your concern, Sir," she says to Richie. It's designed to calm the air and for them to move on. Richie understands this and tips his hat.

"I wish you a safe journey, Sir and Miss." Richie steps off the road so that he is not in their way.

"A word of advice," says Lieutenant Pike. "Watch that tongue of yours."

"I'm sorry, Sir, my ears are not so good. What was that?" Lieutenant Pike digs his heels into his horse, and it trots on, Elizabeth follows behind. Richie watches them go and when they are ten yards away, Elizabeth turns in her saddle and gives Richie a big, beaming smile. He smiles and waves back.

Richie grins. She's made his day, again.

CHAPTER FOUR

It's early summer evening. The bell from St. Michael's rings for the sixth time as Richie and Bess come out of Elier's field and round the corner towards the church. Somewhere inside will be Adam Gamble, yanking on the long rope attached to the bell in the tall tower, so that it swings from side to side and the big clanger hits the metal. It's how everyone in the village knows what time it is.

Richie passes the Pennyman House with its big, iron gates open in front of a long drive. It's a red bricked building with an imposing black front door, big windows with rectangle glass panes and pots with pruned bay trees that stand guard outside. Nothing like where Richie lays his head. He wears his general wide smile as he passes. Somewhere in his mind's eye is the tall ginger lass he saw half an hour earlier, her smile makes his head lightly spin. The musket is in one of his big hands and there's a noise from the driveway, a voice calling to him:

"Richie." It's Mr Farthing. "Miss Charlotte has asked you to visit." The man wears his best Sunday suit but without a necktie. You're not allowed to work on the lord's day, although he will have attended to the horses, fed them and made sure all was well.

"I'm on my way back to check on my Nana, Mr Farthing and I'll be up to the house after that."

"Not so, Richie. Miss Charlotte needs to see you sooner than later." The tall lad cannot refuse an order from someone who has more authority such as Mr Farthing. He walks over to the older man who is standing next to the wheels of the carriage, the one that was robbed a few weeks previous. "She's in the library in the house," he adds. Richie winces in the haze of the early summer evening, he's never been in the great house past the kitchen and, apart from the other morning, he had only been in there to thieve food.

"I'm to go into the house?" asks Richie.

"Aye, you'll go to the kitchen and Mrs Heather will take you in." Mrs Heather is the big cook with enormous breasts and a red face who wears a permanent scowl. Nana says she used to work up at the Pipe and Glass pub, but was caught with her apron pockets full, so they sacked her. In truth, a house like the Pennyman's should have a great deal more in the way of servants but there aren't that many folk to work the land out here, better jobs are to be had in the tanneries of Beverley or even on the coal boats that sail out of Kingston Upon Hull.

Richie walks round to the back of the house and to the kitchen, he bangs on the door and Mrs Heather opens up with her red face under a white frilly skull cap.

"You've taken your bloody time," she's usually foul mouthed is Mrs Heather. Richie will not give any account of himself to this lady. He walks into the kitchen. "And what's that sodding blunderbuss you've got in your hands?" Mrs Heather is like a weak version of Nana, her words don't have any real barbs and besides, Richie has weathered that kind of talk all his life, so he doesn't bother to answer.

"I've been told that Miss Charlotte wants to see me."

"You're not bringing that gun into the house," says Mrs Heather. "And that dog's to stay outside." Bess is too intelligent to attempt to follow Richie into the kitchen. She looks up at him with her big, dark and mournful eyes. He's not afraid to leave her anywhere in North Burton.

"I'm to go to her in the library, Mr Farthing said."

"Not with that musket, Richie Jackson." He's going to take it anyway.

"She'll be cross if she doesn't see me." Miss Charlotte enjoys being angry with Mrs Heather for the smallest reason. The fat cook beckons Richie through the kitchen and into a dark corridor. This is as far as he's ever been into the great house and his boots feel foreign on the polished wooden floorboard. He follows Mrs Heather across the hall, over a bright blue rug with the Yorkshire rose embroidered in the centre and goes down past three closed wooden doors to the room at the end. Mrs Heather pauses in the darkness of the corridor and raps on the oak with her red and swollen knuckles. Her eyebrows are up waiting for the signal to come in. It shouldn't be Mrs Heather doing this job, there should be a butler or a man servant, someone with a bit more gravitas than a burly cook. A high voice comes from inside.

"Come," and Mrs Heather turns the handle for Richie to step inside. Sitting in front of a large desk against the wall, is Miss Charlotte. She wears a ruffled white dress that covers her shoulders and is tied up tight at the front over her corset. Her thin face sags and there's a frown carved in her prematurely wrinkled face. Her once beautiful dark hair is scraped back into a bun on top of her head.

"Richie," she says, and in this word there is just the faintest trace of warmth. Mrs Heather closes the door and leaves the two of them alone. "Did the magistrate speak to you, Richie?"

"Aye, he did Miss."

"I have some papers for you to make your mark upon here."

"I'm not good at writing my name, Miss," says Richie. She raises her eyebrow. He has yet to learn the art of not telling the truth. She pretends she doesn't hear.

"This is the musket you were given by Porter?" Richie holds it up in his hand, nervous as to what he has. Miss Charlotte narrows her eyes at it and swallows. "Doesn't it have a strap?" she asks. Richie shakes his head. "Did you get ammunition also?"

"Aye." There's a moment of silence between these two. They are worlds apart of course, but linked, curiously. It's clear as a summer Wolds day that Richie does not really know how to carry a gun. "Miss Charlotte, do you think it's the right decision to make me the constable of the peace, at my age?"

It is Richie saying the obvious that many would be afraid to say. She looks down at the paper that has been prepared for Richie to sign.

"I don't know, Richie Jackson," she answers. "You have no experience, you're too young, have no status by birth, you're poor, uneducated, tatty around the edges… and yet, you have qualities that are not regular to men in general." Richie looks around the large study, the hundreds of leather books in the cases along the walls, the green studded armchairs, and the plush rug in front of the dark fireplace. He has as little right to be here as his dog, Bess, and he feels as out of place as she would were she standing in his stead.

"Am I to be made a fool of, Miss Charlotte?" he asks. "I went out of my way to help you and your father, that night."

"I'll speak candidly, Richie, if I may." She examines his smooth face with a soft youthful bum fluff moustache, and his thick brown hair.

"Do you mean you'll tell the truth?"

"Yes," she replies. "My father has not been up to running this estate for a good few years and I have taken it upon myself to make decisions about the upkeep of it. I have also made some errors of judgement, especially in terms of money. Now, I or we, my father and I, find ourselves in debt somewhat to men who we would rather not be in debt to."

"How does this concern me, Miss?"

"We have few in our employ who we can trust, Richie. You are both intelligent and brave, qualities that are not usual in men of your stature, and if I am to be honest, not to be found in men or women of any stature in our present age. If you act as the constable, Richie, I know that we can trust you." Richie has begun a light sweat on his back, the air in the study is stuffy and the sunlight streaming in through the tiny windowpanes makes the summer particles dance.

"I've cheated at dominoes, and cards, Miss Charlotte, more than a few times as well," Richie senses that he must go further than he did with the magistrate, in order for her to question his truthfulness. "I have trapped and hunted rabbits and even deer from the Pennyman Estate, I've pinched buns from the kitchen behind us, and I once stole a pair of your knickers from the washing line and sold them to a lad I know on Lairgate, Beverley town." Miss Charlotte's face is impassive.

"Anything else?" she asks.

"I've been drunk a plenty, I've fallen asleep in church, I don't say my prayers, I'm not allowed in any pub in Walkington for fighting. I'm not the right lad to be the constable of the peace, Miss Charlotte." He wishes he were a better speaker, Richie's mouth has gone dry and his throat feels tight. Miss Charlotte considers him with her hands on the paper he must sign before his position can be legal.

"You could have let us die that night, Richie," she whispers. "Who else in this estate would do that?"

"Peter Dawson, the coachman did, he died for you that poor sod."

"He was up to his neck in it, Richie. Who do you think told the highwaymen where we would be? Who else would stick up for my father and I? The folk who work the fields? The sexton at the church? Philipson the landlord down at the pub? These people hate us, Richie. They hate me the most because it's me who makes the important decisions." Richie had never considered that the Pennymans would know they were hated. He thought they were too stupid to understand that. "We know that working folk hunt rabbits and steal bread, that they sometimes get into the cellar and pinch bottles of what they think is the finest spirit. We know this, and just like you think we are too foolish to realise, we pretend we are. All the best liquor is under lock and key upstairs." Richie is at once scared of Miss Charlotte. She seems to see the whole of the world as it is and from all viewpoints at once, almost like a less intelligent version of Nana. Miss Charlotte removes her hands from the paper and indicates to a quill in a pot.

"You'll get a shilling every quarter, Richie and will be relieved of some of your work duties, but not all. You can stay in the cottage with your Nana. Keep your eye on the pub across the road, look out for anyone going in and out that you don't know. Talk to the folk around here, keep your eye out at night when you go walking to Dalton Park Estate. You'll have to turn a blind eye to some things, however, like the sexton Adam Gamble and his card games for money, and where Philipson gets some of his ale, and how barrels go missing from the deliveries to the larder here sometimes. These things happen, it's the bigger irregularities that concern me." Richie swallows again. His hand grips the stock of the musket with sweaty palms. He hasn't yet had chance to inform Nana about the position. It has happened too quickly.

"Think about what you could do with a shilling a quarter, Richie lad," she says. He could buy everyone a drink in the Bay Horse, he could afford a new coat for Nana and new stockings for her too, he could get himself a fine and dandy hat.

"Does your father know that I'm to be the constable?" he asks.

"He's not as quick as he used to be, Richie, but he's entrusted North Burton House to me and its welfare, he'll be happy someone who was born on the estate is to become someone who looks after it. In the last few months, he has rather shriveled up, he barely leaves the house." Richie stares down into her blue eyes. He sees the slight curl from the side of her lip, and her finger noiselessly tapping on the dark stained and polished oak table. You should never stop for a chat with a Pennyman, says Nana, nor share a drink with them neither. Richie has not heard Miss Charlotte talk in such a way for a long time, there is a knot in his stomach, the back of his left leg itches and he has the urge to check behind him as if there may be someone approaching. Danger is near. Miss Charlotte stands up and her long dress creaks against the corset that is bound around her body and chest, but she is nimble despite it. She pushes in her chair and walks to the far end of the room where there is a long table in front of the window. She picks up a clear glass decanter and removes the stopper.

"It's customary for us Pennyman's to have a glass of wine at this time on a Sunday. Would you join me for a drink, Richie, to seal the appointment?" Richie's face wears signs of worry. He'll heed the solid advice he's been given.

"I cannot, Miss Charlotte, I ought to get back to my old Nana. It's been this afternoon since I last saw her." Miss Charlotte pours herself a glass of the deep red liquid with a steady hand.

"You know that cottage is Pennyman property, don't you Richie?" Her voice has lost any quality of warmth that it may have had earlier. "It would be a terrible shame for a woman like Nana to be thrown out into the street. She'd end up in the poorhouse, no doubt. Have you heard of the one in Beverley?" Richie knows there's a rundown workhouse near the Minster and has seen the wretches that live there.

"A man like you could find work, Richie, but your Nana. Well... what would become of her if she had nowhere to live?" Miss Charlotte turns and puts the glass to her lips to take a sip keeping her eyes on the tall lad standing in front of the door. Richie has heard stories about this woman, how she was a friend to all, once upon a time. He was there at her wedding in St Michael's opposite to the handsome lawyer, with her white dress and beaming smile and her long sleek black hair and high cheekbones, she was like an angel. Time and events have withered her, the full lips have become thin, the wide and caring blue eyes have narrowed, her disposition has become cruel.

"I am a busy lady, Richie. You came here to make your mark on the paper – there it is. See, there's your name written in a steady hand." Richie leans over to look at the document and reads his name as clear as day: Richard Jackson of North

Burton. His long hand goes out to the quill and he takes hold of it with his finger and thumb, then taps off the ink just like the Pearlman showed him all those years ago. Under the words, he signs his name in the way he was shown, though he has never been to a day of school in his life. Without a single drop spilt, he places the quill back in the ink pot and looks up. Miss Charlotte has not taken her eyes off him.

"There is more to you than meets the eye," she says.

"Yes, Miss Charlotte," he answers, but not in arrogance.

"May I offer to tell you a little of your future, Richie?"

"Yes, please, Miss."

"You won't always be a lad who works in the fields. You might be a gentleman one day. Now, close the door on your way out," she says. Richie stares at her with open and fearful eyes for a moment before he turns and finds the handle to the oak door. He steps through and has come over a light sweat as he closes it behind him. What will he do as a gentleman? He makes his way to the kitchen and Mrs Heather is pulling the guts out of a plucked chicken on the big table, she's red faced and grotesque.

"You look like you've seen a ghost," she snaps. Without thinking, Richie asks the old woman a stupid question:

"They won't make me a gentleman will they, Mrs Heather?"

"Ha," she scoffs, "you can't polish shite, Richie Jackson, your Nana will tell you that!"

It's eight when Richie finally leaves the livery yard. After a chat with Mr Farthing about his new musket, the man took it upon himself to fashion Richie a strap from an old horse rein. He's tied it around the stock and halfway down the barrel, it's a job that Richie could have easily done himself, but Mr Farthing has a newfound respect for the lad. Now he has heard Richie signed the paper and is the new constable of the peace, his social position has been elevated. Mr Farthing likes Richie.

The sun still has an hour or so in the sky and Richie heads down the hill with the musket on his back and the satchel full of bullets and powder at his side. He passes the pond and the water pump and the little blacksmith that is all shut up at this time and before he knows it, he is standing looking at the sign for the Bay Horse pub swinging above him in the light summer breeze. His cottage is but a few yards away across the street of dry mud.

Richie should see Nana and tell her all that has happened, out of respect if nothing else, but, the alehouse has a pull to him – not for the beer, but for the voices from within, and the warmth of comradery, the clack of dominoes on the worn tables and someone starting with a fiddle for a song, friends he has known all his life and the warmth of belonging. He taps his satchel. Black powder and the finest bullets from Porter's of Beverley will be enough to buy something, he'll have one and take a bottle back across the road for Nana and the old woman will be happy to see him. What can it hurt? There's more also, Richie is now a constable of the peace, why shouldn't he have a drink at the end of a long day? Perhaps someone will even see fit to buy him one.

As Richie goes round to the back entrance of the pub and opposite the little stable that Philipson keeps, he feels a pang of remorse. There is his Nana, all alone in the tiny cottage with her garden out back that she tends too, her knackered hips and her rattling chest as she coughs. It is not right to come here and sup while she is there. It's not the right thing to do at all, and Richie is one who does the right thing, whatever that may be. He pauses at the backdoor to the pub, and looks down at Bess next to him, her wide and dark eyes are mournful.

"I know," he whispers, "I'll have to go home." He takes a deep breath and his shoulders drop, then, there's the sound of the fiddle starting up inside the pub and the clap of hands. It's Nana's favourite song, the one about the bear, and he can hear voices he knows join in with the first verse. It will be a good night Richie is to miss. He turns and there, from inside he hears a voice more familiar than the rest, a kind of rasping.

It's Nana.

Richie flings open the ale house back door and walks in with purpose. The fiddle stops. Heads turn. There's Nana, sat in a chair against the bar with a big wooden cup of something in her red fist and a dumb look across her face. Her cheeks are bright, and her hair is messed up with sweat and her big flabby boobs rest on her stomach covered by her thin shirt. The pub is in mid revelry. She beams when she sees Richie and shows the gap in her mouth where her two front teeth should be.

"Richie lad!" she exclaims.

It is about eleven when Nana finally passes out in her chair, her arms hang to the floor, and her fat body is peaceful with her mouth open and lightly snoring. Richie and Philipson have thought about putting her in a barrow to take her across the street but it would be too much trouble and she is too heavy. The old woman sleeps in a chair most nights anyway and it's summer, if they throw some old sacks on her she will be okay till the morning. Sunday night is not meant to be a night for drinking in such a way, but Nana promised everyone that, now her Richie was the constable of the peace and earns a shilling a quarter, the drinks were on him. Philipson had little choice but to give out the ale and take the payment later, this will be Richie's problem, nobody drank more than Nana anyway. They both stand over the old woman looking down at her with her nostrils flared as she snores up into the late summer night. Richie glances at Philipson next to him, and the landlord's smooth face looks tired. Nana is a bit of a handful in drink and now the Bay Horse is quiet, the few last customers have drifted off home and the light from the lamp flickers from the corner.

Richie takes the wooden cup from Nana's hands and sits himself down on a rickety stool at the bar. There's a bit of beer left in the bottom, he glances to the corner and there is the musket that Porter gave him leaning against the wall. Bess has curled herself up in the corner also, away from all the noise. Philipson appears at the bar in front of Richie.

"That's your last one, I'm afraid," he says. Philipson is calm. He just wants to get some sleep. "Will your Nana be alright there for the night?" he asks. Richie nods.

"She could sleep through a stampede of horses when she's got enough drink in her." Philipson agrees.

"It'll be ten pence for the beer, Richie," he says with apology.

"You'll have to wait, landlord, for I don't have it yet but when I'm paid, you shall have your money." There has been no time for serious talk during the evening, but now Philipson's lips are pale and straight.

"If you live to get paid," he says. Richie glances into his eyes. He expected this sort of talk from Nana, not from Philipson the landlord. The man is not rude with his advice, more world weary.

"What makes you think I won't?"

"There are some bad folk on the road, Richie. Men back from war with gun madness, men who are so poor as to do any task and then there's men that like the evil they can do. You're a brave lad, but it wouldn't surprise me if Miss Pennyman has put you in the firing line." Philipson is from Driffield and he may look like he has got nothing better to worry about than how clean his tables are, but this is not the case. Richie finishes the glug of beer in the wooden cup and sets it down on the bar with his long fingers.

"How would you know, Philipson?" Mary appears from the backroom and begins to collect cups from the tables and stack them on a tray. She is small, stocky and has a smooth face under a headscarf that covers her hair. She moves to the front of the pub and out of earshot.

"Mary and I have had our fair share of troubles, Richie. I have a feeling about such things. I've heard whispers about strange people visiting the Pennyman House in the dead of night, Peter Dawson getting shot, I thought things like that didn't happen around here – that's why we came."

"Things like that don't happen around here, Philipson," says Richie, the lad is tired. Nana sleeps in her chair, her mouth has lolled open, and she has begun to snore loudly. Philipson looks down on the old woman, at her huge swollen body and her head back snoring through wide nostrils. He sighs.

"Just come and get her in the morning." Richie fits his floppy hat to his head and tips it at the landlord. He walks to the corner, picks up his musket and makes a double click with his tongue to wake Bess.

"Will you help us, if things get bad?" asks Philipson. Richie frowns.

"What do you mean?"

"I mean, people like Mary and me, we're not the same as everyone. People talk. Folks talk about where we've come from and why we came here." Richie considers this. He's not a gossip but he's heard things about the landlord and his feeble-minded sister. He has heard also how Philipson was hounded out of Driffield because of the whispers that gathered about him. Richie takes people at face value.

"You've looked after me and my Nana, Philipson. You know I'll do the same for you, if I can, but I won't need to. Folk around here work together, and you're treated as you treat people." Philipson shakes his head and smiles. This is the kind of village attitude he likes in the lad, maybe he is in the right place after all.

"You sleep well tonight, Richie."

"You too, Philipson."

CHAPTER FIVE

Richie pumps the handle of the well and fills the bucket half-way. It's early evening but there is still heat in the sun. He squats, and scoops water on the back of his head, it has been a powerful hot day. Bess sits in the shade of the hedge with her tongue out and panting. He smiles at her. It was a job to get Nana back from the pub this morning, she was all swear words and noise. After Richie had helped her to the latrine, Philipson gave her a half pint of his bitter beer and it lifted her mood. She struggled home and Richie put her to sleep in her chair.

It's been a hard day of graft. Jonny Low has already cleared off home to his place behind the pub. He and Richie have been at work cutting the hay. It's murder on your hands. Richie's palms sting from handling the curved scythe and his legs ache. The two of them will turn the grass and dry it in the summer sun over the next few days, it's a tough job, but not tough on your brain. Jonny is a stout lad with a wide grin and as strong a back as there is, he can drink a bit as well. Bess has spent most of the day under a tree and out of the heat, but Richie and Jonny have felt the full bore of the sun all afternoon. The tall lad puts his hat on and stands up wearing his big smile, like he always does.

Horses' hooves sound on the gravel and a carriage pulls past the iron gates at the end of the Pennyman drive, atop is a coachman with smart white socks, a long whip, a tricorn hat on his head and a smooth clean face. His employers must have a mild amount of wealth, possibly the passengers he carries. The driver guides the two horses up to the front of the house and pulls them up, then clambers below, putting a box down on the gravel so whoever comes out won't have too far to step down.

Richie moves round the corner so he can see who gets out and Bess follows, he wonders who would visit at this time when there's not so much light to get anywhere else. The driver opens the door and a tall lady in a large white dress steps out onto the gravel, she has ginger hair in a bun and a light shawl around her bare shoulders – it's the same lady he saw on the road to Beverley the day before, Elizabeth Pike. Richie swallows in mild panic. His heart flutters. Outside the front door is Miss Charlotte, wearing a green day dress. Her stern face breaks into a smile when she sees Elizabeth and they greet but don't actually touch, the difference in their size is clear with Miss Charlotte a good foot shorter. Richie moves back around the side of the house so Miss Charlotte does not see him and considers where he can go to avoid being spotted. He hears their footsteps coming around the corner and suddenly, he is aware of how he is dressed, with his mucky shirt and breeches and rolled up trousers. He removes his hat as the two women walk around the side of the great house and puts it to his chest as he has seen gentlemen of Beverley do when they meet ladies. He does not know what to say and so he smiles.

"Well met, Richie," says Miss Charlotte. She looks a little uncomfortable that he is here and glances to her guest. "Richie is one of our working lads at the farm," she explains. Elizabeth nods.

"I met him yesterday on the Beverley Road as I was out on a ride with my father. Richie Jackson, is it?" Elizabeth does not have the condescending tone others of her status may have for Richie. She has smooth pale skin and a level, intelligent look in her hazel eyes. "He told me he was the constable of the peace here and saved your life from highwaymen." She is playful with her story.

"Richie, this is Elizabeth Pike of the Reformation of Manners Society. She's here to give us some advice on ending the evil of drink and most especially gin." Miss Charlotte turns to her guest. There is no irony to her. "Richie, did indeed save my life and we have appointed him to the position of constable, however, he has yet to fully grasp the finer details of the role and how he must dress to function in such a position." This is meant as a dig and the smile drops from Richie's face.

"I've heard about this lad," says Elizabeth as she looks Richie up and down. "I think it's a noble thing, Miss Charlotte, that you're not afraid of promoting someone of character above their station because of their ability. Just because someone is born poor does not mean they are not worthy of becoming better. My father is a military man, and he swears by the bravery of the working folk of Yorkshire, he says they are our salvation." Elizabeth speaks with conviction. She's tall and beautiful. Richie is transfixed. "Does your dog follow you everywhere, Richie Jackson?" she asks.

"Aye, Miss, she's a powerful friend." Elizabeth smiles down at Bess and the dog's tongue hangs out of her mouth.

"I have preparations to make in the study, Richie, why don't you show Elizabeth around the livery yard and farm?" Richie blinks back at Miss Charlotte and smiles to cover his nerves. It is not a job he wants to do. Richie is happy to cut hay all day till his hands bleed, or to mend hedges, to muck out cows or walk behind the great horse Patrick with a metal plough, he will carry water up to the house, sheer sheep till his shoulders burn, dig trenches with a wooden spade – anything, any job he will happily do, but not this.

"I'm not dressed to speak to a lady, Miss Charlotte," he says.

"Am I not a lady, Richie?" she answers.

"Aye," he backtracks.

"Elizabeth here has done much with worse dressed folk than you, Richie, she frees poor souls of the poison of drink from Beverley to York." Elizabeth nods as if this is the truth. "You'll be fine to show her around, speak as clear as you can and keep your shoulders back. You're a young lad yet, but you need to learn how to speak to your betters. If that is satisfactory with you, Elizabeth?"

"Of course, I'd be happy to follow Richie and Bess here."

"Very well then, Richie, bring her to the back door and the cook, Mrs Heather will show her through to me when you're done." Miss Charlotte nods, steps backwards as she turns to the house and leaves them alone. The sun is still hot in the sky and the birds in the hedgerows natter, insects hum overhead and the sharp sunlight makes Elizabeth squint. Richie's mouth is dry again and his legs feel weak. It's as if he is about to have a boxing match.

"Do you not have your musket today?" asks Elizabeth.

"I've left it with my Nana, Miss. It wouldn't do to take it out into the fields."

"Quite." They stand in silence these two, Richie looking down on the lady in front of him and she looking back. In his dreams he could not have imagined a situation like this happening, he does not know what to do or say, and would rather the world ate him up whole so he did not have to face her.

"You are to show me around, Richie Jackson," she says. He nods and turns towards the livery yard behind him, she steps up beside, and they begin to walk. She is four inches shorter than he, but tall for a lass, and she walks as quick as he does, on sure feet, he looks down at her boots peeping out from under her long dress and they are sturdy and a little worn, like she walks a good deal. At the gate to the yard, Richie stops.

"This is the livery, Miss," he says.

"Are we not going inside?"

"You can see all of it from out here, Miss. I think there are twenty or so, geldings, a stallion that's a right bugger and a few riding nags."

"You're not a horseman then, Richie?"

"I confess I'm not fond of them, Miss," he answers. It would be rude to use her name.

"A country lad who doesn't love his horses, how so?"

"I've never ridden to be fair, these horses are for Miss

Charlotte and the like. We use the big shire horse Patrick for ploughing but otherwise, my sort isn't to go into the yard."

"I thought you were the constable of the peace?"

"I'm new."

"You don't ride at all then, Richie Jackson?" There's a way she says his whole name that makes him seem like a child.

"I'm not sure they're meant to be ridden, Miss. I mean we need the bigger shires to pull carts and such, but running up and down the country on a poor beast's back, for your own amusement, doesn't seem fair." This is what he's heard Nana say before, but he thinks it's true as well.

"We have power over all the animals, do we not? Isn't that how God intended it?" She has the manner of a school mistress leading you into a trap, not that Richie has had even one day in school.

"I don't know much about God, but I treat my animals like I treat folk, the same as I'd want them to treat me." Bess stands at his legs and her tongue is still out, she would rather be in the shade, but she needs to be as near to Richie as she can. Elizabeth looks down at the animal.

"If you don't know much about God, Richie Jackson, then you ought to learn. He's put you in charge of the beasts and likewise he's put better folk in charge of you, with him at the top." Richie considers this woman, with her high cheek bones and lightly freckled skin under her ginger hair in a bun, he can't work her out, the words seem more like something she has learned by heart rather than a message of conviction. Richie is a village lad and does not know when he is meant to just agree.

"I don't believe that, Miss." Richie wants to say that Mr Pennyman can't even wipe his own arse, but he's wise enough to stop short. Elizabeth looks at him and her clean expression has taken on a kind of interested frown.

"You don't think that God has power beyond measure over men, as it says so in the bible?" Richie swallows, he is striding, blind, into a conversation about which he knows nothing, with just his feelings to guide him, then, from the back end of his brain comes some idea that must have hidden itself away while he sat in church. Maybe he remembers it because he thinks it to be true.

"There is neither slave nor free, for you are all one in Christ Jesus," he quotes. The smile from Elizabeth's face drops and the pious look in her eye dims, replaced by a sharpness that seems more in keeping with her manner.

"Are you a non-conformist?" she whispers.

Richie frowns. He does not know if this is a trick or a question, or what he should say to make the situation right. He has heard of non-conformists before but always in a negative way, he would happily be one for Elizabeth Pike. He would be a nonconformist in a heartbeat.

"I heard it from a sermon, from the Rector here in St Michael's," he replies in some sort of defence. She keeps her stare, but it is one of consent and understanding rather than accusation.

"Of course," she whispers as if this is some sort of code. "I knew there was something different about you. I did not know there were more of us out in the villages, but you are well met, Richie Jackson of North Burton, who is now the constable of the peace and who does not know how to ride."

"It's not that I don't know how to ride, Miss, it's that I don't care to or have the chance." This is not true. Richie was bitten so badly on his arm as a young lad that he doesn't like to go near the animals. Jonny Low who lives behind the pub always leads the big shire horse Patrick when they're at ploughing. "They're flighty things," he continues, "errant and willful too." Elizabeth smiles back at him.

"A bit like me," she says.

"What's a non-conformist?" asks Richie. He should not pose questions like this, but Nana has always explained that if you don't know, you have to ask. Her smooth face is stern and calm with her hazel eyes level.

"We dissent from the church in our worship, Richie Jackson. The power of the organization made by men diminishes the light from God. Are you one of us also?" She is defiant. If she asked Richie to put his head in a beehive, or thrust his hand into a red-hot fire, he would do so. He nods at her question though he does not understand when he is agreeing.

Mrs Heather approaches from behind.

"Miss Charlotte will be ready for you now," calls the cook in a high, affected voice. She has left the kitchen and walked up the path. Mrs Heather tries to sound more ladylike when she addresses anyone above her station. Elizabeth smiles and bows her head slightly, her hazel eyes go back to the way they were previous, all pious and kind, Christian with the sweet tang of devotion.

"Of course, Richie Jackson here was just telling me about the livery yard."

"Well, Miss Charlotte will receive you now in the study if you'd like to follow me."

Richie watches the two women walk away from him towards the house and the kitchen in the sunshine, when they get there, Mrs Heather holds open the wooden door and Elizabeth manages to turn away from her and look back at Richie. From fifty yards away, she gives the slightest wink and then disappears inside.

Richie isn't sure if his blood runs cold or if his heart skips. He thinks about her as he walks back down the hill toward the cottages in the village with Bess padding next to him. He thinks about her smooth neckline, her high cheek bones and those hazel eyes looking up at him. His stomach churns. If she is a nonconformist, then Richie might have to be as well. Not in all his seventeen years has he ever seen anything so amazing as she.

Nana is in a bit of a mood. She's made a tiny fire and has a pot over it, but the water isn't getting hot. She sits in her chair and pokes at the carrots and swede chunks she's got swimming in the dark water. Richie closes the door behind, and she doesn't look up.

"You've taken your time," she snaps. She does not want to see his face, if she does, she will not be able to be as mean to him as she wants to be.

"I've been cutting hay, Nana. What have you got in the pot?"

"It's you should be fetching food," she grumbles, "you and that bloody skinny dog there." Richie sits down on the bench in front of the fire. It seems dark and cold in the cottage when it's so bright and warm outside. Nana will have a hangover but she will not mention it. She continues prodding at the vegetables in the pot below her, and Richie pops another piece of wood on the fire. It takes just a few fluid movements for Richie, but it would take Nana perhaps two minutes of struggle with her hips and joints all stiff.

"I see you left that blunderbuss here," she says nodding at the gun that stands with its stock against the floor and the muzzle resting on the wall. It's not a blunderbuss. That kind of gun is much bigger.

"It's a musket, Nana," he answers.

"It's a dead man's gun."

Nana continues on at the water with her stick although it will neither make the fire burn quicker or the water boil faster. Bess is nervous by the old woman's voice and makes her way to Richie, she sits inside his open knees and his hand rests on her thin head.

"What do you mean by that?"

"You know what I mean." She does not dare look at him. "Why couldn't you have asked me before you accepted being the constable of the peace? Why couldn't you have told me? I would have told you straight."

"You didn't seem too bothered in the ale house last night,

it'll cost me, all that beer."

"Aye, well, it was already on everyone's breath that you'd said yes and been off to Beverley to collect that monstrous gun. What else could I do but make the best of a bad situation? I've told you, the Pennymans aren't to be trusted, Richie, you might as well be in league with the devil himself."

"It'll be fine Nana, a shilling a quarter I'm to be paid."

"A shilling a quarter," she scoffs. "You know why they put you in that position, Richie, don't you, you bloody fool? You know why they want you with a gun in your hand, why any of them dandy sweet-smelling bastards want a young lad with a gun in his hand? Do you?" Nana is really driving this one home, she has raised her voice. Bess has her ears down in terror and moves her front feet in worry. Richie does not say anything, he's learned to let the silence do the talking in such situations over the years. Nana's flabby face and her bloodshot eyes turn to him, they are wide and fierce.

"They put guns in men's hands so they can die, Richie," she whispers. There's reason and emotion in her voice. This is not a rant because she wants to make him feel guilty or worry about her, it is from the bottom of Nana's stomach, the hollow truth. "If you take up that musket and defend the Pennymans again, Richie, you'll be killed."

"I've already said I would, Nana."

"You're all I have left in the whole world," she says.

The sun is going down over the hill beyond North Burton. Richie sits on a stool at the back of the tiny cottage and looks up to the fields of golden grass stretching to the horizon. In the days to come, he and Jonny Low will cut the hay, let it dry and then bale the lot, it will be hard but good work and it's not like they haven't done it before. Richie has been doing it since he can remember, certainly he helped as soon as he could walk.

Nana is in the cottage and Richie has put a wet flannel on her head to keep her cool, after her initial and emotional rant, she has gone back to low level moaning about her aches and the heat and other bits and bobs, like Adam Gamble's card games at the Bay Horse and that the Thorne Farm is empty and there are good fields and food going to waste.

Richie has turned his attention to the musket that he took from foul faced Porter the day before, unlike most village lads, Richie has some knowledge of guns. That man who lived here when he was a boy had a few of them, there was the pistol that Richie has yet, and the big, heavy musket that he said had belonged to his associate Carlos. It was much heavier and cruder than the land pattern musket Richie examines in his long fingers, but the principle is the same. Ram a lead ball down the muzzle, pack it with black powder using the ramrod, aim it and light it with a spark from a flint. Richie has cleaned the stock and oiled the mechanism, rubbed down the pan for the black powder and adjusted the sights. He loads the gun, just like the man who called himself the Pearlman showed him all those years ago. He takes a gunpowder packet from his satchel, rips it open and taps a little of the powder into the muzzle, then adds a ball and more powder and the paper, takes out the ramrod and hammers the contents down, replaces the long rod under the muzzle, then, puts it to his eyes and squeezes. There's the flash bang of the powder in the pan and the gun recoils as the ball fires off into the field behind North Burton. Richie lowers the gun from his eyes and Bess looks up at him with her sad brown eyes in fear. Through the black powder smoke from inside the cottage comes Nana's voice, sharp.

"Richie!" she bellows in anger.

CHAPTER SIX

It's dark outside the Pennyman House but there are soft lights coming from inside the windows. The air is hot and there's the smell of peat burning from the forest behind the estate. He has his gun on a strap over his right shoulder and beside him is Bess. At night, you can hardly see her at all. Richie has been asked to be there tonight, after dinner, at the request of Charlotte Pennyman. He crunches up the stone of the drive and past the great house to the door at the back, but it strikes him suddenly, that perhaps he should go in through the front door now he has a position of authority. Peter Dawson, the old constable of the peace, never entered through the back door. Richie keeps walking and the darkness of the summer night seems blacker somehow for the lamps that light the kitchen. He taps on the wooden door and Mrs Heather opens up with her steady grimace.

"What do you want?" she grunts.

"I'm to see Mr Pennyman," he says and takes off his floppy hat. Mrs Heather snorts. This information may be true and so she ought to at least find out.

"Come in," she says and Richie steps through. "Not that dog, Richie Jackson, I shan't have that dog in my kitchen." Richie goes back outside and squats down in front of his Bess.

"I won't be long, my lass, you just be as quiet as you can," he whispers. "You just wait out here and I'll be back, I promise." Mrs Heather watches him from the doorway.

"She'll not know what you're saying," she says. Richie stands and towers above the fat cook, but not in a threatening manner.

"She knows what I mean," he replies. Mrs Heather tuts and turns back into the kitchen.

"Follow me."

Richie goes after the big woman and into the kitchen where the fire is burning low now the cooking and washing of the day has been done. She goes through the kitchen door and into the same wide hall Richie entered before, this time, they do not go to the study but left and to the dining room. A servant girl scuttles past carrying plates and Mrs Heather stops at the door to put her head inside, there is an exchange of words with someone and then she ushers Richie to step in.

It's the first time a Jackson has been in the dining room of the Pennyman House. The room is not as large as he would have thought and the table just big enough to take four chairs around it. At one end is Miss Charlotte Pennyman with her hair down over her shoulders and wearing a simple white dress, at the other, Mr Pennyman himself. The old man's head is wrinkled and slightly yellow and his eyes are dim, he has a stiff jacket and black breeches with white socks and smart new buckled shoes, in truth, old Mr Pennyman looks like a corpse that has been dressed for the occasion, although he is not dead, yet. He has a knife in one hand and a fork in the other, but the food on the ornate plate is untouched. Richie does a little bow and stands up straight. Miss Charlotte does not look at him, although she knows he's there.

"Father, this is the Jackson lad, Richie," her voice is loud for him to hear and the old face glances upwards for a moment but there does not seem to be any understanding. "He's to be the new constable of the peace here in North Burton." Mr Pennyman nods in agreement as if he can't be bothered to say any more. "Do you remember, Father? We talked about this?" The old man makes a kind of huffing sound that could indicate a 'yes.' Miss Charlotte looks up to Richie.

"He does know you, Richie Jackson, he's just tired at this time of night."

"Yes, Miss Charlotte," he answers.

"I see you have the rifle with you. I'm surprised Mrs Heather let you in with it still strapped to your back. This is North Burton, Richie and in polite company we do not carry firearms, we're not on some frontier colony. You'll leave any weapons outside." Richie does one of those polite smiles instead of saying anything, the gun on his back is a smoothbore musket, not a rifle, it's less accurate but quicker to load. "What's that tucked in your belt?" she asks. Inside the waist of Richie's battered leather breaches is a pistol with a smooth Mahogany handle and a dark mechanism that he has polished and oiled. Now he has bullets and powder, Richie has restored it, he's sanded the stock, filed down the action and fired it a good few times to get the barrel into shape.

"It was my father's," says Richie. He wishes he had not said this as soon as it is out of his mouth, for the man who gave it him was not his father at all, only perhaps in duty and in manner, but certainly not by blood. He was Nana's son, John, or the Pearlman and it was he who showed Richie how to load and fire a musket quickly, how to box and wrestle and how to play cards and cheat without anyone noticing. Richie has sworn he will kill him, if he ever sees him again.

"Your father's gun?" asks Miss Charlotte, there is a wry smile to her lips, like she is repeating the punchline of a weak joke.

"I mean Nana's son, John, the one who returned back from the war when I was a boy."

"I know of him, Richie, well, but he was not your father, it was Nana that took you in after your mother, that Turpin girl, died in childbirth on the stable floor. The good lord knows who your father is, it could be anyone from here to Driffield." She pauses to watch how her words affect the young, oddly tall man standing in front of her with his wide shoulders and mousey brown hair. They do hurt him, she can see him smart without moving. John married a lass from Etton, the next village over, and within a few months, he left for the war and did not return for many years; when he did, he was a different man somehow. He stayed for perhaps seven or eight years before he took off again, and poor Meg who had waited for him once before, decided she would not wait again. It was enough time for him to teach young Richie what he knew, and for the young lad to remember it.

"He left Meg, didn't he? He left her again?"

"Yes, Miss, she went back over the hill to Etton and she's the cunning woman there yet, just like her mother was." Meg's mother was a fine healer, she could set bones and deliver babies, cure and treat cuts and burns and make fine tinctures that rich ladies of Beverley would pay handsomely for. Now Meg is as good as her mother was and the daughters of the ladies from Beverley ride out to get her ointments and advice and pay well for it too.

"I wonder if it was having a bastard in the house that made him leave, with Meg as barren as a desert and Nana drunk as often as she could be." Miss Charlotte is cruel. Her father has no idea what she is saying but it's not the kind of thing a lady would let pass her lips. "Perhaps he did not like the idea of bringing up a bastard?" The big grandfather clock against the far wall ticks as she looks up at him, she is drunk, but not deeply, the words are her own. She wonders how far she can push him as she cocks her head. Richie swallows. There's nothing that Miss Charlotte can say to him that has not already been said by someone before, even by Nana, or that has been considered by Richie himself. It's not nice to be attacked for who you are, but Miss Charlotte's tongue is in no way equal to even the little working lads at the cowshed on Etton hill. In any tavern in Beverley, Richie could get worse, even from people who don't know him.

Miss Charlotte herself was married in the church opposite the great house on a full summer day some eight years back, dressed in white and with a veil, Richie was one of the little lads who threw petals over her as she left the church. He was a Londoner, the man she wed, not a fine city lad but a landowner from the suburbs with smooth skin and good teeth, he was as handsome as Charlotte was pretty and Nana said they were a match. It did not last more than six months before they caught him with his pants down in the Pipe and Glass pub of Dalton, soused on gin and with three whores in one of the rooms. Everyone knew about it. That man left a baby inside Miss Charlotte too, a real wriggler that made her sick after he had gone and nearly killed her as she had it stillborn. Richie waited outside the house that day too, he helped Meg carry the buckets of blood red rags to a fire in the horse field, and they burned whatever had come out of her. Miss Charlotte began having wine for her pain, and she never did stop. That's why Miss Charlotte can stand in the same room as Elizabeth Pike from The Reformation of Manners Society, because the drink is for her agony, not because she is a drunk. There are different rules for those with money.

"There are men, Miss Charlotte, who run away from those they do not love, it's their way," says Richie. They both know this could mean Miss Charlotte's husband as well as John. His blue eyes are smooth and calm as he watches the words fall on her. She grins. Miss Charlotte cannot be hurt easily anymore. She likes the pain when someone gets to her, at least it makes her feel something.

"I asked Mr Farthing to send for you tonight." There is a reason for Richie standing in the dining room with Mr Pennyman drooling down his jacket and Miss Charlotte a few glasses off drooling down her dress. "Mrs Heather says she saw light last night, over by the drain in the fields behind the estate. She says she saw faerie rings. I know she's a rum woman, but not two nights' back, I saw fire there too. If there are folk staying in our wood, Richie, I'd like you to find out."

He looks a little unsure for a moment. It's thick black night outside with just a weak covering of stars above, he's heard talk of a faerie ring as well, and even though Nana says all that stuff is rubbish, it scares him all the same. Miss Charlotte sees him hesitate:

"You're not afraid of ghosts are you, Richie?" she beams.

"Not at all, Miss," answers Richie a little too quick. "My

Bess and me will look in the woods this night."

"I don't want you doing anything foolish with that gun, though, Richie. If there is anyone in there, best let them alone and tell me. You'll do that, won't you?" Richie nods. There seems to be a look of concern across her face, but he can't be sure, perhaps it's the same concern she may show to one of her expensive stallions.

"I'll not trouble anyone, Miss," he replies.

"You're a hot head, Richie. I've heard about you fighting in the pubs at Walkington, you can't act like that now, you're the constable of the peace here and you get paid a shilling a quarter not to be such a person, do you understand?" What is lost on Richie is that, as the constable of the peace, he does not have to follow any Pennyman or their orders, he upholds the law of England only and the laws of God and parliament. This is his duty.

"I'll be about it tonight, Miss Charlotte," replies Richie.

"Be careful then, Richie Jackson," she adds. He stands in the glow of the lamp light a little too long, and hears the ticking from the grandfather clock, listens to the wheezing breath of old Pennyman, smells the aroma of the wine from Miss Charlottes thin red lips.

"You're dismissed, Richie," she says.

It's a warm night, and the sights, sounds and smells out on the path through the fields behind the Pennyman House are much more familiar to Richie than those of the dining room. He hears the shrill bark of a dog fox in the distance and the undergrowth rustles beside his feet, he has been in the forest at night a thousand times. Behind him with her long face close to the back of his legs is Bess. Mrs Heather says she saw a faerie ring out here in the night, a circle of light in the darkness where she says the little people dance and drink and play. In front of a fire or in an alehouse, Richie is scared of these stories, but out here with a musket over his shoulder and the

Pearlman's pistol tucked into his belt, it seems impossible to believe. At a big oak growing the other side of the hedge, he stops, puts his foot on one of the lower branches and hauls himself up. Richie climbs a few steps more till he is some ten foot off the ground and looks down in the darkness at Bess below, it makes her nervous to have him far away and he shushes her from his position with his finger to his lips. Inside the tree, Richie stands and peers out through the foliage at the woods in the distance, he scans the horizon. If there's a fire, he might see it from here. Richie is careful and methodical, like a poacher, and after a sweep one way and then the next, there's nothing to see in the woods at all, not a faerie ring neither. He gets down from the big branch and Bess greets him with her thin tail wagging like it does. It means he'll have to go into the trees to see if there's anything there. Richie is about to say something to Bess in the darkness, but he stops himself, silence is his friend out here. Part of his ear hears something and Richie listens, frozen in time for a moment.

A cough. Muffled but not too far away.

It takes him a few seconds to gather Bess to him and huddle into the hedge below the tree in the darkness, and they wait to see if they hear the noise again. In another minute there's the cracking of a twig coming from something up ahead of them on the path, nearer than the cough. Someone approaches. If Richie goes for the musket on his back, he will make too much noise, instead, his palm goes to the handle of the pistol at his belt and his long thumb rests on the flintlock, ready to cock it. His other arm is round Bess, so that she knows not to make a sound, and as long as she is with Richie, she will not. They wait, the two of them, under the cover of the darkness of the tree trunk with just the faintest suggestion of footsteps approaching.

There's the scuff of feet and that cough, much closer, then a whisper.

"I just need a rest," it's the same gruff voice that Richie

heard months past when Miss Charlotte and Mr Pennyman were stopped up at Dalton Park. Richie's teeth grit in the darkness – he must control his temper.

"We're to be there at eleven," whispers another voice. This is Mr Woodhatch, the man Richie belted in their fight previous.

"How to I know what hour it is, there's not light to see," this is the tone of the fat Mr Rail. He sounds like he is out of breath, the men must have been moving at speed. At once, Richie's mind races, they have been told to be somewhere, again, and now that Peter Dawson is dead, it cannot be he who told them. Richie swallows as they approach, and his hand gently strokes the fur of Bess so that she will not make a noise. He could kill one of them now, he could stand, level his pistol, and pull the trigger, then fight the other but he remembers that Miss Charlotte told him not to engage anyone he found, and to report back to her.

"We'll get there when we get there," says Mr Woodhatch under his breath. The men are at such a pace that they do not notice Richie or his dog as they hide under cover of the oak. They don't expect anyone to be out at this time either. Richie keeps hold of Bess next to him and watches them pass, first, fat Mr Rail with his big clumpy boots, and then Mr Woodhatch with his long coat and the collars up next to his hooked eagle nose. Both of the men have handkerchiefs over their mouths already. Whatever they are here to do, they do not want to be known. It takes the two men a few minutes to walk away down the track towards the Pennyman house.

Richie and Bess follow.

They are so noisy, these two, noisy and rude as they trudge through the night. Just like last time Richie heard them, with their big steps and whispered curses, over dressed for the countryside as they make their way to the darkness of the Pennyman Estate. The two men stink of sweat and spirits, black powder and tobacco. Behind the wall of the livery yard, they stop and so does Richie, he lays down on his front in the stubble of the hayfield, and his brow is sweating. Bess sits also with her wide eyes looking into the darkness and her ears pricked up. One word from Richie and she will be off, out here, Bess is alive and ready, her muscles shiver in anticipation.

"Easy lass," says Richie. He can hear the two men whispering in the darkness. Richie guesses they will be here to steal the horses, they're on foot after all and, the animals will be easier to escape on and sell than anything else they could take. Despite Miss Charlotte's words, Richie will do something if he has to, he cannot stand by and let them take what is not theirs and strangely enough, it is not the honour of being the constable of the peace for North Burton that makes Richie think like this, it's just the right thing to do. The smell of the drying hay is sweet and the sounds of the countryside rise up as they listen, a horse moving somewhere behind the wall of the stable, the silence of the stars twinkling in the night sky above, the scratching sound from rats in the chicken coup at the other side of the livery.

They wait and it does not take long for the men to make their move. Richie sees the shape of Mr Rail as he creeps across from the livery yard and to the great house. In his hand is a long musket with a bayonet fastened to the front. Mr Woodhatch follows, he too carries the same type of gun. Richie's heart quickens – you do not need a weapon such as this to steal horses, there is something foul about these two and less comedic than their appearance.

They are heading round the side of the house in the darkness and to the big front door. Richie gets to his feet.

Time to run.

Time to give it legs.

Mr Rail gets to the large door first. He wastes no time, finds the handle and turns the mechanism to open up. It's unlocked, just like they were told. He keeps half quiet as he goes inside to the hall, they have a job to do there, and in a few moments when they have done it, the whole house might be awake anyway. Mr Woodhatch appears behind him and, just as was explained, a big staircase stretches up and round to the first floor. They know where they are to go, right to the top and through the second door on the left.

It's all been planned.

Inside, the top step of the stairs creaks under Mr Rail's oversized boots. These men are moving a little too quick to be quiet. In the starlight from the window to the hall, they find the second door, and again, just as planned, it is unlocked. They have been told the jewellery will be in a silver box on the dresser, and that once they get it, they should make as much noise as they can as they leave. It's been planned that way by someone they know and it will make the episode look like it was nothing to do with Miss Charlotte. Mr Rail goes in through the big door to her chambers, there's at once the smell of sweet perfume and alcohol and his muddy boots leave a print on the carpet as he looks back and forth in the darkness. Behind the screen with the oriental pattern, Miss Charlotte stands, fully dressed with a tiny pistol in her hand should the robbers get too close. She does not like the plan but there was no backing out of it, and the man who she owes has a keen sense of what is good for his business. It seems to him, that having his men rob a country house will make people of the East Riding more afraid at night, more worried in the day, less likely to want anything to change and keener to have soldiers protect them.

Mr Woodhatch steps through behind the fat man and sees the silver box on the dresser, twinkling in the light. He grins and shows his missing tooth as he steps forward to pick it up.

He stops. There's a sound from outside. Mr Rail frowns and turns his head to hear. Miss Charlotte from behind the screen takes a breath in through her nose and closes her eyes.

There's a dog barking and someone shouting.

Mr Rail tries to look at Mr Woodhatch in the darkness. They hear the barking closer now and a loud bellow coming from near the front door of the house.

It's the lad.

"Burglars, bloody burglars!" he yells as loud as he can.

It's Richie Jackson.

Richie is running through the front door of the Pennyman Estate when Mr Woodhatch fires his musket. The tall robber stands halfway up the stairs and aims at the grey of the open door below, he fires at the blur of movement. There's a blinding flash of light, the stock recoils against Mr Woodhatch's shoulder and the ball flies from the barrel. At this range, fifty yards or so, a musket is accurate and one of the balls can tear through a person's head. Richie feels the ripples in the air as it whizzes past his temple, he's moving too quickly to stop, and bellowing too hard to know what is happening. The solid figure of Mr Rail smashes into Richie, lifts him and pushes him outside in a tackle so that the tall lad falls backwards into the gravel of the driveway. If Mr Rail had ever been a soldier, he would have driven his bayonet through Richie and killed him outright, and although the fat man is not at all stupid, he has never considered the art of fighting, as a soldier has. The fat man stumbles forwards and the smoke from the gunshot is heavy in the air already. Richie scrambles to stand before the man can get to him in the darkness, unlike Mr Rail, Richie has had many aspects of battle and fighting explained to him, in detail, by someone who knew them well, and he listened. As he gets to his feet, Richie brings his long musket up, handle first into the oncoming man, and the heavy stock connects with the fat man's chin for the musket is not just a gun but a heavy bit of wood too. Mr Rail's jaw cracks. It's a lucky shot and the man staggers to the side, but he does not fall, rather, uses the momentum to continue running around the side of the house. Mr Woodhatch runs down the stairs as this happens and with a swoosh of his long over coat, he is off on clever and fast feet around the side of the Pennyman House also, slipping on the loose stone, already calculating that if Mr Rail is dead or captured it will mean that he gets to take both their share of the payment. Richie senses the movement through the door, and sees Mr Woodhatch in the dim starlight, as he makes a run for it.

"On it, lass," bellows Richie and somewhere to the side of him, Bess, the black hunting dog springs into action. Her back legs power her forward, and she is off, around the side of the house on the heels of the robber smooth and quick. It takes Bess just a few seconds to catch up, it's easy to sense where he is in the darkness, with his smell and the sound of his feet on the gravel. She rolls her head as she opens her mouth and catches the back of his calf, a nip to harry him. Mr Woodhatch calls out as the dog bites him. Richie hears where the man is too, senses where his footsteps fall and crunch on the gravel, he has only a second to shoot before Mr Woodhatch is out of range. Bess nips him again and Richie has shouldered the musket, he hears the man cry in pain from the dog's teeth, pulls the trigger and the pan flashes with light and smoke, the stock jumps as it shoots.

He can't be sure he's found his mark, but standing in the darkness, there's Bess looking up at him, wagging her big tail so the whole of her backside moves to and fro.

"Good lass," he whispers.

She has a piece of his long jacket in her jaws.

It's first light.

Miss Charlotte sits opposite Richie. They have been here before, these two. It's half past five perhaps, just after dawn. At the table in the Pennyman kitchen, Miss Charlotte's face looks black with fatigue, she has none of her white makeup on, and Richie can see spots on her cheeks and chin. Her lips are just a line across her face. She should not look so wrinkled so young, but fate has dealt her a series of blows hard for her to take, or at least, that's how she sees it. Despite the relative life of ease, she has punished herself for things that were not her fault. Because the world has done evil to her, so, she will do evil to the world. She takes a sip from the glass of clear liquid in front of her. Richie can smell that it's gin. Her silver jewellery box sits on the table in front of her, the side of it is muddy where Mr Woodhatch dropped it after Bess bit him. On the other side there is blood.

"Mr Farthing says that you shot the man running away," she says, "but it didn't stop him running." There are just the two of them, and Miss Charlotte has asked Richie to sit down in one of the wooden chairs. He feels out of place looking over the table at this young, old woman with bags under her eyes. After Richie had shot at Mr Woodhatch, the Pennyman house erupted in shouting, with the handful of servants running here and there screaming, and Miss Charlotte screaming also. Richie and Bess sat and hid in the bushes and watched as they yelled and called, until Rector Page came and lit a lamp to see what had happened, then Mr Farthing came and lit another, and Adam Gamble who lit a third, and then young Jonny Low. When he was sure they were calm, Richie stepped out and explained what had happened, and, in the flickering light from the lamps the men held up in the darkness, he saw on their faces things he'd never noticed before as he spoke. He saw fear, and respect.

Richie takes a sip on the wooden cup of warm water in front of him and Bess is at his side, her status almost as elevated as his. It's the same kind of morning as when Richie had fought with the two men previous, after they had tried to rob the coach, with a pale blue sky, waiting for the sun to shine and bring the heat. Richie has had time to think. He was meant to go out to the woods on the same path Mr Woodhatch and Mr Rail were travelling upon. There's no point in skirting around the truth.

"I was meant to be killed by them, Miss Charlotte, wasn't I? That's why you sent me out to the woods, because you knew they'd be coming." The expression on her face does not change.

"Kill or be killed, Richie, I wasn't sure. Either way was good for me." Richie still has the musket leaning on his legs and the Pearlman's pistol tucked into his belt.

Miss Charlotte is as rotten as she smells.

"You wanted them to come."

"Not I in particular, Richie but someone. I'm in debt. I'm in debt to an individual who is not at all pleasant. He was meant to rob me some months back, but you stopped his men. He told me the way they would come and the day. I just had to wait, I thought if you went out to meet them, you'd either stop them, or die." She takes another sip on her gin. Richie looks down at his dirty leather britches and his split boots. It is as Nana said. He was only given a gun so he could be shot. It was foolish to think he knew more than the old woman.

"Why couldn't you just give him the money?"

"I don't have any money to give, Richie. This house is my father's and everything in it. I told my creditor he could come and take what he wanted. He thinks somehow, that robbing this house will make people in the villages afraid. That's what he wants. He's a man of power." Richie slowly breathes in through his nose so his chest inflates. He's afraid, it's not the jittery feeling of seeing a shadowy figure in the darkness at night, or the wobbly legged worry when you are having a fist fight, this is a different kind of fear. Richie is afraid for his life and for his Nana's life too. Miss Charlotte is not just a nasty drunk, she is dangerous. Through her father, she owns Richie's house and his job. What would Richie do if she decided to chuck him out into the mud?

"Why are you in debt to him?"

"My husband was, before he left. The man I married in the church opposite burdened me with it, from his gambling debts. My creditor does not so much want to be paid off, not while he can use me."

"Why are you telling me this?" he asks.

"I don't know. Perhaps there's nobody else to tell."

"What if I tell someone, what if I tell the magistrate in Beverley, Mr Middleton?" At the mention of this name, Miss Charlotte scoffs.

"I know you won't, Richie, that wouldn't do any good anyway. You work for me and you have people who depend on you, and, you are a fine lad. There is also something else, something you perhaps did not know." Richie thinks about the musket leaning on his knee. It is not loaded, but Miss Charlotte does not know this. His left hand finds the soft fur of Bess sitting upright by the side of his chair, she looks up at him in admiration.

"You do not know me, Miss Charlotte. You do not know anyone in North Burton." She reaches for the gin and drinks it all in one go, then sets the wine glass back on the table. A glimmer has appeared in her dark eyes.

"Have you ever thought about your birth, Richie? In all these years, have you thought about where you came from?" There is hatred in Richie's eyes and he is not afraid to look at her. He knows the story, he's been told it plainly by Nana, that his mother died as she bore him on the floor of the cowshed not a few hundred yards from where he sits. "Have you thought about how that woman suffered? Alone, cold and afraid, with the stink of cow muck in her nostrils and a bump in her stomach that she had hidden from everyone on the estate. That poor, stupid, wretched Turpin woman, your mother. She died there. She died so that you might live."

Richie's face blackens.

He has thought about this.

Many times.

It has been in his dreams and in words and formless thoughts, it has made him sick with guilt and worry.

"Speak plainly," he says, and the voice he uses is not his own but something darker.

"Did you never wonder about your father, Richie?" She is mocking him. Richie's hand curls into a fist on his knee. "I'm asking you a question, young man." Miss Charlotte's lips are thin and her eyes cold. "If you search yourself, you know who the man is, Richie, if you look hard enough at who you are, you'll know."

"He could have been anyone," says Richie, as he has heard many times from those who would care to tell him. It could be anyone at all, from here to Driffield or Market Weighton or Gilberdyke or York.

"It wasn't just anyone, boy," she shakes her head as if he is stupid. "There have been lasses like your mother who have fallen into childbirth before and since. We send them to the poorhouse up in Bridlington. Why would we let one of our servants have a child in a cowshed?" Richie can feel tears in his eyes. "Have you worked it out?" she is yet mocking. "Your father was my father, Richie, and he wanted you and your mother to die there on that cowshed floor, and were it not for Nana, you would have."

This is new.

He feels sick.

"Last night, I also wanted to see what a Pennyman could do, even a bastard Pennyman like you, and by God, Richie, you gave those two highwaymen hell." There is a wry curl to her lip and a glint in her eyes as she speaks. "You broke the fat one's jaw you say and the other, why you shot him in the dark."

"Will this not make your creditor angry, then, Miss Charlotte, that he has not been paid?"

"Yes, he will be upset, as he was last time. I like it."

"My life is not a domino on a table, Miss, I'm not a piece in some game."

"Yes, you are. Have a drink with me, Richie, the bottle is

on the counter behind you, fetch it over and pour yourself a glass too. You're Pennyman after all, even if you are a bastard one." Richie looks up at her and his cheeks are red.

"I'm not a Pennyman," he whispers. "Not now and not ever."

"Think what you want, Richie, I have presented you merely with the facts. Now, grab that bottle." Richie stands and clasps the end of the musket in his hand, he considers the heavy metal of the action and the long, wooden stock resting on the floor, then looks back at Miss Charlotte, sitting with a grin, already a little drunk. He reaches for the green glass bottle, picks it up and then sets it down in front of Miss Charlotte. She pours herself a full glass, but Richie does not sit down.

"What would Nana think if she knew that you were a Pennyman, Richie? Do you think she would still be your Nana?"

CHAPTER SEVEN

Richie needs air.

Even at six in the morning it is beginning to get hot, and he makes his way out of the Pennyman kitchen to the livery yard. His stomach is a knot of worry. He has thought about his father many times in daydreams and nightmares, he could be a pirate or a robber, an army soldier or a gambler who met his mother for one night in the backroom of the Bay Horse only to leave, not knowing that he had a son. His head aches and pounds. The fight with Mr Rail is an insignificance against what he has learned from Miss Charlotte this morning, that old Pennyman may be his father. The old senior who is so decrepit he cannot wipe the drool off his own chin, and who, even in his prime was as wet and flaccid as a rag, a man with no backbone and a seemingly endlessly full purse with which to buy anything he wanted.

Richie cannot be part of that man. It is impossible. Impossible too that he could share the same blood as the wretched, drunk Miss Charlotte sipping gin in her kitchen that is bigger than Richie's whole cottage. The lad passes through the livery yard and out into the fields that he travelled through the night previous, and the warm sun peeks over the trees in front of him. He follows the track with Bess at his heels and her tongue already out and lolling, at the oak tree that he squatted under the night before, there is a pile of cloth, it is the long blue coat that Mr Woodhatch wore, he must have discarded it as he ran away. Richie picks it up and examines it, there's a rip in the bottom that Bess bit off and a number of holes. Once upon a time it may have been a fine coat, it is good quality light blue cloth with wide lapels and a big collar. It's a good find, Richie slips it on and finds that, unlike Mr Woodhatch, the sleeves are a good fit and it stretches down to his knees. In the right light, it might even look like Richie was well dressed, not in a Pennyman sort of way however, more like a gambler or a spy, or a ruffian.

More like a highwayman even.

Richie and Bess travel through the woods and fields, his musket over his shoulder, and the Pearlman's pistol tucked into his belt. Richie really should be with Jonny Low cutting hay but there is more on his mind as he trudges through the woods at the back of the Pennyman Estate. There is still a lump in Richie's throat, he is going to the one place he knows he will find sense, he is going to see the lass who acted as his mother for so long, the cunning woman out at Etton. He is going to see Meg.

At St Mary's church, Etton, Richie turns right and goes over the path through the graveyard, the sun is up and flowers grow among the stones and along the hedges with the smell of perfume and a fresh breeze. There's a cottage behind, a tiny building with a bowed roof and one window. He goes to the black door and gives two strong raps with the back of his knuckles on the old wood. There's a shout of 'aye' from within. Inside and standing at a table grinding seeds with a pestle and mortar is Meg. She has her sleeves rolled up to her elbows showing her strong forearms and her blonde hair is tied back into a ponytail. Her wise face looks up to Richie and she raises her eyebrows.

"A new coat there, Richie?" she asks.

"I found it," he answers. At once, Meg can see that Richie is troubled by something, normally he is a happy lad with a wide grin and easy-going eyes. Here is someone different with a darkness in his demeanor that is out of character. Meg will let him tell the story rather than interrogate, this is why he will be here. Richie visits most weekends and tells Meg the stories from North Burton, the ins and outs of the pub gossip; she gives him advice about how to deal with Nana, and sometimes a paste to rub on the old woman's swollen legs and ankles.

"I'll get you a drink, Richie." There's a bucket of water on the counter near the window and Meg fills a wooden cup. Richie takes a seat at the table and she brings it to him, returning to the bucket to fill a bowl for Bess. He takes a sip and sets it down. He is usually full of stories, but there's nothing but silence to the tall lad today. Meg goes back to crushing the seeds. She has not yet heard about the attempted robbery at North Burton the night previous, but she will.

"How is your Nana?" she asks.

"She complains about her legs," he answers.

"She's been complaining about those legs for twenty years. She wants to walk around once in a while." Richie does not respond, he looks out the open window at the sunshine and the blue sky through the trees. The only time Meg has seen Richie like this, was when he had a thing with a girl from Leconfield and she kissed him, and he says he fell in love. He's a big lad is Richie, but he falls hard when he gets hurt.

"Did you know my mother, Meg?" he asks.

This rears its head every so often. She'll do what she always does and tell the truth.

"Not especially, Richie. I knew her only in passing."

"Was she a good lass?"

"I believe she was."

"Tell me about her."

"She was tall like you. They called her Turpin. She was polite and pretty and quiet." All of this Richie knows.

"I heard something today," he begins, "I heard someone say that Pennyman the elder had her, and that I was his son and they let her die on the cowshed floor because he didn't want her, or me." The words are difficult for Richie. He feels guilty for being born, if he were not here, perhaps that tall and quiet girl would have survived, perhaps it was because of him that Pennyman was to let her die. Like his big clumsy feet and his long gangly arms, Richie feels out of place as if he is an error. Meg has not heard this one before, and she has listened to a good deal of talk about the bastard lad Richie from folk who like to gossip. She thinks about how to answer.

"Do you think it's true, Meg?"

It might be. Meg will not shy away from the truth. She never has. She stops grinding and looks down at the lad with his blue eyes and light moustache. He's earnest and sad.

"What if it is true?" she asks.

"I'd be half a Pennyman."

"You'd still be Richie Jackson."

"Would I?"

"You'd still be my Richie Jackson, Bess would still be your best lass, and Nana would still be your Nana."

"What would people say?"

"They call you a bastard anyway, do they not, Richie?"

"Aye."

"So, if it were true that Pennyman was your father, those lads in Walkington would still call you a bastard, would they not, and just the same you'd break one of their noses."

"Aye," he answers. He looks out of the little window again. "It makes me different, Meg, if I'm a part of that man, or if I'm a part of that woman Charlotte Pennyman. She's a cow, a horrible cow. What do they say, blood's thicker than water?"

"That's what some folk say, Richie, aye. That's why a king sits on the throne, that's why wealthy men stay wealthy, and they'll tell you that they're rich because they're better than you, or more worthy or more Godly but really, it's just because their father inherited from his father. You're no more a part of that man than Bess here is to a horse. He didn't make you; he didn't stand by you, he didn't raise you. I bloody did." Without knowing so, Meg has become emotional, and her eyes are wet but without tears. "Even if you were his son, Richie, there's nothing to him, he's as wet as a blanket and has never worked a day in his life. You're twice the man he is." Meg is not lying. These are true words for her. She picks up the pestle and slams it down on the table in anger. "You're my lad," she bellows. "Mine and Nana's lad and nobody will change that, not anyone on God's bloody earth. Who's filled your head with such shite?"

"Charlotte Pennyman told me." Meg looks at Richie and frowns as she considers this. She has heard that Richie is now the constable of the peace for North Burton, she knows he has a musket and that he fought off two highwaymen who tried to rob the Pennymans out at Dalton Park. She does not know that he fought the same men the night before.

"That woman is poison, Richie. She's poison and she wants everyone around her to feel the same pain that she does."

"She says I'm her brother."

"There's what's true, lad and what's real. You have to learn the difference. Nana and me, we're your family."

"What about John?" asks Richie, looking at her. "What about your husband, it was because of me that he ran off, wasn't it? I know it was. I wasn't his lad and you're not my mother."

Meg grits her teeth at this.

"Never speak like that to me, Richie lad." Meg is acting like a younger version of Nana. "Not ever do you dare say that to me. He had to go, that man, what he was, he was too dangerous for us, for what he could bring down on our heads, on your head too."

"What?" he asks. Nobody has explained such a thing to Richie. "You told him to go?"

"We agreed he would."

"Did he wish to?" Meg looks back into time in her mind and sees the man she rescued and the man she fell in love with. She sees his eyes as close to tears as they ever were.

"He did not, but Nana and me, we made him pack up, we made him go. It was for the best." Somehow this conversation has moved to a place Meg kept hidden, where she is not sure what to say or what is what. "Things that man had done in days gone by were beginning to catch up with him. He robbed many, killed men even. If folk from his past discovered where he was and that he had a family, why, they'd put a bullet in Nana's head and mine, and yours too. We could not have that."

Though nobody told Richie, he believed the tall man back from the wars in France ran off to the city because he did not want to stay with a bastard son. It will take Richie time to deal with this news but if Meg is telling the truth, then he may not be the reason the man went away. There are other questions now. Richie was taught well by John, he knows how to count and play cards, he knows how to shoot and load a pistol, can fight with his hands and has an understanding that God does not live in a church, these are lessons which have stayed with the lad.

"You sent him away?" he asks, "from his own house?"

"Is that so hard for you to grasp? He was a thief, Richie, a bloody burglar and a robber. He played cards for money, traded horses as far away as Driffield, he sold guns, pinched booze and he didn't know how to do a day's honest work. If he'd have stayed, you'd be the same as him. He was a danger to us in more ways than I can say, and he knew it too. That's why he went."

"Where is he?"

"I don't bloody know, last time I heard he went to Bridlington. He'll be in some alehouse somewhere, dealing cards. It's better that he's gone."

"Not for me," says Richie. The truth comes out quick and hot from his chest. He misses the man or he thinks he misses him. Meg hangs her head and she is calm. She looks down at the old, worn wood of the table she has worked upon all these years. Perhaps she knew she would have this conversation with the lad, perhaps she should have had it many years ago.

"You have to trust me, Richie. It's better that he's gone."

"For you, maybe."

"For all of us."

"Did you not love him? You married him?"

"I did love him. I loved the ground he walked on and everything he said and did. I loved his eyes and his smile and the way he talked and the way he made me laugh. I loved him with everything inside and he loved me back." She wipes her eyes with her palm. "But that didn't make him a good man, Richie, that didn't make him good or right and the love I had for him, it twisted me, it hurt me inside and turned me into something I was not. You see, that's what love does, Richie, lad. It burns out everything inside and leaves you hollow, it drives you mad with sorrow and pleasure and fear, and it will kill you if you let it. Look at Charlotte Pennyman, eight years ago she was married on a fine summer day like today and she loved him like I loved my John. He left her and she's withered up and dried out like a flower left in the sun. That's what love does to you, Richie. That's what love does to all of us." The tall lad blinks back at her.

"What about Nana and me? What about us?"

"That's a different thing, Richie, that's called duty and care, and my love for you is as solid as stone, unmovable and unbreakable for as long as time. It's not the love of a man." Richie sniffs. They have never spoken like this, the two of them. This is the East Riding of Yorkshire; nobody says they love each other. You keep your feelings to your chest, keep them wrapped up inside in your belly and never let them out to see the sun; but Richie is a brave lad.

"I love you, my Meg," he says and stands, walks a few steps around the table and they embrace. Meg puts her head into his shoulder, and he holds her there as she sobs lightly and shivers. It is perhaps a minute before she lets him go and then, she stands to go back to the pestle and mortar like nothing has happened. Richie goes back to his chair, sips his drink and Bess looks up at him with wide and confused eyes, he ruffles her hair.

"What will Nana say?"

"Say about what?"

"If I am a Pennyman?"

"She'll expect you to get what's owed, Richie, if you are his lad. She'll want him to pay up."

"She'll disown me."

"For all your height, you're as daft as a bloody brush with no bristles, lad. You're all she has." Meg always sets Richie straight, always. He watches her go back to the grinding on the table, all the emotion now swallowed back down into her tummy. There's nothing that ever happened in North Burton than Nana doesn't know. He'll need to talk to her.

"It looks daft," says Nana as Richie stands in front of her in his new but battered coat. "You look like one of them rich Beverley folk, from a distance when you can't see the rips. Take it off Richie. Have you checked the pockets?"

"They're empty." Nana does her grumbling face. It's late on in the evening. Richie walked back to North Burton and spent the day in the fields with Jonny Low, they managed to cut nearly half the back field with scythes and they talked about girls and cards and ale. Richie told Jonny Low of his two meetings with Elizabeth and explained her in as much detail as he could, even embellished them too. He added a bit more to his fight with the two robbers the night before. Richie has put thoughts of his father to the back of his mind, for now.

"Take that coat off, Richie, it's the middle of summer," says Nana. He hangs it on the hook behind the door and sits down opposite her on the long bench where he and Bess sleep sometimes. There's a knock and Richie gets up to open it. Outside in the evening is Mr Farthing, he passes a rectangular wooden box to the lad

"That's from Miss Charlotte," he says. Richie looks down at the box nervously. "It's for what you did last night." The man takes off his hat and is earnest, like he's never been before. "It's from all of us, in a way. You're a fine lad. I had my doubts about a boy being made constable of the peace, but here you are, and it's a good job you're doing." Richie looks back at him and wrinkles his nose.

"If it's that Jonny Low come to ask you to go to the alehouse," bellows Nana, "you can tell him to piss off, you're not to go tonight."

"Thank you, Mr Farthing," says Richie.

"You're welcome, lad." Richie closes the door and stands with the box in his hands. He's confused and suddenly worried, because it's from Miss Charlotte. Why would she give him anything?

"Who was it?" asks Nana, "and what have you got there?" Richie pulls the square lid off the box and reaches inside, at the top there's a package wrapped in wax paper, he hands it to Nana.

"It's seed cake," she says. "Who's sent this?"

"Miss Charlotte Pennyman," answers Richie. He pulls out a long, clear bottle and passes the box to Nana so she can look inside. He pops the cork with his fingers and smells at the liquid, it makes his face wrinkle up like a bulldog.

"What's that?"

"It's gin." Nana grabs the bottle out of his hand and looks at the contents with a raised eyebrow, then takes a double swig. Her throat bobs.

"You've earned this," she says. "Seed cake and a good wet of gin, you've paid for this with your bravery, Richie Jackson." She takes another glug. "You best get me a cup."

Richie grabs her one from the shelf next to the fire and passes it down.

"You know, you being constable of the peace might be a good thing, Richie lad, after all. That Miss Pennyman is a sound lass with judgement as befits her station." Nana will say any old shite with a bottle of something in her hands. "You mark my words, Richie, you'll do right out of this."

Richie watches the old lass take another big swig from the bottle and her mouth leaves a pop as it comes off the lip.

He's got a bad feeling about everything, about Miss Charlotte and about the robbers, about who she is in debt to and what she will do to pay it off. He's worried too about who will come to North Burton next and who it will hurt. Then there's his father, which of them is he, the Pearlman with his dandy hat and a dark pistol tucked under his cloak, or the drooling old man withered with age and money up at the Pennyman house.

He watches Nana take a big bite from the seed cake. Crumbs fall into her lap. Whatever will be, it's not the right time to ask Nana now.

CHAPTER EIGHT

Richie and Jonny Low are at work in the fields with Patrick the big cart horse, and they've been turning over the hay to let it dry in the sun. Patrick is almost blind and with a mottle grey coat and big feathers out of his hooves. He's not pretty enough for Mr Farthing or his wife to groom and so Jonny Low is giving him a brush down. They get Patrick to pull the rake behind as they lead him across the field, if they had to turn the hay by hand it might take all day. Richie likes this horse because he doesn't bite or run and you can depend on him to stop and start as you like. Jonny Low uses a brush on the animal's back and great pieces of horse hair lift into the afternoon sun and blow away into the gold of the fields around them. Richie takes a bite from an apple.

"How much do you get paid for being the constable then, Richie?" asks Jonny although he knows the answer.

"A shilling a quarter," he replies with his mouth full. Jonny tuts and shakes his head as he keeps brushing. He's not grooming the animal for the sake of beauty, but because they need Patrick to make their lives easier. They don't want his coat to get ratty or for him to pick up a tick, Jonny feels along the skin where the big rake has been attached to the horse to make sure there are no cuts or lumps. They have to keep the old nag healthy if they want him to work.

"I thought we'd take a trip up to Weighton when you get paid," says Jonny as he works. "There's pubs a plenty and they're full of lasses too, and lads who don't know how to play cards half as well as you do."

"How come it's when I get paid?" asks Richie.

"Well, we'll go together." These two have worked alongside each other for a few years and if one is rich, then so is the other. Jonny Low has the misfortune to live even closer to the pub than Richie, in a cottage in the orchard behind, and he has to pass by the great windows every day. In the summer the ale cools him down and, in the winter, it warms him through, so, there is probably not any man who has built up more debt to an innkeeper. In the Bay Horse, Philipson is too shrewd to cut off credit to a local lad, Jonny is good with a hammer and nails, and if ever the boys from Walkington turn up looking for trouble, Jonny is one of those who'll fight them on the street outside. Philipson has to look after him and, if Jonny ever comes up with a win in a card game, why, the Bay Horse is the first place he'll come for a drink. In his years as an innkeeper, Philipson knows that locals like him are best to keep close.

"Weighton is a half a day's walk," says Richie, "we'll have to come home as soon as we get there. We'll get Philipson to sell us a barrel and we'll roll it into the orchard of a Sunday afternoon, we'll get the cards out and have a chuck farthing session against the cottage wall." Jonny turns to him and grins. This is an excellent idea.

"Will you be off to Beverley at the weekend?" he asks. Richie shrugs his shoulders. In all truth, Richie does not like leaving North Burton at all. "I thought you might be off to see that Elizabeth Pike now you knock highwaymen out in your spare time." Richie may have made his friendship with the tall ginger lass seem more than it actually is.

"They're crooks, Jonny Low, in Beverley, they're all crooks and posh knobs and swindlers." Richie is boasting out into the fine summer afternoon, over the fields where nobody can hear him, where he and Jonny Low are masters of all they see. "Aye she's a fine lass is that Elizabeth, clever and well spoken, educated and with high cheekbones and smooth skin, big hazel eyes and a smile that could stop a Lincolnshire Bull at 50 paces, but she's not for me. I'd sooner have a mug of ale in one fist and a hand of cards in the other." Jonny stops brushing again and looks at Richie, his eyes and face are serious. This is a lie. Either of these two would trade bitter ale and a gaming session for a smile from Elizabeth, in a heartbeat. Richie takes the brush off Jonny Low. "I'll do the other side," he says.

"You've to watch yourself, though, Richie."

"How come?"

"If you're the constable of the peace, you'll have to attend the quarter sessions up in Beverley and, if Mr Pennyman binds anyone over, you'll have to go and fetch whoever it is to the courthouse if they won't go of their own accord."

"When did Mr Pennyman bind anyone over ever?" Jonny Low does his confused face with a frown and a smile. Nothing happens in North Burton. Not until the last few months anyway.

"Who knows what'll pass?" answers Richie. He stops brushing and his face loses all emotion. "We can't go on doing this forever."

"Doing what, cutting hay?" answers Jonny. "Someone has to."

"I mean, being lads like this, working the fields all day and playing cards and you chasing lasses. We have to grow up one day." Jonny Low takes off his hat and wipes his forehead with the back of his hand, it's still hot.

"We're still young, Richie. I'm eighteen, I'm not old enough to be married yet."

"Lads over at Etton are wet and fathers at your age, making a life for themselves."

"Is that what you think we should be doing? Or is that what you think I should be doing, now you're the constable of the peace round here. Do you think you're better than me?"

"I didn't mean it like that." Richie looks off down the golden field of cut hay and across to the still blue summer horizon with the shape of St Michael's in the mid distance. "This is our home, Jonny, we should be making more of it than cutting hay for the Pennyman horses and cows. What about cutting hay for *our* horses and cows?"

"What are you on about? We haven't got horses." Jonny's

mind has not made the same jump that Richie's has. As soon as he was promised a shilling a quarter, he thought not of the ale and brandy he could sup or the bigger card games he could play, but what he could buy, keep and build.

"When I get that brass, Jonny, I could buy four pigs and keep them out the back of our cottage. Nana and me would fatten them up, eat one and sell three, and then we'd buy more." Jonny frowns as he thinks it through. Richie continues. "We could get a cow and, maybe we could rent out a livery at Farmer Thorne's old place for a horse and trap. You and me could work for anyone that could pay us." Jonny Low shakes his head slowly.

"Who's put this into your head?" he asks.

"Nobody. I'd rather not be cutting hay when I'm an old man."

"You're thinking above yourself, Richie. Like God made the sun in the sky and the little mice hiding in the undergrowth, they all have their place, me and you do too. We work the fields, that's what my father did and his father before, that's what I'll do too. You've got different blood in you, Richie, from God knows where, but it's what you should do as well." Richie has heard this one before, that because he is a bastard, this somehow explains his wayward temper, humour and anything else that makes him different, even his height.

"I know what I am, Jonny. I'm not afraid to work these fields either, and I believe God did put things in the way he sees fit, but there's the strong that overpower the weak, by strength or by cunning. See Patrick here, he's stronger than you and I put together and if he so wanted, he could thrash and kick out, then be off into the trees and across the fields, he could be free."

"Who'd feed him though, Richie? Who'd brush his coat, who'd sort out his hooves and keep him inside from the cold." Richie rubs his chin.

"He'd look after himself, Jonny, just like we could. We

don't need a Pennyman to look after us, it's we that look after them." Jonny shakes his head at this.

"You're wrong, Richie. There's a way to the world and a natural order to it, the king at the top and the beasts at the bottom. You and me somewhere in between. The sooner you get your head around that, the happier you'll be." The sun sends thick orange light across the fields from behind the woods at the back of the estate. "We should stick to drinking and playing cards." Richie doesn't believe this, and it is not because he has different blood in him, it's just because of who he has known. He thinks back to Nana's tall son, the man who said he was his father in title only, the tall man who taught him to shuffle and play cards and use a leather sling shot, how to hit a man where it hurts and how to catch a chicken without too much effort.

"Let's get Patrick back to the stables," says Jonny. There's a weariness to his voice, he has heard Richie going on in this way before, he likes it better when the tall lad sups and then fights. "You need a drink, you do," says Jonny Low as he pulls Patrick by his reins to get him to turn.

"Aye," he replies, but this not what Richie thinks. There must be more than the bitter ale that Philipson brews.

It's just past six. They have returned Patrick to his stables and Jonny Low has gone off home to his cottage behind the pub. Richie is at the pump beside the great house. He's filled a bucket of water and is about to take it to the horse who has helped him to turn over the hay all day. He's tired. As he turns to go back to the livery, there is Miss Charlotte. She's in a black dress with a tight bodice and white make up with a wig. There is a black dot on her cheek, her eyes are swimming and crossed already and Richie feels a jolt of fear go up his legs when he sees her. He is frightened by how much he hates her.

"I wish to speak to you in the study, Richie," she's not slurring but he can see she has been drinking. His face loses its smile. Miss Charlotte is bitter poison after a fine working day.

"I'll give this to Patrick first, Miss Charlotte," he says.

"The horse can wait," she snaps.

"Not in this heat," answers Richie. She narrows her eyes, and he can see the white powder crack to give way to crow's feet wrinkles at the side of her face. This is insolence from the lad, however slight, and he knows it too. If she is going to play games, then so is he.

"Put the bucket down, now, boy," her voice is calm but the words are clear. Richie stands in front with the wooden pail in one of his big hands. He looks down on her with his light brown hair a little too long in front of his eyes, his shirt open to his chest showing the swallow scar, and his sleeves rolled up to his elbows. He does not move.

"Patrick has been out in the fields all day, Miss, he's been hard at work and needs a drink. Whatever it is you wish to talk of can wait. I'm sure you'll agree." She flares her nostrils and it's clear that he is going to do what he wants.

She watches him walk down to the livery yard carrying the wooden bucket with ease and wonders what she has created in a boy that week previous would have jumped off the roof if she had told him. She swallows. Miss Charlotte doesn't know what she's said, and which lies are true or which of the truths she's made are now lies. They all blur into one, like the summer days. The anger in her prickles and she strides forward down to the livery yard following Richie. The tall lad is not moving very fast, slower than he normally would, in fact, with purpose to his steadiness.

"Mr Jackson," she calls to him and he turns. "I'll accompany you, after all, what is more important to me than the welfare of the animals on my estate and the people who look after them?" She falls in step with him as they pass the rows of horses. Once upon a time, Miss Charlotte came to the livery yard two or three times a day to check on her favourites, to brush their coats and chat to Mr Farthing and his wife or their daughter. She was free and funny, interested in the horses and the lives of the people in the village. Richie remembers her and her smile. It seems like it was a hundred years ago. The woman who walks with her back straight next to him is cold and prematurely wrinkled. What was it Meg said? She said that love destroys everything. Although he can only look out the corner of his eye at her, he can see the thin pencil line lips on her face and the anger blazing out of her eyes. She was happy before she met that man, and when he left, the girl who pressed a penny into the palms of North Burton children of a Christmas Eve, left with him, to be replaced by a monster.

At Patrick's stall, Richie opens the half door and goes in. He sets the bucket down on the floor and the big horse sticks his nose in it straight away, the lad drops a rag into the water too then fishes it out to wipe Patrick's back with the cool liquid. Miss Charlotte stands at the half door looking in. Richie pretends that he does not notice her there, with her pale eyes glaring at him as he works on Patrick's back with the rag.

"I don't suppose it matters where I talk to you," she begins. She checks over her shoulder to make sure nobody is in earshot, then adds, in a loud whisper, "brother." Richie pretends he does not hear and drops the rag back into the water as Patrick drinks his fill. "You know now that you have gainful employ, Richie Jackson, I have been thinking about a good many things."

"Aye, Miss," he answers as he works.

"Well, as you're the constable of the peace here in North Burton, you'll have to attend the quarter sessions up at Beverley in October, right at harvest time. You might be needed for some errand or other, that would take you away from the work you have here on the farm." Every constable of the peace has other duties. Richie has not considered that he may have to carry out jobs as the representative of the king's law as Jonny Low explained earlier, and he has put thoughts of this out of his mind. Any man may come to Mr Pennyman, the Parish Justice and make an accusation of another, and if the wet old man deems it to be reasonable, Richie would have to arrest and bail him, or even take him to Beverley jail to await trial. These are things he had not considered when Mr Middleton offered him the job.

"I believe I can still do what's needed of me, Miss," he answers. He wipes Patrick's wide back and lets the water run down his coat.

"If you can't do your job, Richie, then you won't be allowed the perks that go with the position." There is cruelty in her voice. Richie does not understand what she means.

"I beg your pardon, Miss."

"Well, that cottage you and Nana have. Why, if you can't work for me properly, then you don't deserve that. I could move a family of seven in there, and they'd outwork you and your Nana a week to your year." Richie stops and looks at the woman from the darkness of the stable, the smell from Patrick is rich and earthy and the horse draws his enormous head from the water and lightly shakes droplets off his nose.

"Nana has rights to that house, as a widow."

"Well, times change, Richie. It happens that I need workers on the farm, not folk who enjoy a restful old age at my expense. You and Nana have had long enough there." Richie steps closer to the woman on the other side of the door and she smiles now she sees she's getting to him. "A fine man like you ought to be able to do well. You've got good blood in your veins, just like me. You should be able to look after yourself. The cream rises to the top, Richie. Quality will always shine through." She is mocking him.

"It would be a shame, Miss Charlotte, if those robbers were to come back to the house again, would it not?" This makes her grin more. She likes the nasty talk, she likes the push and pull, the friction of anger, especially with Richie who is not very good at it.

"I think you'll find that a Pennyman can look after herself, Richie. Like a Pennyman does." He feels one of his hands curl into a fist at his side in the darkness. "I tell you what, let's have a little wager shall we, on how resourceful a young lad with the right blood inside him can be?" There's a twinkle to her ice blue eyes. "I'll give you a fortnight to come up with the rent that I think is due on the cottage, if you don't pay, I'll have you and Nana thrown out into the street. Friday week, there's to be a visit from the Reformation of Manners Society, you met Elizabeth previous. She and her father will be staying on their way back from York at my invitation. There'll be men with them, perhaps even a few soldiers, he was at Blenheim, you know. Those people, they mean to do God's work, and while they'll help the poor on a Sunday, if they find out there's been any sort of devilry, they're happy to beat the sin from a body. I only have to tell them a half of what I know about Nana, and you'd find yourself without a home." Richie steps closer yet, his voice is just a whisper:

"Why are you doing this to me? I saved your life and your father's too."

"Perhaps we didn't want to be saved, Richie and perhaps, there is a man you are supposed to be, and you'll need a bit of fire to bring him out."

"I won't help you again," he says. His mouth is dry.

"You will," she whispers and steps back away from the door. "I'll need a guinea by Friday week, understand? A guinea, not a penny less, for the rent that you owe me, or I'll have that cottage from you and your Nana."

"A guinea?"

"Yes," she gives a little laugh. "A guinea. Sounds impossible, doesn't it?"

"Aye, Miss. It can't be done."

"I believe you, of anyone, can get that money, Richie. You know people, you play cards, you get something from here and sell it there, you borrow it, or you find it. Whichever way, you don't have to tell me how." A grin comes over her face. "Friday week, Mr Jackson, and we'll see what kind of blood runs through your veins."

He does not speak as she turns and walks away. At the gate she looks over her shoulder and gives him a nasty grin.

Richie and Bess walk out behind North Burton and over the hayfields towards Etton. It's past seven but the sun is still out and the night is warm. He needs time to think. When they get to the top of the hill looking down on the little village, he sits with his knees up to his chest. Bess sits close, like she does, and leans her thin body against him. The summer evening sky is a pale blue with clouds along the horizon. It makes him feel small.

Richie does not know what to do.

He looks down on the Etton pub below them, it's much more well to do than the Bay Horse and named the Light Dragoon after a cavalry regiment. There's a carriage with two horses that has just pulled up and, the driver dressed in green with a big hat gets down from atop and sets a box next to the carriage door. A gentleman gets out with fine white socks and then a lady in a travelling dress of lilac. They look out of place, these two rich travellers, in the world that Richie lives in, socks are never white, and lilac is only a colour for flowers. He rubs Bess behind the ears as he watches them.

Ordinarily, Richie would go to Nana or Meg or both and ask for their counsel, but there is something different about this, the deal concerns Nana and, Richie is worried that if he told the old woman, she would stand up on her fat legs, march up the hill to the Pennyman house and box Miss Charlotte around the ears, or worse. There are many paths open. Richie does not have to get the money, he and Bess could take off over these Wolds and north towards York and the rest of the world, he could forget all about North Burton, just like Nana's son John did, the man who called himself the Pearlman. Richie could never do that. He could refuse to do as she has asked and then deal with the consequences, but, he does not believe that Miss Charlotte is bluffing. It is as if she really believes that Richie is a Pennyman, and, because of his noble blood, he will somehow be able to come up with a guinea by Friday week. If Nana is turfed out of the cottage, there will be nowhere for her to go, she might struggle up to the minster at Beverley and ask for pity and alms, but she'd soon be begging and dead when the weather got too cold. Richie wipes his eyes with his thumb and forefinger in worry. He cannot let that happen. Perhaps he could shoot Miss Charlotte and for a brief second this seems like the best option, Nana will keep her cottage, Miss Charlotte Pennyman will have a face full of lead shot and Richie will be taken to the Knavesmire at York and then hanged by the neck until he is dead and his tongue lolls out of his mouth and his bowels empty down his legs. He rubs his eyes again and looks into the long face of Bess beside him.

"What am I to do, my Bess?" he asks. She blinks back at him with her kind eyes. "How am I to find a guinea, and by Friday week too?" If she could help him, she surely would. Richie knows the cards well and he could play for the money, but it would take time, and he would have to find bigger stakes than are to be had in the back room of the Bay Horse. He'd need to go out to the richer places, to the Pipe and Glass at Dalton or to Beverley, where men are wont to gamble more but it would be trouble to play for bigger sums. He'd need a large stake and a reputation to play in games where the winnings are substantial. It is a pity that Nana's lad John didn't teach him anything more useful than how to count and play brag before he cleared off into the world.

Richie looks up as he thinks about the man.

He did teach Richie a few things in the stories that he told him, the tales that the tall man did not explain to Nana or Meg, the ones after he had left the service of the King's army in Europe and returned to England. When he lived on his wits on the roads between Nottingham or London, or Leeds and Doncaster or the stretches of lonely path north of Lincoln. Richie remembers what the man told him, and his face becomes smooth and serious as if he has arrived at a conclusion. He stands, suddenly, he is aware of Meg's worries. Richie understands, clearly, that she did not want the boy to see another path that was not hard work in these fields, or devotion to a wife and family, or God. She worried that the Pearlman's influence on him would make the lad wayward and difficult, lazy and shy to face up to life's problems. Now he realises, why she sent that man away, partly for his business dealings partly because his past associations were a danger to the family and partly because of his influence on the boy.

What if the Pearlman had influenced Richie already and explained all that he needed to know to become a robber? What is there to know? You find a rich man or woman and you hold a gun as close as you dare to their face, then wait for them to beg for their lives with their money. They already stole the money in the first place from the working folk they employ – it would just be a question of Richie stealing it back.

He takes a deep breath as he looks down on the Etton pub in the distance below.

It's time to become that which Meg and Nana wanted to stop him becoming.

CHAPTER NINE

It's just turning dark when Richie comes through the door on Main Street in North Burton. He lets Bess run through first and there, in front of a weak fire, sits Nana. Richie steps through after the dog and pulls off the shoulder bag he carries and sets it down on the floor. Nana will have the fire on for the light and for hot water, there's no need for the heat.

"I've been alone all evening," she says in her best warbly voice. Richie can smell beer on her. He nods. "I'm an old woman," she continues, "with no one to look after me and no one to care, I might as well shrivel up and die." Her eyes are watery in the weak fire light.

"Bess got us two rabbits," says Richie as he opens the satchel straps. Nana shuffles in her chair.

"Pass them up here, Richie and your Nana'll sort it right for the pot." It's unlike Nana to offer.

"Who's been round," he asks as he passes her one of the floppy animals. In the tall fields at dusk, Bess can run as fast as a rabbit can for a short distance, she catches them in her long teeth and with a shake of her head they're dead.

"Nobody's been round," she says. "I've been all alone, Richie, on a summer evening like this. It's not right at my age, there should be family here, young uns and cousins and brothers and uncles. It's too quiet in North Burton these days, I'll tell you, I remember when this house was full to bursting with my old man and John, and the folks. Why there were seven of us living here and we lived here happy too." Nana's old age allows a level of error that is not considered healthy for younger folk. In truth, she does not remember what it was like thirty years ago in the little house, or even how many people bedded down there.

"I can smell the beer on you," says Richie.

"I'm an old bloody woman, if someone came round here with a few bottles of beer, why I'll drink them up and there's no one stopping me, not at my age, Richie lad." He wonders who would bring bottles of beer round to the little cottage, it's not as if anyone has money or beer to spare, even in summer.

"Who was it?" he asks again.

"It doesn't matter now, there were only two bottles, and it took me half an hour to get to the door."

"So, they didn't sit down?"

"It was Miss Pennyman sent them, Richie. She sent them for this house." Richie gives a light snarl.

"You mean she sent them for me?"

"Aye, but I'm your Nana and you weren't here, so I fetched the top off one to have a taste and before I knew it, the lot was gone down my neck, and I pulled the top off the other to have a smell and then that one was gone too. You don't mind Richie; you wouldn't take a comfort from an old woman who's alone."

Richie shakes his head. The truth is, if Nana wanted, she could shuffle across to the pub and yap all night with whoever is there, drinking or not. She stays home for the quiet sometimes. Nana takes a chopping board onto her knee and begins with the sharp knife that she keeps down the side of her chair. She has gutted a thousand rabbits and it's as familiar to her as tying a shoelace or squatting down outside for a wee. She makes knicks in the rabbit's skin so she can begin to remove it.

"I've not had anything to eat all day neither, and I've been here all alone as well. It's not right at my age." She knows she has done wrong, but with a little effort, she can twist the conversation away from her misdemeanors. "You should be married at your age, Richie, or at least courting. When I was seventeen, I'd already met my old man and we were to be wed. There are lads in the village who are getting on with their lives, young ones in Etton too, who are already dads and them are younger than you. That Jonny Low, why, even he's courting away with that lass from Bishop Burton, what do they call her,

Rose or something." Richie did not know this. Jonny has kept it quiet, or it might just be gossip that Nana has heard or even made up herself. She continues on. "You'll be left on the shelf, Richie and it'll be a shame, a right nice looking tall lad like you, all alone, and his Nana too, when there should be bains all around like puppies with their noise and their chatter. It's not right, Richie, it's not." Nana can warble on for a good long time about roughly the same things, especially if she has had and drink and if there are people half listening. It's her way. Richie wishes he could tell her what he has decided, but he cannot, it would do no good at all. He builds the fire a little under the pot and adds more water to boil while Nana skins the animals that twenty minutes before were running across the stubble of the hayfields outback.

"We're to take nothing more from Charlotte Pennyman," says Richie. His voice is low and dark.

"I'll take any drink she sends round, Richie, this is my house."

"Not when the drink is meant for me," he answers. Richie does not argue with Nana as other folk have done. He knows not to. He must present facts that he believes are true. Nana huffs as she pulls back the skin on one of the rabbits.

"Have you got yourself into trouble with her?" she asks.

"No, what have you heard?"

"Only that you're up there at the house, and you go inside and that she was talking with you at the stables this afternoon." North Burton is full of spies and Nana hears everything, somehow.

"I'm not in trouble with her, Nana, she just wants to get her teeth into me. I don't know why. Now I'm the constable of the peace, seems like she owns me."

"They're not to be trusted, them Pennymans. Not at all. They drink too much all of them, that Miss Charlotte most of all, and they don't care about anyone, not even themselves. That Charlotte Pennyman, why she was a fine lass, once upon a time but she's been poisoned by too much drink and money and not having to do anything but sit all day long. You be careful of her Richie, she's not like us Jacksons, if she had to live like we do even for a day her heart would stop and she'd curl up and die." The words are familiar for Richie, but more so, somehow, now that there is a possibility, he could be a Pennyman too. What would Nana say if she knew, really, or had any idea what he may be? It all makes Richie think. Nana has made a quick job of the rabbit and has stripped back the skin, her knife makes quick cuts to get the meat off, she drops the pieces into the black pot over the flames, like she has done hundreds of times.

"I went to see Meg," says Richie. Nana stops cutting.

"What for?"

"I wanted to see her." Nana's face has no expression. Her and Meg went through so much. When the Pearlman left, their arguments raged through the house and made Richie worried as each blamed each other for whatever wrong had befallen them. It did not take long for Meg to go back to Etton, over the hill, where her mother had been the cunning woman before she died and where Meg remains.

"How is she?" asks the old woman.

"Busy," answers Richie. Nana begins at the next rabbit once more with her knife in the firelight.

"She'll make a bob or two," says Nana. "She ought to come back over here to North Burton once in a while, I've got terrible ankles. It's like she's forgotten us, Richie, now that my John has gone, she thinks she doesn't have any responsibility to us and she can do what she likes. She married him you know, up at St Michael's on a sunny day, I was there, I sowed the blooming dress too." She adds the rest of the bones and the bits to the pot, there's no need to waste anything from the rabbit apart from the guts. She tosses the bits down onto the floor and Bess steps into the light to lick them up.

Richie sits on his bum in front of the fire below Nana and

pulls his knees up to his chest. Bess settles down next to him with her long head resting on his knees. The sticks crackle and spit as they burn. It's warm and calm. Outside, they can hear faint noise from the Bay Horse, people chatting and a fiddle drawing back. Far away over the hills there's the hoot of an owl. Richie takes off his boots and sets them against the wall side by side.

"I'm sorry I drank the beer, Richie lad," says Nana. Her voice is soft, without the usual rasping and complaining that is the cover for what she really thinks.

"I'm glad you did. I don't want anything from that woman."

"I know. What's been bothering you, lad?" she asks. This is Nana all over. You think she doesn't see you, she talks all the time, complains as much as she breathes and yet, it's Nana that notices the first leaf that falls in autumn or when Mrs Farthing is walking with a limp or when Rector Page looks red faced on a Sunday morning from drinking too much on a Saturday. Richie swallows. He does not want to tell her what is wrong. He is afraid. He does not want to lose his Nana.

"Tell me about John," he says. Richie has learned to twist the story away from what he doesn't want to talk about.

"Speak plainly, Richie. When it's you and I in front of this fire, together, there's no need for all that fluff and nonsense. What is it you want to ask?"

"I know there was something wrong, with him, I mean. I know he was different after he came back from war."

"You know the story, Richie. My John, the one that married Meg, he went off to war and he did not come home, never again. He was lost in France. That man who lived here, he came here by chance during The Great Frost, came out of the cold with his great coat and hat and a stab wound in his stomach. Your Meg made him well again and he fell in love with her, and he became our John, even though that was who he was not. You know that, lad."

Richie takes a breath in through his nose and watches the fire lick up around the dark pot in the fireplace.

"He said he was my father, Nana." Worry covers the old woman's face as she hears him say this. She has to make the best of these words and bend them, so that whatever bad is in them can be made good.

"He would have meant that too, Richie. He was not really my John, in many ways, he was better. He was more handsome and taller, he knew his cards, could sing a song, knew his guns and horses too. He couldn't handle a scythe or a spade like a working lad should, but he was a trier, and his heart was right. He wouldn't have lied."

"Then why did he go away?" Nana looks down at her big legs in the chair and her swollen ankles in wooden clogs under wrinkled, dirty stockings that go up to her knee.

"I sent him away," she says and her voice is dark. She does not want to admit this to the boy because she knows how much he thought of him. "I sent him away because of what he was doing to you. He was changing you, Richie, he was making you like he was."

"You said he was tall and handsome and knew cards and was a trier."

"He was Richie, but before he came to North Burton, he was a gentleman of the road, who knew how to rob and fight and what it entailed to shoot a man to death. He could be as quiet as the night itself and as calm as the dawn, and though he kept that inside himself, I could see it in him. He couldn't help but be the man he was. There were stolen things here in this house, he played cards as far as York and Leeds. He came into money more easily than a man who was meant to be my John could. I knew he'd mess up this life we have here, I knew he'd make what was simple more difficult. That man couldn't work like you could Richie, and he didn't have the peaceful heart that you do. He couldn't stay here. He had to go. It was me that made him go."

"He wanted to go, didn't he?"

"No, he did not. His past was catching up to him, Richie, even up here in the East Riding. There was a price on his head and it happened once he was recognised, then we knew it was time he was gone, for the best."

"Meg says she sent him away."

"She would say that. She's as brave as they come, your Meg, it was her that told him first, then me. We gave him a week."

"What about me?" asks Richie. "Didn't anyone think to explain it?"

"You were the only one we thought about Richie. He couldn't have stayed."

"He said he was my father."

"Well, he wasn't even if he thought he was."

"You see that's where I'm confused." Richie has done too much thinking of late, and his words come tumbling out. "You see, you say you're my Nana, but you're not, my mother died on a cowshed floor at the Pennyman house, so you're not my Nana at all, just like the man who said he was John is not my father." Nana clicks her tongue.

"You look into my eyes, lad," she says, "you look into my eyes, right now and you tell me that I'm not your Nana, I bloody dare you," her voice is a whisper.

"You told me, that there's what is true and then there's what's real."

"Aye. You might not have the same blood as me, but your spirt and your heart and your guts, they're Jackson, Richie. Meg and me, we love you and we knew this would come, the time when you'd wonder."

This has happened so quickly. How have they stumbled onto the issue that has been skirted over for so long, how has this monster raised its head now of all times?

"If you're my Nana, then he's my father. That's by your reasoning, lass." The old woman looks down at the tall lad in the flickering firelight. He is handsome and his eyes are watering. She has been backed into a corner.

"Aye," she answers. Nana swallows and closes her eyes. Her voice is suddenly soft as she says something she does not want to. "He left you something too, Richie."

"I've got his gun."

"Not that. He knew you'd not be able to shoot it without powder and bullets. Upstairs. Slide out the chest and lift the loose floorboard underneath. He wouldn't go unless he could leave it for you, and he made us promise, me and Meg that we'd give it to you, one day." Richie blinks in the half light. It frightens him, that the Pearlman thought of this moment all those years passed.

"When is that day to be?" he asks.

"The Pearlman said we would know when." Nana looks worn out by it all. "I guess that time is now."

He stands and is at the bottom of the ladder in a few strides, with one foot on the third rung. Nana calls at him in the darkness as he makes his way upstairs.

"But be careful, Richie. It's not the life for you, the way he lived. It was wrong. Do you hear me?" Richie moves quickly to the edge of the platform once up the ladder, he places one of his large hands on the chest and slides it out, then feels for the loose floorboard. His fingers find the space and he pulls. All these years and he did not know whatever the man had left him was just below his head as he slept. He reaches into the darkness and feels deep beneath the floorboards, he feels cloth and pulls out a hessian bag, sets in on the floor then kneels to undo the drawstring.

"Bring it down, Richie," calls Nana. "I'm to tell you what's in there."

By the light from the flickering fire, Richie pulls a hat from the bag, heavy and expensive felt with a smooth well-made rim, a hat as dandy as there is.

"That's from Atkinson's in York," she says. "It's worth two crowns, you pin the sides up and it makes a tricorn hat. It's proper. That man said you were to have it, when you were ready." Richie does not know what to say. Under this in the bag, wrapped in cloth to keep them new, is a pair of leather riding boots, with good wide sides and string laces to tie them tight. "The boots of from Sarrell's of Kingston Upon Hull, crafted to last a hundred years so he reckoned. He said they'd fit you, one day." Richie looks up to the face of the old woman and she blinks down on him in sorrow. "These clothes, Richie, they won't make you happy. It won't make you any different from what you are now. I'm just thankful he left when he did, before he could teach all the ways that went with these clothes, before he could make you into something you're not." Richie sets the boots down on the hearth and looks at the hat in the firelight.

"What if he already taught me, Nana? What if I'm his boy, just like I'm your Richie?"

"I don't know, lad. I only know that if you take up a gun, you'll die by one, and if you think you can rob like he did, you'll swing from the gallows in the end. Choose a life that you know, go up to Beverley the morrow, to the market, sell that hat to the pawn man for a crown and the boots too, bring the money back and buy a drink in the Bay Horse across the road. Look for a lass that catches your eye, pick her flowers, and fall in love, work the fields with your Bess and live a life that's poor but sweet and you'll not regret it."

There's an iron taste in Richie's mouth and a tingle down his spine.

"I'll never be more than a working lad, Nana, but if there's something dark than needs to be done, then I'll be the man to do it."

"Don't you go remembering that shite he told you, Richie. It's the kind of talk that gets you shot and killed."

"I just want to take what's ours, Nana, what belongs to us

and what the likes of Pennyman have taken for too long."

"Taken what exactly? Would you want to end up like old Mr Pennyman, with no friends and three servants who hated you? Or his daughter, a drunk and a wreck because she didn't have enough backbone to get over her husband leaving her? You've no idea what to take if you could take it all, Richie. You've got your nice boots and a posh hat from Atkinson's in York, what more do you want?"

Richie looks into the fire at the flames licking up around the black pot, he works his fingers around Bess's soft ear as she rests her head on his lap.

"I want dignity, Nana. I want us to keep this house."

"What's gone on?"

"Nothing."

"A lad who says nothing has gone on means that something has gone on." He moves Bess's head from his lap and gets to his feet to look at the rabbit stew on the fire.

"I think it's ready" he says.

"You're not to do anything daft, Richie." He takes the pot off the flames using a rag around the handle.

"As if I ever do, Nana."

She wrinkles her nose.

"I can't stop you doing what you'll do, Richie. I just hope that I've taught you enough to make the right choice."

Richie nods in earnest.

.

CHAPTER TEN

It's midday. Richie and Jonny Low sit on the grass verge opposite the Bay Horse, under the light shade of an apple tree out of the heat. Bess is more sensible and sits in the cool grass next to the trunk with her tongue out, she's lightly panting. They've been out in the hayfields again. Soon, and when it's all dry, they will tie it in bales and then bring it into the barns for winter. It's a good feeling to look at a cut field of hay and think that you cleared and baled the lot of it. Neither of the working lads has touched on the discussion they had the day before. They will eat their lunch and wait for the hottest part of the day to pass and then get back to it. Philipson comes out the pub with a bucket of dirty water that he tips into the street.

"I see you're working hard, lads," he calls. There is no heat in this comment. They all know that Jonny Low and Richie's duties are back breaking and that it's too hot to work in the midday sun. He follows up with: "Would you like me to get you a couple of pillows?" Jonny Low beams back at him and Richie lays back onto the soft grass with his hands locked behind his head.

"I'd swap places with you, Philipson," says Jonny.

"You can't count, how could you sell ale?" The young man grins. They like knocking chips off each other. Philipson sets the bucket down and wanders across the mud lane so he can look up to the church.

"What are you waiting for, Philipson?" says Jonny.

"There's a coach passing today on its way to Weighton, should be coming through about now." The landlord pulls a watch on a chain from a little pocket on his waistcoat and opens it to check the time.

"What's on it?" asks Richie.

"Well, if it hasn't been robbed, there should be brandy for the pub, and sacks of sugar too for the brewing," Philipson looks worried, but he always looks worried.

"It won't get robbed in the daylight," says Richie.

"You don't bloody know," says the landlord. "They'll take anything, highwaymen will, sugar and brandy are just the kind of thing they'd be on, and I can't afford to lose it lads, not if I'm to keep this place going." He nods to the pub in front of him with the Bay Horse sign creaking in the light summer breeze. He pats his balding head down with a handkerchief, to wipe away the sweat from the hot day.

Jonny Low points to the top of the hill just below the squat tower of St Michael's church.

"There it is," he says. "There's your wagon right now."

Philipson is fussy with the driver. He gets Richie and a reluctant Jonny Low to carry the three bags of sugar off into the pub and to the storeroom at the back. He takes care of the case of brandy himself. It's not that Richie and Jonny Low are thieves, it's just that temptation might make them become lads they are not. Philipson has seen many a good lad turn wicked when he is tempted. He struggles with the heavy case. Mary, his squat sister, appears to help him, between them, they carry it off the back of the flat wagon and into the building. The driver has got down and relieved himself behind the apple trees, he greets Richie and Jonny Low as they come out of the pub.

"It's bloody hot," he complains. He's red-faced and a little overweight with the arms on his shirt rolled up to his sleeves and a handkerchief around his neck. Richie nods a hello. "Any of you two lads know a Richard Jackson?" asks the man.

"Aye," answers Richie. "That's I."

The driver gets back up into his seat and reaches for a leather satchel.

"I've got a letter for you," he fishes inside and pulls out a square of paper with writing on it. He looks at Jonny Low. "Can you vouch that this is Richard Jackson?" he asks.

"Aye," answers Jonny. Philipson comes back out the pub.

"Landlord," calls the driver. "Is that lad here named Richard Jackson?"

"Yes, that's him," he answers back. The driver hands Richie the letter.

"I'm not paying for it," says Richie.

"You don't have to. The magistrate, Stephen Middleton, passed it me in Beverley last night and said to give it to you. He squared me up already." Letters are paid for by the receiver usually, especially if the correspondence travels a long way, there's no point in delivering a letter you've already been paid to deliver, you might as well put it on the fire. Richie grins. It's the first letter he's ever received.

They watch the horse and trap rattle off down the hard mud track and on to the York Road where it will travel on to a few more stops before it gets to Market Weighton by evening. Philipson seems a little more at ease now he has his delivery.

"A sharp nip of that brandy would see us right for our help, Philipson," says Jonny Low. The landlord pretends not to hear.

"Are you not going to see what's in your letter there, Richie?" he asks, attempting to change the subject. Richie glances down at the rectangle of stiff paper in his hand. He looks up to Philipson and raises his eyebrow.

"He can't read that," says Jonny Low. Philipson grins. It's normal for farm lads not to read, why would they?

"I can read it fine," says Richie. "I just need to sit down and think about it." Jonny Low does a mocking nod. Richie takes a few steps backwards towards his cottage on the corner and he wears a frown.

"I'll read it for you," says Philipson.

"No need," says Richie. If this letter is from Stephen Middleton, the magistrate, then he needs to read it as soon as possible. He leaves the two men standing out in the lane and walks the twenty yards to his own front door.

Nana is inside with a flannel on her forehead to keep her cool. She has taken her long socks off and her bare feet are on the cold stone. They are swollen and fat with sausage toes.

"Get us some water will you, Richie," she says. "I'm sweating like a pig in a fire." Richie does not have time for this.

"I've got a letter, Nana." In the dim light of the cottage, the air seems still.

"Who from?" she asks.

"Stephen Middleton, the magistrate."

"Well, what's that got to do with me?" She sits up and looks at him with a frown.

"I need it reading."

"You've been to Sunday school, lad, and Our John taught you how to play cards."

"Aye, but that's not scribbles on a paper, Nana. This could be important. I'm the constable of the peace here. I need to know what it says."

"You should have tried harder when folk tried to learn you, Richie, and anyway, it's too hot for me to read it now, can't you see my feet have swollen up? It's okay for you young ones who can fetch your own water from the pump, but it's not the same for me, Richie. I'm an old woman. I shouldn't have to go reading any bit of paper that you flap in my face." It would take Nana a lot less effort just to admit that she can't read it either, but that's not how it's done, not in North Burton anyway. Those who can't read are held in lower esteem than those who can, but the truth is, apart from Rector Page, probably nobody can do a few lines of the King James bible justice, not even Miss Charlotte.

"How am I to read it then, Nana?" he asks.

"That's your bloody problem."

"It's our problem."

"You're the sodding constable of the peace not me."

"It was you supping ale across the road on my money the other night, money which I haven't even been paid yet."

"You shouldn't have taken the job if you weren't up to it then, should you?"

Nana is more than a match for Richie. She has been swapping insults and dodging the truth for more than seventy years. She won't admit that she can't read.

Richie turns and goes back out of the front door. He makes sure he slams it, and the whole frame of the cottage rattles as he does. Outside, Bess has been waiting for Richie, her ears go down when she hears the noise, and there's shouting from Nana behind. She will be complaining about Richie's temper. He looks up to the Bay Horse sign creaking, it'll have to be the landlord after all.

Philipson is behind the bar of the pub. Open on the counter in front of him is a very large ledger and he looks down at the pages with a quill in one hand and a little bottle of ink at his side. He doesn't glance upwards as the tall lad walks up to him.

"How can I help?" he says as he continues to look down.

"I need a favour."

"Let me guess, you want me to read the letter."

"Not quite," says Richie.

"What then?"

"I want you to read the letter and not remember anything that it says." Philipson looks up at this.

"Depends on what it says, Richie. If it has anything to do with me and my business or my sister, then I'll have to remember it, if you understand." Philipson has a past, and his sister does too. What if it has followed them all the way from Driffield to North Burton? What if it's in the letter that Richie carries in his big hand?

"I'm asking you, Philipson, as a friend to read it to me and, if it doesn't concern you or yours, to forget it as soon as you do. If it is a matter concerning you, then we'll work through the problem together and I'll do the best I can to help."

"You'd be in my debt, Richie. Do you want that? If I'm to

keep secrets, you'd owe me more than Jonny Low does in ale."
Richie looks down at his big feet in his ratty boots, not a bit
like the ones the Pearlman gifted him that were made by
Sarrell's of Kingston Upon Hull.

"I can protect you, Philipson," he says. The landlord
considers this tall lad looking down on him from across the
bar, with his earnest face and floppy, sun burned hair with a
light moustache across his top lip.

"What can you protect me from?"

"Lads from Walkington who come to smash the place up,
working folk who try to nick your brandy, Bess here will have
a go at rats that come for your sugar and your beer hops. I've
helped you out before," says Richie. "Time for you to return
the favour."

"Like I said," explains the landlord, "if it concerns me, then
I'll have to remember and if it hurts me in the future, I can't
promise I'll forget."

Richie sighs. This is not a good position to be in, but
Philipson is better than anyone in the village to go to. More
trustworthy than the drinkers who would pretend they could
read, and much more worldly and reasonable than Rector Page
up at St Michael's. He places the letter on the bar in front of
him. With delicate hands, Philipson picks it up and tears open
the flap. He pulls out the paper and opens it. Philipson reads
quickly, his eyes tripping over the pen of the magistrate up in
Beverley. He skims the five or so lines and lets out a silent sigh,
there is no mention of him.

"Would you read it me?"

"Richie, a carriage comes through Leconfield in two nights
on the full moon. It's bound from Driffield North to the
Minster in Beverley. Watch it for me. Tell no one. It's signed
Stephen Middleton. August 5th 1722."

He's already told someone else.

Philipson passes him back the note, then looks down at his
ledger and picks up his quill.

"Is that all it says?" asks Richie.

"All what says?" answers Philipson.

"The letter?"

"What letter?" The landlord is already a step ahead of Richie. The correspondence is of no concern to Philipson, so he will forget it. "But you owe me, Richie Jackson." The tall lad taps the hard wood of the bar in thanks.

"I'll not forget this, Philipson," he says.

"See that you don't."

Richie smiles and he is gone, out the front door of the Bay Horse and into the street and off, quick as his legs will carry him. Philipson watches him through the tiny panes of glass in the window of the pub. Mary comes out from behind the bar, he turns.

"You weren't bloody listening to that, lass?" he asks. The woman shakes her head, and her eyes look wide and honest under her white skullcap, she is suddenly fearful.

"I didn't hear nothing," she answers. "Nothing." Her tongue is a little too fat in her mouth and it gives her a lisp.

"You best not have done. That there Richie is a good one, we need his sort on our side."

"Are they coming to take me away?" she asks. Her nostrils are flared, and her eyes are childlike scared.

"They won't take you away, I've told you that, nobody will take you, not from here and not ever. All you have to do is forget. I've paid what's due and that should be the end of it." It is harder for Mary to unremember what happened to them at Driffield.

"I didn't mean to do it. He would have killed me if I hadn't hit him." she says. Philipson turns on her. Through barred teeth he speaks, angry but concealed.

"You're not to mention it, Mary, not now, not ever, not to me nor anyone, not even to God. You did what you had to do and you're not to speak of it again. Your deed has been paid for, over and over." The girl's eyes lock on her older brother, the one who has protected her for her whole life, the one who stopped an angry mother from beating her and dragged the drunken gentleman away after she had smashed a glass into his face.

"I'll not say a thing," she lisps, "not a thing."

Philipson goes back to his ledger on the bar and takes a deep breath as he looks at his accounts.

If only she can keep her mouth shut, it will all be alright.

It's night. Richie has some thinking to do. He and Bess are up the top of the ladder in the tiny cottage, on the sleeping platform, laid on a mattress filled with straw. Richie tried to leave the dog on the ground floor, but she just barks and whines, so he brought her up. A light warm breeze rustles through the wads of thatched straw that make up the roof. It's murder to sleep up there in the winter, but on a summer night, it's cool and still. He looks up through a gap where one of the panels of thatching has come loose and he can see a star twinkling in the sky. He's seen this one before. Richie heard that the souls of the dead live as stars in the sky so they could watch the people they left behind on earth, but when he told Nana, she passed it off as nonsense, and that the stars were pin pricks in the black firmament with the light of God shining through.

Richie knows what he's going to do, but not quite how. The carriage that Stephen Middleton has told him to keep quiet about is his mark, of that he is certain. He is not sure of the ins and outs of it and there is a lot he has to remember, and to prepare, but this will be his target. His fingers work around Bess's soft ears in the darkness, it helps him to think. He has to concentrate. When John the Pearlman lived there, he and Richie spent much time together. If John went out to cut the hay in the fields, Richie went with him. In the autumn, Richie helped him dig up potatoes and turnips with the rest of the farm workers. They fixed hedges at the start of winter and cracked the ice on the pond so the pigs could drink when the snows came. There was a lot that came out of John's mouth in those years. Plenty. Richie heard as many stories as there were to tell and perhaps some of them that were not meant to be told also. The Pearlman was at times a soldier in the army of the Duke of Marlborough in Europe, a horse thief, a fence, a marksman, a bookie, a butcher for poached meat, and a singer and for a time before he came to be in North Burton, a highwayman. It is to the last profession that Richie thinks on, and he works his way back through time, sifting through the memories for the gems of information that he was told, on the operation of how to be a highwayman and how to rob and take from those rich enough to have wealth and not want to give it away.

He recalls the rule of three. For a gang to be a success, there must always be three, like the legs of a stout stool. They must act together, but they have different roles. One must be the eyes, another the heart and the third, the head. The roles may be swapped from time to time but, by and large, these are the three roles to be taken. As the Pearlman, John was the head, he could see the true value of an action, his comrades acted in parts as the eyes that does the shooting and the lion's share of the battling; and the heart, the one who feels if the way is right or wrong. Richie calculates. He shall be the head like John was, Bess sleeping on his chest shall be the heart, and the pistol, laid under the bench downstairs will be the eyes. Three of them. Like the legs on a stool. Though this is not quite what is meant by the rule of three, Richie is beginning to develop Nana's sense of truth, that a body may bend the facts to make a reality that is more suitable for the occasion.

He blinks in the darkness. While they take their rest here under the thatched roof of the run-down cottage, the world outside is alive with animals about the business of a summer night. Just like Richie's mind spins and thinks, so the rats scurry in Philipson's cellar and the badgers roam in the forest behind the Pennyman House, voles rustle through the long cut hay in the fields behind and the frogs of the North Drain croak out into the warmth of the evening.

The Pearlman spoke of circles many times, he said it was the shape that held the whole world together, the circle of the sun and moon, the wide shape of a tree trunk and the inside of a flower with the petals growing around the outside. The whole world is a circle, the birth and rebirth of the plants from winter to spring, the birth and death of people and animals, everything in a circle. Richie did not know where he got his exotic ideas, but they were as straightforward and reasonable as the circles that made up his blue eyes. In the summer they would wrestle, the two of them, shirtless in the fields behind the houses. The Pearlman showed him how to throw a man and swing a punch, and he spoke of circles here too, of how a fight moved like a whirlwind, and how each punch curled and your feet danced in a ring around your opponent. It's why Richie can belt hell out of better fed lads from Walkington or Bishop Burton, and why he likes the feeling of his fist connecting with their cheekbones. It's a dance, just like John, the Pearlman told him it was. He grins to himself, but there's no time to think of these easy lessons that the man taught him; he has to get to the harder memories that are hidden somewhere in the sphere of his brain. He thinks on, closes his eyes and sees the stories of highway robbery the man told him and the advice he gave therein.

Rob at dusk, he remembers the man saying, when there's just a few minutes of light left in the sky. Then you can be off with the money and the night will have set in already. Best not to just jump out of the bushes as they come round the corner either, that will only encourage whoever is driving to either speed up or take a shot with his blunderbuss if he has one. Try to get them on a bend, dig a hole in the road, get them to catch the wheel on a sticky patch of mud and so they pull the horses up and scratch their heads as to what's stopped them. Once all is sweet and calm you can make yourself known, not in a flashy way but in a calm sensible manner. The driver will know what's going on alright because he knows how highwaymen dress, the quality boots and a decent hat with a nice cloak or a jacket with shiny buttons and a scarf tight over his face. He doesn't want to get shot, neither do the people inside, and a highwayman doesn't like to waste a bullet or get into anything unnecessary. As quick and as gentle as a light shower he should be, a greeting, a pistol produced, cocked, a light and polite turn of phrase and for the occupants to step outside and pop their rings in a bag, he reminds them of his friend in the bushes with a musket and another associate behind with a pistol similar to his own, and that he is so sorry about all this and wishes it were not so, but this is the nature of the roads these days. Before the lady and gentleman can raise a fuss, it is done, and the highwayman is gone into the forest or the bushes and the sun has gone down completely to leave nothing but darkness.

That's how Richie will do it.

He knows the road that goes from Driffield to Beverley. Stephen Middleton has told him to watch the carriage at Leconfield which means it will be travelling through the flatlands near Beswick at dusk. He knows a tiny bridge called Mill Beck. He'll stop them there, Bess will be the look out. Richie will wear the long blue coat the robber dropped the other night, he'll put on the tricorn hat and the boots that John left him, and he'll cover his face with a black scarf and they will know his business.

If he runs fast enough, through the fields, he can meet the road again, hide the boots, the hat and the coat and be Richie Jackson, constable of the peace with his long muzzle loading musket and earnest face. He will be shocked about the robbery, shocked and angry that he did not stop it.

It will be easy. He will rob enough money to shove down Miss Charlottes throat and keep Nana from being kicked out into the lane.

CHAPTER ELEVEN

Richie has tied the boots, coat and the hat up into a sack and he carries this over his right shoulder gripped tight in his hand. The muzzle loading musket is strapped to his back and it clacks as he walks. Bess scampers along just behind his heels. They are outside North Burton, and the bell of St Michael's has just rung out the seventh low dong for seven in the evening. He and Bess cut out over fields that he does not know as well as his own and towards Leconfield. It's a village much the same as North Burton but without an alehouse.

Richie and Bess must move quickly if they are to get to Mill Beck before the carriage does. They must make their way through the darkness of Bygott Wood and through the swampy ferns of the forest behind and then, onto the wide-open fields where the farmers grow barley and wheat for the breweries in York and Beverley. They stick to the tall hedgerows do Richie and Bess because, even though they are out in the wilds of the East Riding, there might be someone to see them. Richie will not change his clothing until the last minute possible.

It takes an hour and a half to go round the long way to get to the bridge at Mill Beck. The going is not easy when you cannot use the paths and ways that normal folk go. There are bogs and little ponds to go round, squawking herons call at them through the undergrowth, he climbs tree stumps and squeezes through gaps in the bushes with Bess following behind and her fur full of sticky buds.

They stop twenty yards away from a tiny stone bridge on a bend, just big enough for a cart to pass over. Mill Beck is a trickle at the moment, but some summers, it can be ten yards wide, so the gap under the bridge is big enough for Richie to hide under without being seen. He lays his musket on the grass and sets down the sack before stepping towards the water next to Bess, the thin dog drinks with big laps and Richie squats to scoop up the beck into his face with two hands. It has been a hard road so far, and it's not going to get any easier. He opens the sack and swaps his own battered boots for the ones inside for the first time. Richie has big feet, and boots are hard to find but these things, heavy riding boots made by Sarrell's of Kingston Upon Hull, fit over his long toes like gloves. As if they were made for him, like John the Pearlman would have known what size the lad would become all those years ago when he left. Richie takes out the blue overcoat and unrolls it before slipping it on over his shirt, then fits a black handkerchief around his neck. He examines the hat and makes sure that the rims are pinned tightly to the sides to make the tricorn shape before putting it on. The fit is good. He takes the pistol from his satchel and loads it. His legs feel like jelly with anticipation. In bed the night previous, the idea had seemed like a game, a fancy thing to do in his mind that would be an adventure. He remembers what John the Pearlman said to him from atop the horse, that life was a dance, and it's only now that Richie realises, as he packs the black powder down into his pistol, that he has never danced before, not really. He does a jig with Nana at the Pennyman barn every year and swings his legs at Christmas in the Bay Horse, but dance, like he imagines a gentleman or a highwayman to dance, why he has never done that. His lips are dry. Darkness is beginning on the horizon as the late summer sun begins to sink to his left in the direction of North Burton.

"You're not to come with me," he whispers to Bess below him. "If they see you, then we're both as good as hanged." The dog blinks up at him with wide eyes, Richie knows she does not understand him, but she will. The two of them come up out of the steep bank of the little beck, they look around. Here is the Holderness Plain, as flat as one of Nana's pancakes and smooth to the eye, with a wide-open sky and a cool wind blowing from the south. Richie walks a good two minutes in the direction of Beverley and then squats down to look his dog, Bess, in the eyes.

"Stay," he whispers and he holds her nose lightly in his big hand. "Wait for my call. Stay." He keeps his eyes fixed on hers. Bess does not like to be away from him, but she knows this order, she's been doing it for months.

Richie walks back along the mud path towards the little bridge at Mill Beck. He feels the expensive hat made by Atkinson's of York over his thick brown hair, the quality boots that cover his feet and the long blue coat, a little battered, but certainly something a man of means would wear. He sees in the distance, the carriage that he has been told to watch in Leconfield as it makes its way towards him, and he steps into the shadow of the bushes with his hand on the pistol at his belt.

He does not feel like Richie at all.

The man he is, stands as steady as the chalk hills, and as calm as the light breeze coming up from the Humber Estuary, as gentle and as languid as the birds wheeling in the fading light of the summer evening. He is something other than the farm lad who works the fields at North Burton. Perhaps the man he is now, with his expensive hat and loaded pistol, perhaps this man knows how to dance. Perhaps holding up a carriage at dusk is in his blood.

Lieutenant Pike sits opposite a short, scruffily dressed man with shifty eyes and mousy brown hair. Elizabeth Pike is next to her father on the same side but against the window. The driver atop the carriage keeps the four horses steady and they are moving at an acceptable rate, not too fast to tire the animals unnecessarily, but certainly making ground. Either way, they are late. This is not so bad because there is to be a full moon tonight and the sky is clear. Lieutenant Pike looks out of the carriage window over his daughter's shoulders and Elizabeth smiles back at him. They have been to Driffield on their business, the Reformation of Manners Society takes up a lot of their time as they try to establish themselves in the towns and villages around the East Riding. The older man watches the starlings as they wheel and follow each other in the sky in a great summer dance before they go to sleep. He smiles back at his daughter. He's lucky to have her, especially at his age.

Men get the wrong impression of Lieutenant Pike. He is aging, but not yet old, big, but not overbearing, his manner is calm and polite, and he is good at conversation, listens as well as he talks and is educated such as gentlemen should be, but he will not lord this over you. Those in polite society would never call him boorish or overbearing, he does not state his views over others, he is charitable and welcoming, his shoes are clean and his socks pulled up neat, and, while they are not the best quality silk, they are a good standard. Men who do not know better, might think Lieutenant Pike is pushed around by his high cheeked, tall daughter with her fine ginger hair, beautiful and slightly upturned nose, and smooth, almost porcelain skin, but this is not the case. Pike bought the rank of lieutenant in Lancashire for six hundred and fifty English pounds when he was twenty-six, and that was everything his father had. He fought in Europe under Marlborough. He has commanded men in war, and the hands that rest gently on his lap have choked a man to death, they have held a whip and fired pistols, cannons, they have shot horses, cut open a man's eyes and stabbed a body right through with a bayonet and felt the ribs pop. Lieutenant Pike is not to be pushed around, not by anyone. Indeed, those men in Beverley who are loud and well-dressed, with the finest of handkerchiefs and wigs, these are the men who do not know hardship, and in some ways, it is these men who can be taken in by the Lieutenant's quiet and steady confidence.

Pike has not spoken to his daughter about the meeting in Driffield. They will wait until they get back to Beverley before they discuss matters. He would not want the other passenger to hear what they have to say, the driver neither.

"How long till we get home, father?" she asks.

"An hour at most." Their business has not been successful. The Reformation of Manners Society is not always welcomed, not least by those who like a drink, and there is a lot more to it than the boozers in The White Horse in Beverley or the King's Head would credit. Of course, Lieutenant Pike wants poor people to live a better life and not gamble and fritter their hard-earned wages on gin or gut rot wine imported in from Holland, but this is not quite the reason behind the group. There's more to it. Pike and his daughter want influence, they want the freedom to express the way they read the bible and not the way the established church does. In his younger days, the Lieutenant served with an Irish minister who spoke to him of the scriptures in a way he understood for the first time. However much the rich and the church tried to cover it up, they could not hide the truth written by God in the pages of the King James bible – that all are free in His eyes. Over in Driffield, inside the cold walls of the All Saint's Church, neither Lieutenant Pike or his daughter were well received, and the Curate informed them, in certain terms that the only body capable of giving alms to the poor was the church, and that anyone who thought otherwise was a non-conformist.

That's a dirty phrase.

Elizabeth would have smiled inside when she heard it.

The man opposite in the carriage has been taking nips on a little bottle of something he keeps in his breast pocket. He rests his head back on the seat and closes his eyes as his body rocks from the bumpy road below them.

Outside, the day is just beginning to fade, there is perhaps only five minutes left of good light before the summer evening will draw in proper and the wheeling starlings in the sky will disappear into the trees. They approach the little bridge at Mill Beck and the driver slows the horses so they can pass over the stone path just big enough to fit a carriage.

At once, Lieutenant Pike frowns. It could be intuition or

he may have noticed something different, the driver pulls up the horses to stop them and Elizabeth looks to her father as if there is something wrong. The air is not quite right.

A face covered with a black handkerchief under a tricorn hat appears at the window and a smooth mahogany pistol points at his daughter in a steady hand. It has happened with no warning, nor drama nor noise, just a masked face looming out of the dying summer day.

"Toss your purse out of the window there, Miss and Sirs." His voice is just a whisper, but there is mettle in it. Pike feels a rush of blood to his head as he sees the pistol trained on his daughter's chest, electricity shoots down his legs and his mind races. If he were younger, and less wise, he may have grabbed for the pistol to wrench it from the highwayman's hands, but a number of things stop him. He's not as quick as he used to be, and, he has already noted the pistol, the flint mechanism well-oiled and dark, obviously cared for; he has seen the tricorn hat the man wears, black and heavy felt, excellent quality probably from some milliner in York or Leeds. This is no common footpad. There is also the hand that holds the pistol, it is as steady as a rock. In Lieutenant Pike's experience, those who shake when they hold a gun, even a fraction, are those that do not know what to do with it. A steady and fixed grip indicates that the holder is proficient in its use, this is dangerous and means that he may, and can, kill her. These are the reasons Pike does not react and reaches his hand to the inside pocket of his jacket to remove his purse. He takes it out slowly to show the highwayman that he does not have anything more dangerous.

"Toss it out the other window, Sir," he whispers. Pike does so and the coins clink as they fly through the air and there is a splash as the leather pouch hits the water under the beck below. The man opposite Pike has gone white as a sheet and holds his hands up. "Yours too," says the robber. The man fishes in his pockets, pulls out whatever is there, and lobs the bits and bobs out the window. Elizabeth's face is stone, not frightened, but angry and her lips are thin, her nostrils flared. She looks at the highwayman's blue eyes and her stare is bitter.

"Thank you," whispers the robber, as he begins to withdraw.

"We need folk like you," says Elizabeth. To hell with it. When will they get the opportunity to speak to such a man again? "The church always has a place for you, Robber, whatever you believe and wherever you've been. There is an Inn down the lane from St Mary's Church, Beverley. The White Horse. Tuesday night in the back room. Those who want to change the way things are, they meet there. Tuesday night, Robber." Her eyes are fixed and strong. Here is a woman who will not be scared by highwaymen, or guns, or men who tell her she has no place in the world. The face of the highwayman disappears into the darkness, and he bangs on the back of the carriage twice to indicate it should move. The wheels start up again and the carriage rolls forward. There's a loud, deep voice from outside.

"Don't stop till you get past Leconfield. My lads are not as kindly as I."

It has all been so fast and a minute later, they are once more bumping along the lane, just as they had been previous. Elizabeth's face is flush red, and she puts her handkerchief to her mouth with the stress. Her father puts his arm on her back to comfort her. She lets out a sigh. There's a whistle from behind them in the darkness. A signal to someone.

"Should I have said that to him?" she whispers. Her father nods. He is the kind of man the Reformation of Manners Society would do well to know. The little fellow opposite takes a long drink on his bottle and his throat bobs.

"Good God," he says in relief.

"Keep moving driver," yells Lieutenant Pike. "There will be more. Keep on till we get to somewhere with a light on."

Richie moves quickly.

Once the carriage has got out of sight he whistles for Bess, and jumps down into the water, onto his hands and knees in the shallow beck to fetch the purse the rich man tossed out the window. Richie's heart is thumping out in his chest. It was over so quickly, and he dare not think of the fear in the faces he just robbed. He comes across the leather pouch and spirits it into the pocket of his pants. On the bank, he strips off his long blue jacket, the hat and the handkerchief. He takes off the boots. All this, along with the pistol, he stuffs back into the sack and ties the drawstring tight, then picks up the musket and swings it over his shoulder.

He needs to get to Leconfield faster than that carriage. Bess appears looking up at him in the fading light. Her tail is wagging.

Richie grins and a tingle goes down his spine.

He's a highwayman.

Just like his father.

CHAPTER TWELVE

There's no point in sprinting, Richie will be exhausted after a few minutes and so, he begins at a steady jog down the track following the carriage. The musket rattles on his back as he runs and somewhere just behind him, following in the new evening darkness, is Bess. Richie has not thought this next part of the plan through to completion, his mind was only focused on the robbery, and, now that's gone well, he has to consider the future. He picks up the pace. He must dump the sack somewhere nobody will find it, but he does not want to lose the disguise or the expensive boots or the hat, or the pistol. The road will swing out, past a hamlet of a few houses and a tiny church before going on to Leconfield.

Richie slows as he hears voices from up ahead, it's the driver from the carriage, they must have already stopped. He is talking in low tones to the passengers and Richie can see a spark of light in the darkness, and a match going to the lamp that is beside where the driver sits. The carriage is some two hundred yards in front, and the lamp an orange glow. In another minute, the driver clicks his tongue and they are off again down the track. Richie is far from out of danger, the passengers will now be in a heightened state, perhaps Elizabeth will be armed, her father most certainly will be, Richie knows he is a lieutenant and he can hardly believe he kept his cool in front of these two.

He swallows down his fear as he follows the cart at a distance. The carriage moves slower than it has been, in the darkness the horses are less keen to trot when they cannot see in front of them, and Richie keeps up but well behind. There's another short but wide bridge over a beck, the carriage rises and the light disappears as it moves out of sight round the corner. The moon is climbing slowly up into the night sky and Richie can see a little better, he must move swiftly if he wants to get ahead so that he can pretend he has been waiting for the carriage in Leconfield as he was instructed to do by Stephen Middleton, the magistrate.

It must only be a few more miles and Richie does not have long to hide the sack. He follows over the bridge and sees the light of the carriage moving ahead, now further away, the road is straighter here and the driver will be more confident to let the animals go faster if they dare. He will also be more willing to get to Beverley now they have been robbed at gunpoint. Richie must run if he is to keep up and yet he must also be as quiet as he can, he begins a sweat, the realisation of what he has done comes over him as he jogs. If he is found out, he will be hanged, either on Gallows Lane Beverley or at The Knavesmire in York, hanged by the neck until his face goes blue, then where will Nana be? What will happen to Bess? He moves on. There's no turning back.

The moon is high in the sky now, the light makes the shadows darker and there is no wind in the still summer evening. There's the rustle of something in a hedgerow, and the call of some bird far away but everything is calm. The carriage has stopped just outside Leconfield on Old Road near a white farmhouse, on the same side of the lane there's a tumbled down barn just off the dirt path, and Richie squats behind one of the rotten beams that once would have made up the walls.

He watches through the overgrown bushes at the light on the side of the carriage. There are voices from the farmhouse and the scuff of feet. Somewhere in a livery yard, Richie can hear horses being readied. His heart quickens. He has done a grave wrong, the driver or the Lieutenant must know someone here and they have stopped to explain the issue. They will be ready to hunt robbers down, unlike North Burton, there are small holdings in Leconfield with families of means, who own the land they work and the animals they manage. Highwaymen are not heroes to families who have even the slightest amount of wealth, they are vermin like foxes to be rid of. Richie pulls his head back in behind the wood of the rotten bark, he takes the sack from over his shoulder and stuffs it into the undergrowth – better to hide it near, where they might never search. He looks at Bess in the darkness and puts his finger on her long, dark nose so she won't make a sound. The clatter of hooves comes from the little white farmhouse in front, and two horses make their way at relative speed back up the way towards Mill Beck where the robbery happened. Richie listens to the sound of them getting further away. He must make his move.

He crouches low and runs at the same time, back out onto the dirt track, to the other side of the road and into the long grass. From here, he makes his way up the lane and past the little white farmhouse so that it may look like he came from the direction of Leconfield when he approaches the carriage. There's a lump in his throat as he considers what he is about to do. He could take off back to North Burton and be in his bed within the hour, with the money he has robbed safe under his pillow and Bess sleeping at his side. That's what he should do, but he comes out of the long grass, and stands on the moonlit track with the farmhouse in front of him.

He can't afford to do that.

If he doesn't make contact with the carriage then Stephen Middleton will think he wasn't there, after he has been sent a letter instructing him to do so. Talking to the Lieutenant will also give Richie and alibi, sort of, and as the constable of the peace for North Burton, Richie Jackson would never rob a carriage at gun point – he's not that sort of lad. Just as Richie felt different as the highwayman he became, the lad he really is, the one who looks after Nana and cuts the hay in the back fields, he is returning. Richie feels his heart beating in his chest and he looks down at Bess next to him.

He's afraid.

Richie knows how to react to a situation. He can do the right thing if he's to stop a robber or belt a Walkington lad around his jaw when he's cheating at cards, but this is something different. He has to walk towards the carriage some hundred yards away, and lie. Richie thinks about the silver tongue that John the Pearlman was meant to have. He remembers some of Nana's wisdom, suddenly as if he has never considered that he may need to bluff his way out of a situation. The only way you can get along with the world is if you believe that which isn't true. Nana is not his Nana, but she is his Nana. Meg is not his mother, but she has always been his mother. John, the Pearlman is no relation, but of course, he is Richie's father, just the same as a fox calls to the silvery moon above. There's what's true and what's real and these two can exist side by side without issue. Richie was born a bastard by the Turpin woman on a cowshed floor, begat by a Pennyman – this is true, but it's not real.

He has already made his way to the carriage just outside the white farmhouse and the driver notices him come out of the darkness.

"Who the bloody hell goes there?" barks the man. His eyes are wide and, in his hand, he carries his horse whip, ready to strike if he has to.

"Richie Jackson, constable of the peace at North Burton."

"What in God's name are you doing here?" As Richie carries on walking, he sees that Elizabeth and Lieutenant Pike are standing on the other side of the carriage. Their faces look grey. The driver steps towards Richie and Bess gives a low growl, he swings his musket from over his shoulder to his hands to be ready.

"What's gone on?" he asks.

"Why do you want to know?"

"I'm the constable of the peace at North Burton a few miles away."

"You told me that, so what business is it of yours?" Richie frowns. This driver is as quiet as a church mouse when there's a pistol to someone's head.

"Let him come through," says Lieutenant Pike from behind. "Come through, lad," says the older man. Richie and Bess step into the wide circle of light thrown off by the lamp on the carriage. The man considers Richie with his wrinkled face and crow's feet from the side of his eyes under his hat.

"We were robbed," he says.

"Who by?" This is the kind of daft question Richie is glad he has asked, for if they knew who the culprit was, they would not look quite so upset.

"How does he bloody know," calls the driver. The Lieutenant holds up his hand to quieten the man. Elizabeth steps forward and recognises Richie's face from a few days earlier.

"You work for the Pennyman estate, Sir, do you not?" she asks.

"Aye."

"What's your business here tonight, Sir?" The Lieutenant is a few inches shorter than Richie, but he has gravity and authority in his voice and by the way he stands.

"I was told that a carriage would pass through Leconfield this night, and I was told to watch out for it." The older man seems to nod at this.

"Mr Middleton?" questions The Lieutenant. "What would his concern be for us?" Pike knows the magistrate and they are not at all friends; he considers them outsiders with their liberal views on the church. In fact, The Lieutenant has been warned by Middleton, in a round about gentleman's way, to stop his efforts with the reformation of Manners Society. He returns his stare to Richie.

"How much did they get?" asks the lad.

"Plenty more than you would expect," is the reply. Richie does not smile, although part of him wants to. The leather pouch that The Lieutenant threw from the carriage window, even as they speak, is pressed against Richie's leg in his inside trouser pocket.

"What happened, Sir?" The Lieutenant draws in breath through his nose.

"It was a professional job, quick and light. A masked man with a quality hat stopped us on a bridge back there, pointed his pistol at my daughter and we were asked to toss our valuables out the window."

"Do you know how many there were?"

"I'd say there were at least two. I saw the glint of a musket down on the riverbank as he approached the window." This must have been Richie's weapon that he laid on the grass. "He also gave a whistle to signal to his associate as the carriage began again." This was Richie's call to Bess. "Professionals. The gang wanted it done quickly, and, I believe they would have killed any one of us if we had not given him what we had." None of this is true, but it certainly sounds convincing as the older, wiser man explains it.

"They would have had horses," says Richie.

"Yes, lad, but kept some way off I'd imagine. I have an associate here in Leconfield who I called on as soon as we arrived and he and his son have gone off to see if they can catch up with the buggers, but they'll be long gone now. Are you the lad who faced up to the Pennyman attackers? Twice now, I believe."

"That's I," says Richie. The Lieutenant nods at this.

"In a way, young Sir, it is a mercy you were not there. You'd have been shot defending us."

"I may have shot them back, Sir," answers Richie. Elizabeth looks down on Bess and then back up to the tall lad's blue eyes under the warm light of the lamp.

"Is it just you and your dog, Mr Jackson?" she asks. Richie swallows. She remembers his name. He feels his stomach knot as it did previous when he spoke to her near the Pennyman House a week or so previous.

"Just us two, Miss Pike." Richie is not going to explain that he is too poor for a horse, it's already obvious. Elizabeth looks across at him with a mixture of pity, mild contempt and delight, like one would some curious dog or exotic animal. Richie catches her eye. An hour ago, he held a pistol to her throat.

"Well, Richie Jackson, it looks like we are to carry on out journey to Beverley," says the Lieutenant. "Will you join us? Your musket will certainly be a welcome addition to the carriage." Richie does a false smile. He does not want to go with these two and the little gentleman inside the carriage, or with the angry driver on top. He would rather he and Bess cut back through to North Burton to think of what they have done.

"I'd be honoured to accompany you, Sir," he answers. The Lieutenant nods at this and signals to the driver.

"What about your friends?" asks Richie.

"They'll return soon enough. They're more worried about the trouble robbers could present to their livelihoods as much as they are about a carriage being robbed."

"Right," says Richie. The Lieutenant opens the door and his daughter goes up the step and into the wooden carriage, Richie removes his musket so he can climb in next and he sits inside with his head by the window, looking down at Bess outside. The Lieutenant climbs in and shuts the little door behind him before finding a seat opposite his daughter.

"Keep up, Bess," says Richie to the dog down below. He does not like to leave her outside but with such people as this, he can hardly bring a thin hunting dog into the carriage, besides, Bess is more than capable of matching the pace. The carriage rocks as the driver clambers up to his seat, there's the crack of his whip outside and the horses move off into the darkness with the big cartwheels clacking on the cobblestones of the farmhouse yard.

There are four of them in the carriage. Opposite Richie sits the Lieutenant and next to him, the little man that did not get out at Leconfield. He looks pale and gaunt and his hands are shaking, the episode at Mill Beck must have scared him. Next to Richie, is Elizabeth, in the middle seat, away from the windows. A part of her pale pink dress is touching Richie's leg and the sensation of it, just a tickle on his knee, sends electricity and shivers up the side of his body and to his head. Her perfume is rich but not overbearing and even though he has not looked to the side to see her, he feels that she is the most beautiful creature he has ever seen, even in the dark. The curve of her neck, her high cheekbones, the clear, intelligent voice and proud eyes. Richie swallows in fear. They have not been going more than a minute, when he looks through the open window outside and down, to make sure Bess is following. There she is, in the orange light from the driver's lamp, running along. Richie gives a click with his tongue and the dog looks up and her tail wags – she is fine.

"You are concerned for your dog, Mr Jackson?" asks Elizabeth.

"Aye, Miss. Bess is like our family."

"Dogs are loyal," she comments. "Would you say they were more loyal than people?" Richie thinks for a moment. He thinks of John the Pearlman who left Meg and he and Nana, and of Miss Charlotte Pennyman's husband who left her also.

"I think some are more loyal than others. If you fed my Bess for long enough, she'd follow you." It's a lie. Bess and Richie have become like stitches next to each other in a jacket seam, they both hold each other tight. Elizabeth smiles in the dim light of the carriage lit by the silvery moon outside.

"So, if you pay a man enough gold, you can get him to follow you, is that what you're saying?" Elizabeth's voice is a little nervous, clipped even. Richie feels the cool barrel of his musket in the palm of his left hand where he holds it between his knees. Elizabeth has a way of getting to the heart of a problem, of getting inside him with a question he does not know how to answer. Of course, men will not do anything for money, Richie knows this, but he is not sure how to put this into words.

"I don't think men are dogs, Miss. They don't just work for food or money." Elizabeth shifts her weight and looks out of the opposite window.

"Those men who just robbed us did," her voice is like ice, as if, it were Richie and his kind who just robbed them. Which, of course, it was.

"Now, Elizabeth," says her father as if admonishing her in some way. "You'll need to watch your tone of voice with those you do not know. My apologies, Mr Jackson, the events of this evening will have shaken her somewhat. She's not been threatened before, I'd say our guest here hasn't either," the Lieutenant motions to the little, shabbily dressed man next to him whose knee is jigging with nerves.

The carriage bumps up and down beneath as the horses pull them along the straight road towards Beverley. Richie frowns, he has not considered his actions, he did not, for a minute, think that there would be real people inside the carriage that he was to rob, real people who would be affected by what he did. The Lieutenant has a wry grin:

"You'll have been in situations before, Mr Jackson, won't you?" Richie looks puzzled, even in the dim light of the carriage.

"I'm not sure what you mean, Lieutenant Pike, Sir." It's the first time Richie has used this man's name. The old soldier grins.

"I mean... your first fist fight stays with you for a time, just like the first time someone shoots a gun at you or the first time you are in a situation where you could lose your life... do you know what I mean?" The Lieutenant is not speaking in arrogance, he just wants to share his experience with someone and perhaps, with one of his eyes on his daughter, he wants to make her feel at ease.

Truth is, Richie doesn't really remember his first fist fight, the fire in his belly wiped out the fear and he does not know the breathless, sleepless nights that a pistol pointed at your face can bring, because it has never happened to him before. There's a sudden realisation, that this version of himself, the version that is the constable of the peace for North Burton, is in more danger than the robber he was a few hours before, and this conversation with a wealthy and powerful man who he has just robbed, could cost him his life if he plays this wrong. It's easier to tell the truth in situations, so Nana says.

"I'm usually too afeared to recall them, Sir," he answers and at once the Lieutenant smiles. This is the kind of answer he was after.

"The fear passes, does it not, after a while, Mr Jackson?"

"Aye, in the end," Richie doesn't want to say too much.

"I've heard a little of you, young man, I heard that you faced off two highwaymen over on Dalton Park and scared off two more who were in the Pennyman House. You're getting a reputation. I feel better that you're here. Is that musket loaded?"

"Aye Sir." This is why Richie holds it with the barrel pointed upwards, a well packed ball can fall out in time. The Lieutenant nods.

"Good lad. Does it not make you feel safer Elizabeth, to know that Mr Jackson rides with us, and that we're only a few miles from Beverley?"

"You told me the driver had a blunderbuss when we left Driffield this afternoon," she snaps back.

"That's what he told me."

"Next time we travel father, you ought to bring the sword that hangs over the fireplace. If I'd have had that, why, I would have sunk it into that bastard highwayman's neck." Her words are icicles in the warmth of the night. This time, it's Richie who feels the shiver of fear across his chest and he wishes he could tell her not to be afraid. For the pistol was not loaded, and, the steady hand that the Lieutenant understood to be experience, indicated only that Richie would not, and could not hurt anyone of them inside the carriage, why else would he keep the pistol on Elizabeth?

Richie remembers Bess and leans his head over to look out of the window. The dog is not there. He pulls his head back in and his face empties of all expression. The Lieutenant senses that something is not quite right with the lad. Richie sticks his head out the window again, the hairs on the back of his neck stand up, he puts his finger and thumb to his lips and gives a sharp whistle. Despite the rattle of the wheels on the hard mud road below them and the clattering of the wooden frame of the carriage as it moves, Richie can feel the night around him, smell the rabbit droppings and the fox dung. There's a dull, muffled bark from the side in the darkness, Bess somewhere outside matching the pace of the carriage. Richie pulls his head back inside.

"There's something ahead," he says in a whisper. Lieutenant Pike frowns in confusion. They have already been robbed once. It can't happen again. Elizabeth's nostrils flare and her teeth grit. The little man opposite raises his eyebrows and puts his hand to forehead in fear.

"Not again," he calls.

There's the dull crack of a gunshot outside in the darkness, something big, a rifle perhaps. The first horse of the four pulling the carriage is hit in the neck. The beast pitches forward, and stumbles sidewards, the tack drags on the other horses, and the carriage tips upon two of its wheels. The driver jumps free. Spokes buckle and snap and the little cabin where Richie and the passengers sit, turns sideways, crashing down into the hard mud of the road.

Inside, Richie feels the carriage tip, he manages to move so that he doesn't fall through the window. Opposite, Lieutenant Pike is crushed by the other passenger and Richie feels the body of Elizabeth fall onto him in the darkness. It's more of a shock than pain. One of the carriage wheels spins in the air as the whole thing comes to rest somewhere between Leconfield and Beverley.

Richie regains his senses quickly. He lifts his head, and she is on top of him, almost in his arms. He can feel her breath on his face. It's as if time stops. He can smell her perfume in his nostrils and see her hazel eyes in the moonlight, feel the soft material of her dress against his arm, and the weight of her on his chest. Though he has thought of Elizabeth many times in this way, the reality of it, now, here in his arms, it is almost too much to take. She struggles to get up.

The brief second is over. Richie's mind races. This is why Stephen Middleton asked him to come to Leconfield, because either he knew something would happen, or he had planned it. There will be highwaymen outside, even now stepping closer to the carriage on its side with the horses fretting in front. Richie thinks of his own calm robbery, just like the Pearlman had explained, quick and painless, this job has the bluster and violence of men who do not know what they are doing. Richie is suddenly angry.

He's robbed this carriage already.

He'll be damned if anyone else is going to.

There's another gunshot as Richie pokes his head through the window and into the moonlight. It was a struggle to get around Elizabeth's body but the people inside the carriage are more shaken than hurt. The real danger is in the darkness. Richie opens the door upwards and clambers out, he sits and puts both legs over the side then reaches inside to pull his musket up next to him. He glances back down at the three frightened faces within, and there's a coarse shout from somewhere in front.

"You'll jump down off that carriage, you lanky bastard and drop that musket while you're at it." Richie has heard this voice before, back in Dalton Park a few months since. It is the fat, Mr Rail, who he has crossed paths with twice before, three times now. Richie turns to where the sound is coming from, somewhere off in the dark scrub, he slips forwards and lands in the mud but he does not drop the musket. He brings the weapon up to his shoulder and levels it into the bushes, his finger goes to the trigger, his teeth are barred and his face is red. He is not going to let the fat highwayman off for this one, he's going to shoot him once and for all and that will be him done for. Somewhere within Richie, there's a nagging sensation, under his temper, a calmness, perhaps it is the voice of the Pearlman. This intelligence already knows that Richie is doing it wrong, he's red hot and angry, it's not a way to deal with a situation unless you're in an alehouse full of drink. Richie does not know, that, while he points his musket into the bushes in the moonlight, a figure creeps around the side of the fallen carriage with a pistol in his hand, a man dressed in black with a handkerchief over his face.

"You've bitten off more than you can chew this time, Robber," spits Richie. The dark figure slips out of the shadows and clobbers the tall lad around the back of his head.

He goes down like a sack of potatoes.

CHAPTER THIRTEEN

Richie is used to hangovers. He doesn't complain about them because they are his own doing, besides, complaining doesn't get anything sorted. He opens his eyes, and his brain assumes he must have drunk a great deal the night before because of the pain. His mouth is furry, he is laid on his back, sees the dull light of dawn above him and hears the birds singing at the joy of it. His legs are stiff and his shoulders hurt against the cold ground under his back. At his side, nestled into his armpit, is Bess, she feels warm and one of her ears flaps as Richie comes round.

He remembers holding the musket. Then nothing else. Richie sits up and Bess raises her long head watching what he does. The scene is much the same as it was the night previous in the grey of the summer day just beginning. The carriage is still on its side, but the horses are gone. Sitting a few yards away resting his back against the underside of the carriage, with his wig off and his head scuffed, is Lieutenant Pike. The old man looks like he's been roughed up considerably. Richie sits full and tries to get to his feet.

"You're lucky you're not dead," says the Lieutenant. His face is grey. The voice is flat.

"What happened?"

"After they hit you, they dragged us out of the carriage. One by one. If I'd have been ten years younger…" The Lieutenant has his eyes fixed on the ground in front of him. He is exhausted.

"Where are the others? The driver? The man who sat in the carriage, Elizabeth?" Richie manages to get to his feet. He feels unsteady and his head throbs, there's a bruise just above the back of his neck where someone hit him with the handle of the pistol. "Where are they?" he repeats to the old man.

"The driver ran off to Beverley to bring help. The little man said he was from Bridlington, he went East, just ran."

"And Elizabeth?" asks Richie. Lieutenant Pike looks up to the lad with red rimmed eyes, sorrow and regret across his face.

"You attacked too quickly, lad. You should have taken your time. All fire and anger and no thoughts. They went through our pockets, rough, without any manners at all. They took my rings and my cane. They would have had your musket too, but that dog wouldn't let them near you. Then they untacked the horses, apart from the one they shot." Richie looks over to the front of the carriage and there is the body of a horse on its side, he can see the stomach breathing up and down yet. He returns his gaze to Lieutenant Pike.

"What about Elizabeth?" he asks.

"They took her, lad. They took her, screaming and flailing till one of the men slapped her round the face and tied her hands behind her back. She's a fighter all right." Richie steps closer to the man.

"Didn't you try to stop them?" he asks and knows at once this was the wrong thing to say. He can see a fresh bruise on the top of the lieutenant's bald head and a scuff on his cheek. "How many were there?" he asks to cover his first question.

"I saw three but there would have been more."

"How long ago?"

"Four hours, maybe more."

"Which way?"

"Back the way we came towards Driffield."

"Was one of them fat and ugly?"

"Yes," answers Lieutenant Pike. This will be Mr Rail.

"And the other?"

"Small, quick and his face covered. He's the one did for you. I thought you were dead." The Lieutenant looks up at Richie and the face he wears now is one of disgust whereas before there may have been admiration. If they had thought they were safe with Richie along, then these gentle folk were mistaken. It's like the man can see right through him. "You're all bravado and bark, like your dog, Mr Jackson. If you came across these highwaymen before, then it was only by luck that you frightened them off, you're no soldier, I can see by the way you hold a gun that you've shot one before, but you've never killed a man, never needed to." Richie takes a deep breath and looks around them. The dawn is coming fast and soon the sun will be up and hot on their backs, he hears a snort of pain from the horse some yards away from them. This is Richie's fault. If he hadn't tried to be some sort of hero, he might have been able to keep them from catching Elizabeth.

"You'll help me up, lad," says the Lieutenant. "We'll make it back to Beverley and to my study. I'll send correspondence to men that I know at the barracks in Kingston Upon Hull and they'll dispatch a brigade to get her back. I'll have men who know how to fight hunt them across the wildlands here, but it will take a day for them to get the message, and then half a day for them to get after the highwaymen." Richie listens to the words and the tone of a man who has lost his daughter. He knows the game. They will ransom Elizabeth back to Lieutenant Pike, just as they did before to the girl from South Cave, just as Stephen Middleton explain to Richie in the back room of the Bay Horse. They will treat her as badly as they did the girl pervious.

"If you want to make yourself useful, Mr Jackson you can help me, if we get on the way to Beverley right away. It's the least you can do, after all the bloody help you were to us last night." Lieutenant Pike keeps a lid on his anger. Richie stands to his full height and looks off to the countryside, there are paths that lead to the Eske pond off the River Hull and plenty of places to hide there, deep in the forests.

"Are you listening to me?" barks Lieutenant Pike. "Help me get to my feet."

"I'm sorry, Lieutenant Pike," he says.

"They shouldn't have sent a boy to do a man's job."

"I won't be helping you to your feet. Someone knew this

was going to happen to me and you. I aim to find out why, and if that mean's getting Elizabeth back, then that's what we'll do." Richie checks his belt for the things he'll need. He still has his satchel, the bullets and the black powder, also the long-patterned muzzle loading musket and Bess at his side. He moves to the top of the carriage where the driver would have sat and there is a saddle bag open. Richie pulls out the contents and there's a package wrapped in cloth. The driver's supper. He undoes his own satchel and slips it inside.

"You're a bloody fool," says The Lieutenant. "A bloody fool. They'll kill you as soon as you approach. And then you'll be dead and she'll be worse. The best you can do for her and me, is to get me back to Beverley as swift as you can. It's madness to follow them. They've already bested you once, lad, and they'll do it again."

Richie has had practice with those of a higher status. He has learned to say no. He removes the musket from his shoulder and sets it on the ground with the barrel pointing upwards, pulls out a packet of black powder and rips it open with his teeth, then pours the contents into the nozzle. Richie has learned something that he should not at all know, it's something the Pearlman, John, taught him and Nana too, Meg as well. Confidence. It's the currency that the rich wield over the poor, what they are taught by their school masters and what is confirmed in the eyes of those who have never been successful, and work for food so that their loved ones don't starve. Richie's confidence is different, it is pretend in many ways. He knows if he dances, he'll look a fool, but he'll dance anyway. He adds a bullet down the barrel and withdraws the ramrod, spins it and inserts it in the hole to pack the whole lot down.

"Bess and me are going after her," he says.

"You'll be shot."

"You understand, Lieutenant Pike that it will take your men at least a day to get here. They do not know the area like

I do, and they don't know how to hunt either, like you said yourself, they're soldiers. Bess and I track deer in these forests. We know them. You may know how to fight wars, Lieutenant but you don't know the East Riding like we do." It makes sense. Richie also needs to get back to where he dropped his gear, partly so it is not found and also, the boots and coat give him more of the confidence he has to pretend he has. The Lieutenant considers him with more education, this lad with his big hunting dog, battered boots and a wide smile.

"You've loaded the gun twice," says the Lieutenant. Richie nods. He did not fire it last night.

"For the horse." It's a kindness. Two bullets will get through the dying animal's head better than one. The Lieutenant's eyes soften. The lad is maybe the only chance he is ever going to see his daughter alive.

"Don't shoot the horse, lad."

"Why not?"

"You might be the constable of the peace, but you're still a farm boy. You go shooting someone else's horse, even if it does need shooting, you'll be charged with something, best not mess with another man's property. And also, Mr Jackson, if you don't get those highwaymen, then someone will be to blame for all this - don't give them any more excuse to point the finger at you." He nods. That is good advice. The Lieutenant rubs his bald forehead and his voice is calm, suddenly more reasonable. "I wish I were going with you. Ten years ago, I'd be on my way now, if I hadn't shot them already."

"You're sure they went towards Driffield?"

"Yes. There'll be horse tracks. They will have cut off the road somewhere. Elizabeth will not go easy, Mr Jackson, she'll be the worst prisoner they've ever had." The two men stare at each other and the light from the summer sun peaks over the horizon of the golden fields to the east. Richie finds his floppy hat and sets it on his head.

"You be careful, Mr Jackson, and by God above I hope to see you again." Richie tips his hat and smiles.

"You can call me Richie, everyone else does."

It's a fine morning. Richie is on the road most used between Driffield and Beverley and moving quickly north. Bess is in front with her nose to the ground and tail wagging. Richie jogs behind. There are tracks on the mud but these could be anyone from a week or so past or even their own carriage. Richie and Bess are looking for a path off the road, broken undergrowth where three horses in a hurry would have made a bit of a mess. They pass the farmhouse where the carriage stopped the night previous and there is smoke coming out the chimney even though it is just light. There's no need for Richie to stop here, there would be too many questions and like the Lieutenant said, time is important if he is to get Elizabeth back. At the ruined barn further down the road, Richie stops and steps into the fallen timbers where he squatted the night previous. He finds the sack he hid and swings it over his shoulder, looks around, from the road to the fields to make sure there are no eyes on him. Bess looks up with her tongue out already and he smiles down on her, then, they are off again.

It's eight o'clock already and it's going to be hot although to sky is overcast. Richie jogs, the musket in one hand, his satchel clinks as his legs move. They have not seen any obvious signs of people leaving the road at speed yet, and Richie is worried that they may have already lost the trail. Bess slows at various points and sniffs the ground, she's not a breed known for their sense of smell, but the two of them have tracked deer before through Dalton Park and the dog gets the idea she is following something.

At a corner, next to a wide-open field of corn, Richie can see that the tall stalks have been flattened as if something has crashed through, Bess does not pause but goes straight into the field following. This is it. The highwaymen are rude and stupid, anyone can see where they've been and where they're going. There's relief that Richie is following the right way but his heart is also nervous. He has not had time to plan what he is going to do nor unpick the events of the night previous. He sees flashes in his mind as he looks into the carriage dressed as a highwayman, sees the soft curve of Elizabeth's neck and shoulders, bare above her dress. There's fear too, the bruise on the back of his head is fresh, and while he is wary of Mr Rail and the tall Mr Woodhatch, the little one who clobbered him seems to be more dangerous, devious even, whatever he is called. There are questions too about other issues, why did Stephen Middleton send him to Leconfield, did the magistrate know it would be attacked? He must have. Why did he want Richie to be there? To stop the highwaymen, or to be killed by them? What have Elizabeth Pike and her father got to do with all this?

The way becomes more difficult as Richie follows Bess through the bashed down corn plants, they are taller than he is, and he loses the dog as she disappears up in front. The crushed path breaks at the other side of the field and Richie can see where the three horses have jumped a low hedge, it looks like one ploughed straight through it. They are at the top of a very gentle hill and can see the line in the wheat field opposite that the riders cut a few hours before. Further in the distance, over some scrub there is a dip and what he knows is The River Hull. The river snakes its way from North Yorkshire and through the flatland here, through Beverley and on towards the great Humber and the North Sea and the world, so Richie has heard. He stops and squats down within the confines of the tall corn plants, suddenly conscious that he will be out in the open when he steps into the wheat field. He sets down his musket and sack and wipes the light sweat from his face, Bess returns to him wagging her tail and her nose goes to his hands.

"Let's take this a bit slow, lass," he whispers. From inside the satchel, Richie pulls out the cloth package that he pinched from the driver's seat a few hours before and begins to unwrap it. Bess pokes her nose at him as she smells the food. "You'll get some lass," he says. It's half a heavy pork pie with a thick crust and pink meat inside. Bess does her daft yelp in excitement as Richie breaks off a big bit.

"You're smaller than me," he says. He tosses about a third of the pie off into the undergrowth and Bess bounds off to eat it. Richie chews on the pastry and the gristle of the meat. He considers the horizon in front of him. The three of them would have had to cross the river somewhere, the nearest place from here is Wilfholme Landing and that will be busy, it's where farm lads load grain and livestock onto boats bound for the market at Beverley. It's not the sort of place that three riders can clatter over the river in the dead of night. The other crossing would be south at Hull Bridge in Tickton, busier even than Wilfholme landing. Maybe they didn't cross at all. Richie scans the horizon; to his right is the open plain of fields and flat land under a wide and overcast blue grey sky; to the left a thick wood of perhaps a hundred or so trees. Richie looks to the birds wheeling overhead and then down to his chest, his shirt is open and there's the swallow scar just over where his heart should be. The highwaymen won't have crossed the river. They'll be here, waiting, before they move onto somewhere safer with the horses.

Richie eats his pie as he watches the summer morning ahead, he knows the gentle and flat curves of this land and the sweet breeze coming from the east. The men he follows are rude and arrogant, the path they've left is like an arrow pointing to their position. They're nothing like highwaymen should be, nothing like Richie's Pearlman explained. He thinks back to what he knows of the two he's faced before, Mr Rail and Mr Woodhatch with their funny accents and charmless ways, if they cross Richie this time, he'll kill them and there's no doubt. The pie sticks in his throat as he considers this, but he knows that he must eat if he is to have the strength to do what must be done. A working lad is fit for nowt without breakfast. Bess returns with her head down, licking her lips and she positions herself next to where Richie is, leaning on him as she sits on her bum with her front paws out. He runs his hand down her sleek back and she looks over her shoulder. He's lucky to have her. He's lucky to have everything: these strong arms and powerful lungs, keen eyes and wide broad feet, a Nana who loves him and friends, and to live opposite a pub. He should be at work in the fields now, Jonny Low will be cursing his name some ten miles away.

He's not really sure how he will do this. There's no getting out of it neither and no going back. He robbed a carriage last night and now it's time to set that right. Isn't that what he always does? To hell with Miss Charlotte Pennyman and her money. He'll take Nana somewhere else if he has to, and that woman can have the battered cottage they live in, and she can find another poor lad to cut her hay and answer her beck and call. He opens the sack and pulls out the tricorn hat.

There's someone else Richie has to be.

His new boots crunch through the undergrowth and into the woods, in a strange way they make Richie feel taller, certainly the sturdy quality gives him confidence. He wears the tricorn hat low, and his light brown hair peeps out the back with the black handkerchief over his nose and mouth. The long blue coat is too hot for this weather, but no matter, it gives him the weight that he needs. The loaded pistol is tucked into his belt and in his right hand he carries the long musket, oiled and loaded also. By his side, Bess walks close. She senses somehow that this is not a hunt like the others she has been on, Richie makes no attempt to hide, he does not crouch, is not downwind and does not move silently. He wants to be spotted.

It does not take long for him to find them, they aren't woodsmen. They have decided to camp in a wide and open clearing. Richie can hear the fat Mr Rail talking in his loud angry sounding voice. He's looking through saddlebags that are strapped over one of four horses they have tied up to a line of trees. Richie stops and listens to the man as he calls over his shoulder to someone making a campfire, the smaller Mr Woodhatch. Elizabeth is on her knees with her hands tied in front of her by some sort of rope and a handkerchief gag around her head. Her eyes look down. She is truly frightened now. Richie stands as he is, motionless and looking across at the highwaymen in the clearing, busy about their business somehow without seeing that he is there. Bess growls low and mean and without turning, Richie senses that there is someone behind them, his hand goes to the pistol at his belt, but his thumb just touches the stock.

"I mean you no harm," whispers Richie. Initially there is no answer and Bess growls. She has turned to look at whoever is behind them.

"Drop your musket then," comes the answer. The accent is as funny and alien as that of the other two, perhaps cockney. He's not going to drop the weapon.

"That's no way to treat a guest," he answers. Richie takes care to keep his voice as low as he can, to give him a little more majesty.

"I'm telling you to drop that musket or I'll put a bullet in the back of your head." Meet strength with strength.

"Do that and you'll never get the money."

"What money?"

"The money I'm going to give you for that girl."

"How much is that going to be then?"

"You tell me." Richie has not yet counted the coins he stole from Lieutenant Pike the night previous. They are still in the purse stuffed in the inside pocket of his pants.

"What's to stop me killing you and taking the money?"

This highwayman is a cut above Mr Rail and Mr Woodhatch. Richie can smell him even though he cannot see him. The man stinks of rum and sweat, wet leather, mud and dried blood. Bess has not stopped growling.

"Nothing," answers Richie. "You're not from round here, are you?"

"Observant?" There's sarcasm on his voice.

"I'm not here to chat, I'm here to buy the girl."

"We're having this conversation at your request, you're the one who walked in on us. What do you want with the girl?"

"The carriage you hit last night, I robbed it first. With a little more finesse than you did. I'll get more for returning the girl than you will get for ransoming her."

"Is that so?" Richie feels different with the scarf over his face and the tricorn hat tight on his head. The words he uses are not really his own, nor is this confidence.

"Take my offer or leave it. The man inside the carriage you robbed is a former Lieutenant. Whatever you do to me, in a few days, once he has contacted his associates, there will be soldiers here. You'll not outrun them." Richie hears the mechanism on the pistol behind him uncock and the smaller man walks in front and lowers the weapon. The man is perhaps five foot, with long greasy black hair, an ugly pointed nose and a scowling face. He wears a brown tunic fastened tight around a pot belly with a wide belt and a golden buckle. He smiles and there are a few teeth missing.

"My name is Mr Swan," he says, "on account of my good looks." Richie does not alter his position. "Who are you?"

This is not an easy question to answer. Not right now. He is not really Richie.

"Turpin," he says. It's his mother's name. The woman who died in childbirth on the cowshed floor some seventeen years before. It feels right.

"Follow me," says Mr Swan and he begins towards the clearing where the other two men squat next to a little collection of sticks they are trying to light. Richie and Bess move after him.

"This fella here was about to walk right into camp," barks Mr Swan at the other two. They turn and the fat one, Mr Rail, jerks the pistol out of his belt in surprise when he sees the tall figure of Richie standing behind Mr Swan. Mr Woodhatch turns and his mouth gawps open. Elizabeth, shaking on her knees, looks up with her eyes wide. Richie knows these two already. He has seen them twice before and there's a knot in his stomach at the situation. What does he think will happen? Did he just expect to walk up to them, hand over the pouch of money he stole and take the girl? Mr Woodhatch narrows his eyes at the tall stranger, his lip curls in a snarl.

"Who's this?" he asks. They will not know Richie because his face is covered. The coat looks familiar to Mr Woodhatch though.

"Says his name is Turpin. He wants to buy the girl. He tells me that there'll be soldiers here soon enough and that the old man in that carriage last night was a lieutenant." There's a jokey quality to Mr Swan's voice as if what he's saying is foolish. Mr Rail levels his pistol at Richie's stomach. Mr Swan steps behind the lad once more.

"Does he know who we're working for?" he asks. It's a rhetorical question. Richie does not know this information. There's a glint in Mr Swan's beady eye and a half smile.

Richie has made an error.

A man who has ridden many country lanes and fired a pistol many times would not have put himself in this position. There are three of them and whatever happens in children's stories, men are hard to fight and stop. Richie knows this from the brawls he's had in pubs with drunk, strong working lads. These men are different. They seem cruel, nasty even, with hands that know violence, even if they don't know hard work, men who have no problem with tying up a young woman and gagging her too. Richie is on a path where he does not know where to step, he can see how the conversation will go from the grin that fat Mr Rail wears across his greasy face. They will intimidate him some, and Mr Rail will not drop his pistol, they will circle him like vultures before something will go wrong. Richie has been talked to like this before and he hasn't got time for it. The boots on his feet feel strange, the handkerchief tight across his nose hides his raised lip, the tricorn hat covers his eyes that blaze with anger. He can see that Mr Rail's pistol is not cocked; it's probably not even loaded. That's the gamble.

Standing behind Richie, Mr Swan has the security of companionship and his associate's gun trained on the stranger. He's not expecting anything to go wrong – it hasn't so far. There they are, Richie standing in the middle, with the ugly Mr Swan behind, Mr Rail in front pointing a pistol at his belly and next to him, small Mr Woodhatch, with a grin on his daft face. He doesn't recognise Richie even though he's wearing his old coat.

Sometimes it's better to start a fight, just so you can get the first punch in, maybe that's the only one you'll land. Richie's nose is covered by the black scarf, and his hat is tight over his head, like in a game of cards, they will try to read his face. Perhaps they can see Richie is about to show his hand. Mr Rail's fat thumb reaches out to cock the pistol he holds; the mechanism is stiff because he has not bothered to look after it.

Richie is swift.

There's no plan, just the rage of spirit in his chest, like always. Richie steps forward and swings the handle of the land pattern musket up towards Mr Rail's chin. The pistol is not loaded after all. He pulls the trigger to no effect. The stock end of Richie's musket connects with the man's jaw. It snaps his head back and he falls. In the same movement, Richie spins the musket and brings it to his shoulder, pointing at Mr Woodhatch a few yards away to the side. Unlike the pistol, Richie's musket is ready to fire. It has happened so quickly. Mr

Woodhatch holds his hands up and does a false grin. The lad is swift, make no mistake.

It's not over yet.

Mr Swan comes at Richie from behind. In his hand is a knife, the same one he uses to cut meat and pick his teeth. With a thud, he sinks the blade into Richie's side under his arm, right up to the handle. The heavy coat takes much of the steel, but there's still a very deep stab into Richie's ribs. It's a shock. His finger squeezes the trigger and the gun bursts in smoke and flame as the bullets leave the chamber and shoot down the barrel. It's double loaded. At long range, muskets are not so accurate, but this close, a bullet will normally hit what's intended. The heavy lead balls strike Mr Woodhatch, one just below his throat, the other into his shoulder. They make a mess. The collar bone shatters and the soft tissue of his neck rips and splits apart, he staggers as he falls backwards, his mouth open to gasp at the air. He will never get up again. Mr Swan pulls the knife out to stab it in once more. Richie spins and hammers the handle of the musket into his cheek, the bone cracks with the force of it. The man's eyes widen with fear. Richie falls on top of Mr Swan, driving the handle of the musket into his ugly face. He smashes the head into the mud below three more times, till he is tired from the effort. He stands and staggers but keeps his feet.

Now it's over.

Richie steps back away from the man's body and Bess comes to him, nervous as she tries to lick his hand. The lad feels shaken and his legs are weak. He pulls down the scarf so he can take a deep breath and looks across. Staring at him, with her wide hazel eyes, is Elizabeth with the gag still fitted and her hands tied in front of her. She shakes her head when he looks at her. Emphatic. She is trembling. Richie stands up and collects the knife from the motionless fingers of Mr Swan. As he approaches her, he crouches. Bess follows.

"I mean you no harm, Miss," he whispers. The blade goes to the knot on the bonds that have been tied so tight her pale fingers are purple, and he cuts it open. He retreats and she removes her gag, coughs and splutters between deep breaths. She is a mess, her face bruised and dirty, the ginger hair ruffled and her dress ripped. Elizabeth's eyes stream but she is not crying as she looks up at Richie.

"You saved me," she croaks. She saw him fight, saw him whack Mr Swan and beat him with the musket, saw him shoot Mr Woodhatch in his neck, watched him knock Mr Rail over and she heard his name too.

"Thank you, Mr Turpin," she says. He takes off his hat so she can see his face properly.

"Not really Mr Turpin," he answers, "It's me, Elizabeth, it's Richie Jackson. Richie Jackson of North Burton."

CHAPTER FOURTEEN

It's been about half an hour.

It's like a nightmare.

The horses have bolted and there are two men, dead.

A few minutes ago, the fat one, Mr Rail, came round from the blow Richie had dealt him with a groan. He sat up, felt his chest and stood, on his unsteady flabby knees, while Richie and Elizabeth watched. Bess growled low and mean, and then, he stumbled and ran into the trees and away, leaving them in silence with just the insects chirping in the hot summer morning.

Elizabeth has vomited a few times and Richie has found a waterskin next to the fire that was never lit. She's drunk something at least. They've done something to her, one of her ankles has been clobbered so the bone is out of line with the rest of her foot, and she can't walk properly. They have not spoken but the injury was unnecessary in Richie's opinion, to prevent her from running, he wishes he had done something worse to them. Mr Woodhatch has had his shoulder and neck blown open and he lays on his back with his eyes wide to the canopy of leaves above him, dead as a broom handle. Mr Swan's face is nearly split in two. The heavy handle of Richie's musket cracked his skull at an angle, and his face is warped, his body on its side and unmoving.

Richie has killed two men and he ought to be shaking like a drunk now but he's calm. He can't change a thing about what has happened. Elizabeth takes a drink on the water skin and coughs into her hand. She looks exhausted, sitting on a log with her dress ripped.

"So, it was you that robbed us first then, Mr Jackson of North Burton?" Her voice is level and steady. She recognised the tricorn hat. There is steel to Elizabeth evident when you first see her, but clear too now that events of significance have had an effect. She has had her ankle nearly broken and been robbed, twice, tied up and now saved. This is more than happens to most Beverley lasses in a whole lifetime. "Was it you than robbed us?" she repeats.

"Aye," says Richie. He stands opposite looking down on her. "I'm sorry for it too."

"Do you have my father's money?"

"Aye."

"I'll have that back."

Richie fiddles in his pants and reaches the pouch of coins that he has yet to count. He tosses it over to Elizabeth and there's a clink as she catches it.

"You'll hang for that," she says.

"For coming back to save you?"

"For putting a gun in my face. My father is a soldier. He'll see you flogged from the Market Cross to the North Bar for what you've done."

"I came back for you."

"But you robbed us first, Mr Jackson of North Burton, you and your lads robbed us, you made my father go white as a sheet."

"There were no lads, it was just me."

"My father knew there were more of you."

"He was wrong. It was just me and Bess here keeping watch. Just like it's just Bess and me here now." Elizabeth is not done being angry with Richie yet.

"Regardless of what you've done subsequently, you held a carriage up, Mr Jackson, you'll swing for it. I'll see to it myself." She attempts to stand from the log she sits on, and pain shoots up her leg from her ankle, she winces as she sits down once more.

"You can't walk."

"I know very well what I can and can't do, Sir," she snaps.

"It's not so far back to Beverley, perhaps a few hours, I can help you."

"I think you've done enough."

"I'm not going to leave you here," he says. Richie is concerned. He may well be hanged for what he has done, highway robbery is as serious a business as there is. He cannot just leave her for a number of reasons, firstly it's wrong and also, Elizabeth knows that he robbed the carriage. If she doesn't say anything, it might go away. He wipes the sweat from his brow and takes off the long blue overcoat, the heavy material took most of Mr Swan's blade, but not all of it. Richie's white shirt is thick with red blood and he winces when he sees how much there is of it. Elizabeth takes a breath when she sees how bad it is.

"He got me under my arm, I think." Richie's fingers go to the wound on his side under his armpit.

"Take off your shirt," says Elizabeth. "You'll bleed to death if it isn't seen to," she's half joking. He struggles to get the material over his head, and he tosses it onto the ground in front of him. It's sticky with blood. Richie's chest is smooth and toned from working every day of his life, but his lips and cheeks look pale.

"I'll need to stop it bleeding," he says. The wound does not seem so big, but it looks like he has lost quite a bit of blood. Richie casts around the bushes behind Elizabeth. There's a patch of dock leaves and he rips some of them off and stuffs them in his mouth, chewing up the bitter foliage. He stands and then applies the green paste from his mouth to the wound. He picks up his shirt from the floor and passes it to Elizabeth.

"Would you tie this around me, to keep the poultice in place?" She stands on her good foot and wraps the shirt, wet with blood, around his thin but muscular torso. There's no drama in this lad. He's been stabbed but what else can he do but try to fix the situation? This is how it works in the East Riding; you can cry all you like, but it doesn't get things done. As she works, Richie glances to the forest behind them where Mr Rail escaped. There's no telling if there are more of them, or if the fat man will come back.

"There's a healer woman in Etton, not far from here," says Elizabeth. "She might be able to help you." Richie smiles.

"She might be able to help you as well." Standing in front of him with all the weight on her good foot, Elizabeth looks up into his blue eyes and sees steadiness there. He does not wince as she ties the shirt around him tight, neither does he complain, a smile comes to the side of his mouth. He saved her and her anger is gone. She sees the young man from North Burton and not a robber.

"How long have you been a highwayman, Mr Jackson?"

"Not even a day."

"So you've never asked a lady to stand and deliver."

"Not yet, Miss, but I'd have a mind to."

"Really? Would you ask me to stand and deliver if you robbed me again?" Richie swallows.

"I would Miss, aye," he whispers. She holds his gaze in her hazel eyes.

"Thank you for coming after me, Mr Jackson." Her voice is soft with her breath on his bare chest. It feels divine. "If you were to rob me again, what would you do with me?" She is playful.

"I'd have a mind to take you far away from all this, Miss, far from Beverley, north to Scarborough perhaps."

"You'd capture me then?"

"Not capture, you'd come of your own free will."

"We'd be married," she says. "In secret." Richie looks at her with one of his eyebrows raised, she's taking it a bit too far. Perhaps it's all the emotion of the robberies, the violence, the terror as the men captured her and the relief of this big lad, Richie Jackson. "Does Mr Turpin have a secret hideaway?"

"Aye," he answers. "Out at Dalton Park, the big forest north of Etton, follow the little stream from the road to the West. There's a wide and old oak in the forest, Bess and I rest there when we go poaching." Elizabeth does not look so impressed.

"I rather imagined a tumbled down cottage on the cliffs, Mr Jackson, something with a little romance in it."

"I just told the truth."

"A highwayman ought to keep the truth close to their chest."

"Men who are afraid tell lies," he says. She considers this and her clever hazel eyes look at the man in front of her. She likes this. She likes him.

There's a shout from the wood behind them, a man calling out to another. The moment changes and Richie looks at where the noise came from.

"We have to get moving," he says. "There may be more of them."

"I don't think I can walk," she answers.

"I'll carry you." Her eyes narrow, the playfulness gone, the serious tone returns:

"I'm not a child."

There's another shout from the wood behind and rustling coming from within. They look at each other in fear.

"Please excuse me for this, Miss," says Richie. He scoops her up into his long arms and steps over the log she sat on, carries her past the body of Mr Woodhatch and over the lifeless form of Mr Swan, in a minute they are away from the clearing and Richie dips his head under a branch so they are out of sight. Bess follows. The three of them crouch in the darkness of the foliage. Richie in the middle, Bess on one side and Elizabeth at the other. He reaches out his hand to the black dog to calm her, they need to be as silent as they can, for in their current state they won't be able to outrun whoever is coming through the woods towards them, and Richie doesn't have the stomach for another fight.

Some fifty yards away, crashing through the undergrowth is the figure of Mr Rail. This time he carries a musket in his hands but his face is red and hot with fear, he looks up and down the clearing, and then back to another figure that joins him from behind. The new man is dressed in clean black pants and riding boots and a wide brimmed hat. There's blonde hair spilling out of the back. The two of them walk to the body of Mr Woodhatch and look down on it. The man in black shakes his head then takes off his hat to wipe his brow.

Richie draws in breath sharp. He knows this man. It is the person who sent him the note to be at Leconfield. It is the venerable magistrate who employed Richie as the justice of the peace for North Burton.

It is Stephen Middleton.

Elizabeth touches Richie's arm and he looks at her in the darkness of the bush where they hide, she knows this man too and her eyes are wide and frightened. This is more than just a robbery, Elizabeth and her father are targets, Richie is aware, more suddenly, of his insignificance in this story and that it is as Nana said, he was given a gun so they could shoot him. Miss Charlotte Pennyman must be mixed up in this somehow too. Richie feels his stomach bubble in terror as he watches these men in the clearing, now looking down at the smashed face of Mr Swan. If Richie thought he was going to hang before, now he is almost certain. What's the reason Stephen Middleton wanted him to be with the carriage at Leconfield, to be killed? Either way, the village lad has been made a fool of. The two men in the clearing talk together and Stephen Middleton shakes his head and waggles his finger as he explains something important to the fat man with his back turned to Richie and Elizabeth. Mr Rail points in the direction of Leconfield as he replies. They will know who they are searching for.

In the bushes, whatever indignation Elizabeth felt previous has melted away. If it were not for this tall and brave lad, she would be in grave danger. Richie taps his shoulder and turns his back to her to indicate she should put her hands around his neck. She takes a deep breath in fear. He will carry her piggyback.

Things have taken a turn for the worst.

It's a struggle for Richie. Elizabeth is not so heavy, but he can't run as well as he could normally. In his right hand he carries the long musket, on the other shoulder is his satchel, heavy with the pistol and the bullets he carries within. He has cut through the woods and into the long grass by the side of the River Hull, running as quick and as silent as he can, he's confident they have not been followed, there's none of the noise and bluster that men like Mr Rail bring with them. Besides, Bess would hear them if they did.

He runs through the grass that grows up taller even than his own head till he comes to the banks of the river. Here, Elizabeth's arms slip from around his shoulders, she tries to stand on her good ankle but pitches backwards onto her backside and into the soft mud. Her ginger hair falls over her face to cover the agony and indignation of it. She does not try to get up and Richie squats next to her. It's as good a place as any to rest and she looks pale.

Here, the river beside them is perhaps twenty feet wide and a rich brown colour, it's not dirty, just muddy. If they follow the water south it will take them to Beverley, but Richie is not so sure that's the best way to go, given that there are people who are looking for them. He takes the waterskin from his satchel and offers it to her. Her face is red and worried, those hazel eyes not so solid or calm. They have been quiet since the clearing some twenty minutes previous. She does not take the drink.

"You know who that was with the robber, don't you?" she asks.

"Aye," says Richie. "It was Stephen Middleton, the magistrate, the man who asked me to look after your carriage. What does he want with you?"

"It's the Reformation of Manners Society, Mr Jackson. My father and I are not exactly welcomed in polite affairs of Beverley." Richie frowns. He does not really understand.

"How could he find fault with you, with charity?" She rolls her eyes.

"It's not about passing food to wretches, Mr Jackson, or stopping men and women drinking themselves to death because it's ungodly. We're trying to free people from the grip of the church. We've been threatened before." Richie squats and takes a swig on the waterskin.

"Do you think they want you dead?"

"Not dead," her face takes on a bitter quality like the word is rude and somehow distasteful. "It's probably a warning, my ransom would be a signal to my father to stop what he is doing. That may have changed however, you upped the stakes when you killed two of them."

"That's nothing to do with you."

"It's not how anyone who doesn't like my father and I will see it, Mr Jackson. We're non-conformists. We want an end to the church as it is, there are many of us in Kingston Upon Hull, men whose fathers stood on the side of God when the civil war started, men and woman who oppose the king. People who believe in the freedom of everyone, even the poor, we want the land given back to them." Her eyes blaze with passion. Richie has heard this kind of talk before, not as eloquently explained by Nana, and with less fervor when recounted by the Pearlman.

Bess comes out of the tall grass, she wags her tail and puts her head down as she goes to Elizabeth. She rubs the back of the dog's head and her eyes soften.

"I'm in real trouble," says Richie.

"Yes, you are," she adds.

"I'll not see my Nana again, nor the pub where I grew up, nor my Meg or Jonny Low or the chapel at St Michael's neither." Richie looks out across the water of the River Hull. He does not sound quite as upset as he should do.

"You won't see anything at all when they hang you."

"I'll not be hanged," he says. "Once we follow the river

down to Beverley, I'll deliver you to your father, and then, Bess and I will be off. To the north probably."

"Of course," there's a touch of sarcasm to her voice. "You've been a highwayman for almost a day. What's the name you used? Turpin, is it?"

"Aye."

"Where did you dream that one up?"

"It's my mother's name."

"Richie Turpin. You'll be the scourge of the north, feared and loved in equal measure." Richie winces. He's not sure about that, none of it and even less about the way Elizabeth speaks.

"Everyone knows me as Richie."

"You'd have to change it to something else. Richard. Rick. Hitch, or something." He cocks his head, he's not sure about that either.

"I think we have bigger worries right now," he whispers.

"Really?" Elizabeth has a cruel streak a bit like Nana but worse, somehow. He sees her sitting between the reeds where the ground is soft and damp. She's frightened, perhaps this is what brings out the harsh tone. Richie leans forward, he drops his voice.

"Will you be safe if I get you to your father's house in Beverley?" She nods. "If Bess and I are to get you there then you'll have to help us, you'll have to be on our side and keep that sharp tongue steady. Do you understand that, Elizabeth?"

"Do you mean not mention that you robbed my father and I last night?"

"Aye," he answers.

"Why did you come back to save me, Mr Jackson?"

"You'll call me Richie."

"Why?"

"I did wrong when I robbed your carriage. Now I want to do right. That's what I always do." Her smooth eyes consider the lad in front, and she hears the light whoosh of the water as the current takes it south, in the sky there wheels a seagull. Without this man's help, she will not get home, the robbers that captured her would not have killed her, they would have done things, unspeakable, given the opportunity. Mr Swan broke her ankle with the back of a hand axe, cruel and straightforward like he was snapping a branch to put on a fire. They meant her harm and she was afraid. She too knows the story of the girl from South Cave. With Richie, she feels safe, somehow. He has a quality to him that Elizabeth cannot quite put her finger on, her father might call it character, he's capable too of standing his ground. Like her father, Elizabeth sees the bigger picture, thinks of what such a man as the highwayman, Mr Turpin, could do if he were under the employ of the Reformation of Manners Society. Now it's Elizabeth's time to move her face forward so she is just an inch away from him. He can see her smooth skin and her light ginger hair falling over her eyes.

"If you get me home, Richie Jackson, I'll forget everything that I know about you, but Mr Turpin, that man will owe me a favour." She puts her hand up to his face and lays a palm on his cheek gentle and soft, the sensation sends shivers down his back. Richie maybe six foot four but he is also a seventeen-year-old boy and he has only ever kissed two girls, only one of which he remembers. "Is that a deal?" she asks.

He nods.

If she had asked him to guide her home from hell, he would have agreed that.

It's not far off the truth.

Richie knows this flat land. If they keep along the banks of the River Hull and among the tall grass then they won't be spotted. The going is hard on the soft ground. Elizabeth is heavy on his back, and he feels weak from the wound under his arm, it's more a dragging pain that leaves his muscles limp and weak and his forehead with a frown.

This can be a busy river. Farmers north of here all the way to Driffield use it to transport their animals and crops to Beverley. If they were to walk the side of the same river at harvest time in October, there would be shallow bottomed boats up and down with farm lads shouting from the uneven decks. Thankfully, it's quiet.

Elizabeth struggles with her arms around Richie's shoulders. Bess walks in front. They are bound for the village of Tickton. The river widens and there is a wooden bridge that leads to Beverley. It's far, perhaps four miles. Ordinarily, this distance would take Richie a lot less than an hour at a dawdle but with the ground underfoot so bad, the reeds to push through, and the weight on his shoulders and back; this journey will take Richie most of the day. If they get to Tickton and then walk to Beverley, they'll be spotted by someone who knows them. Elizabeth is a figure around town, along with her father, and word will have quickly spread that there was a robbery at Leconfield. Like in North Burton, gossip is wildfire among working folk, so they'll have to move into the town when it's dark if they are to get to Lieutenant Pike's property on Toll Gavel without anyone of note spotting them. He has explained his plan to Elizabeth and told her to keep her eyes and ears open while he carries her, she has been quiet for the last half an hour, the pain in her ankle is hurting her too.

The river bends off to the left and in front, opens up to a wide body of water ringed with trees and a mud island in the middle. This is Eske Lake. A dragon fly buzzes past Elizabeth's head and, on shimmery haze in the water, a heron turns its head from far away, sees them, and takes to the blue sky on huge white wings.

"Now you be easy," says Richie down to Bess. She'll chase the birds if he tells her too or if she gets too excited.

"I need to rest," says Elizabeth from above. Her head is just behind his, he turns to see her eyes are thin in pain.

"We must keep moving to higher ground, Miss," he

answers. "If there's a high tide, we could get stranded, or worse. I know a place, not too far."

"We're miles from the ocean here," she says. This may be so, but the kickback from the North Sea washes all the way down the mighty Humber and into the River Hull, stretching many miles up into the East Riding, past Dunswell and Thearne. River folk know how to use the tide to carry their boats much further than the wind could, but what would Elizabeth know of this. They press on, Richie looks up to the sun in the sky and tries to see how far away from midday they might be. The water level will rise slowly and they must keep moving if they don't want to be up to their waist in it. There's a tiny wood ahead and where the trees grow the ground is higher than the river. Richie makes his way towards a twisted dogwood, the bloom will have faded months ago, but the branches are thick with green leaves. Under the canopy, Richie sets Elizabeth down and she struggles to sit with her back against the twisted trunk. Bess comes to her and she grins as the face comes to lick her. Richie takes off his waterskin.

"He's a good dog."

"Bess is a girl," he answers.

"She's a comfort to you, is she, Mr Jackson?"

"Aye, but she's more than that, she's a fine rabbiter and we've hunted deer before now, back up at Dalton Park." Elizabeth's face, now gifted with the wisdom of weariness has understanding. If she and Richie were to pass each other at Wednesday Market, Beverley, of a busy afternoon, she would perhaps consider him wretched with the nobility of Christian goodness in her proud nose. Now she sees the virtues of his strong hands and his friendly Bess, the humility in his smiles and that he looks pale even though his skin is tanned from days and days out in the fields. Her father taught her never to look down on the poor, but she never considered that she may look up to them.

"They won't hang you, Mr Jackson," she says. "Your cause

is just. I don't believe those men were going to let me go, now I come to think about it. I heard them talking. They were going to take me north, to Bridlington. I heard talk of boats and of the bay up at Flamborough Head."

"If they catch me, Miss Pike, I'll be hanged, we both know that. That's what they do to lads like me. I'll carry the blame, we both know."

"Not if I can help it, Mr Jackson. That's what our organisation wants, for men like you, who have done nothing wrong to have the protection of God and the law."

"Good luck with that." He takes a drink on the waterskin, and his eyes are weary, his lips paler than they should be. Richie has done plenty wrong which she has forgotten about.

"Have you already decided what your actions will be, Mr Jackson." He has told her to call him Richie.

"I have, Miss Pike. I've explained that I will get you to your father in Beverley."

"I mean after that?"

"I think I have."

"You'll go back to North Burton?"

"Aye, one last time." The world around them is still and green, blue-sky peeps through the green dogwood tree leaves and the sunlight warms Elizabeth's ginger hair and face. They could be on a summer walk these two, with a picnic and sitting in the shade for a rest.

"You said about your Nana, you said you robbed my carriage to pay for your Nana's house? What of her?"

"I'll take money to her, somehow and then, I'll leave, and I'll never come back."

"Just like that? You'll leave everything behind?"

"Aye," his voice is flat. It does not sound like much of a plan to Elizabeth.

"Where else have you been, Mr Jackson? Where do you know to go?"

"There's someone I need to find, Miss, a man who left

North Burton a time ago." He looks at her hazel eyes. "I need to find him."

"Who?"

"My father." Elizabeth has heard tales of working folk and their families, how the drunk stray and there's a new father for the children every week. Richie does not seem like this, somehow.

"Where's your mother?"

"A long time dead."

"Mine too," says Elizabeth. "What will happen when you find him?"

"I thought I'd kill him," says Richie, "but now I'm not so sure." She rests her head on the bark of the tree trunk as she considers the young man, he's not as carefree as he looks although he hides it well.

"What made you change your mind?"

"Now I know that it's for the best, for someone to leave and never come back."

"You could stay and fight, Mr Jackson, fight for your name. You're a brave lad, you would have my father and I to help you, you'd have the love of your Nana to stay for."

"You don't know my Nana," says Richie.

"Is there nobody else, no girl you have eyes for?"

He shakes his head.

"What about you, Miss Pike? Will you be wed?"

"I court men. It's not for love or for the want of anything but influence."

"You don't believe in love?"

"It's not that. I do, but the man I'll fall in love with, why, he'll be tall and brave, rich in manners more than coin, someone who would look after me as I would look after him. I'm in no rush to find him, either, Mr Jackson, and if I never find him, then so be it, but I know I will love one day." Bess has nestled next to her long dress and put her head into Elizabeth's lap while the lady strokes her soft ears.

"You've never been in love then," says Richie, his voice is dark and suddenly faraway. "That kind of love destroys everything it touches and it's better to be away from it, if you know what's good for you." Richie uses the long musket to help him get to his feet and his face looks strange now it is serious and bleak.

"You're wrong, Mr Jackson," she says. "Love heals us and makes us more than we can be."

"That's for your story books, Miss. Love makes those who can see blind, makes a bight person dull, cripples one who can run." She is suddenly sad for this lad who stands in front of her under a dogwood tree, in a swamp next to the river with his kind pale eyes. Of anyone she has seen, he's been brave and warm, tall too and rich in manner more than coin. There's a change in the light somehow as he reaches his hand down to help her up.

"We have to keep moving. If we keep to this side of the river, we'll make it to The Crown at Tickton soon enough. We'll wait till dusk and then, I'll take you home." Elizabeth nods as she stands and her hand goes out to rest on his bare chest just over the bandage that is wrapped around it. Tall Elizabeth is a good few inches shorter than he and her hazel eyes stare into his. She is not used to looking up to men, being this height.

They are too close.

She can feel his heart beating within him and the strength there, and the sorrow too. Perhaps she would be dead if it were not for this man.

"Love will come to take you, Richie," she says. It is the first time she has used his name, "and it will set you free."

"Not I, Elizabeth," he answers with conviction. "I have told you; love destroys everything it touches, it destroyed my mother when she died as she bore me, and it destroyed my Meg, and it destroyed the man who told me he was my father too. It will not destroy me." There's water in this young man's eyes as he speaks these words, truth he has known but did not dare speak. He's not afraid of drunks in Walkington pubs or highwaymen with pistols and knives or the hangman's noose even, but he is afraid of this woman looking up at him. He is afraid that he would do anything for her, he can feel the darkness of passion slipping through his veins, making the hairs on the back of his neck stand up and the touch of her palm on his chest burns him.

It cannot be.

Not now and not ever.

Not after what Meg told him.

"You'll not be able to stop it," she whispers up to him.

"You don't know me, Miss."

"I know you well enough already, Richie. You came back to save me, and if you need me to, I'll do the same for you."

Richie turns away from her. He has to believe this is not true. He's not worth it.

"We must keep moving," he says.

This is the way it starts. One half of the two sees something they did not notice previous. There's at first a kind word and perhaps a smile. There could be a touch, an accident maybe. Another kind word. This is the way it plays. Between these two the process in the summer wetland is charged, like the dragonflies that buzz by their heads and the frogs that chatter in the tall reeds by their side. They are already closer than they should be, as he carries her through the reeds. Elizabeth's arm is across Richie's strong chest, her head peers over his shoulder and her legs are wrapped around his waist; tighter than before.

CHAPTER FIFTEEN

It's just turning from day to dusk.

They are on the bank of a gulley, laid on the soft grass not half a mile away from the Crown pub at Tickton. Richie is on his side looking out over the open fields and Elizabeth on her front looking towards the pub, this way they can see if anyone is coming. Bess lays in between them with her body snuggled in close to Elizabeth. They are waiting for night proper to come, and the sky is orange red across the horizon turning blue further up and the long clouds are dusted with bronze. There's the smell of summer in the air, cut wheat from far away and the noise of starlings wheeling around each other in a dance before they settle in the trees. Elizabeth has changed the dressing on Richie's side using a strip she cut from the bottom of her dress. She's not so much in pain with her ankle unless she stands on it. Richie says it will hurt more as it gets better.

They have discussed much in whispers, for in the situation they face, the normal rules of the East Riding have melted away. It does not matter that Richie is a farm lad, and is only just able to write his name, or that Elizabeth can speak Latin and until recently had a lady who helped her get dressed in the morning. Out here, as they lay waiting for night to fall, they are just two young people who share the same purpose of getting Elizabeth home. Bess wriggles between the two of them on the slope and her head goes to rest on Richie's chest, she smacks her mouth lightly and yawns.

Elizabeth has told Richie much about the Reformation of Manners Society and about the might of the organised church, how men with money buy positions of power and influence. There are those, in Kingston Upon Hull, merchants of wealth, non-conformists, who want change and to be able to worship as they see fit. They could use a man like Richie Jackson, she has told him. The talk goes over Richie's head a lot of the time, but he watches the way her lips move as she speaks, and the ginger hair falling in front of her face, and her high cheek bones, and her smooth skin with a dusting of perfect freckles. At times she has reached out and touched his hand as she explains, in earnest, and in these moments, Richie feels his stomach tremble and his head buzz at the enormous perfection of her. How will he ever explain this to Jonny Low?

"It'll be dark within the hour," he whispers.

"Good," answers Elizabeth. She does not mean this.

"We'll move past The Crown as soon as it's dark enough and then cut over the moor to the right, and to Beverley itself." He can still see her eyes looking across at him in the half light.

"Then what?"

"Do you have any people you know this side of the town?" She shakes her head.

"Why?"

"If I have to carry you down the lane we'll stick out like a sore thumb. Everyone from here to Wetwang will know about the robbery at Leconfield by now. If I could leave you at the edge of town, it'd be easier. If I could leave you in that pub over there, it would be much better. You could ask someone to ride you into town – you're known here." Elizabeth frowns in the darkness as if this is a bad idea.

"I don't think you'd be safe, Richie. At my father's house, he'll offer you the reward you deserve and protection also. You have to get me there." Richie frowns back. "It's over two miles to the Minster at Beverley from the Crown, it would be worth your while, I promise it." She takes out the pouch of coins that Richie robbed from her father, and that he gave back to her.

"Take this," she says and the coins clink within.

"What for?"

"It's payment, for bringing me back?" Richie takes the leather pouch in his palm and spirits it into his pocket.

It's dark enough now for Richie to sit up and his hand goes

to his temple, he has a throbbing headache. The last twenty-four hours have taken a toll on him, in every way. The stab wound on his side stings and his muscles feel sore and weak, his vision is blurred and his stomach gripes. Richie Jackson is not sure he can carry Elizabeth to the pub half a mile away, let alone right into Beverley. Elizabeth sits up also.

"Richie," she says as she puts her hand on his leg. "It will be worth your while and what you have done for me so far, I appreciate. I don't say this lightly. I hold you in high stead." Her brow is clear and the words are earnest, thoughtful, designed to get to him; for now Elizabeth has spent time with Richie Jackson, she wants to see more. Here is maybe the tall and brave lad who has more manners than coin.

Under them, Bess suddenly wriggles and gets to her feet, her chest growls low as she looks towards the darkness of the way they travelled that afternoon, but Richie catches her, and whispers for her to stay calm in the darkness. The two exchange a look.

Who has followed them?

In silence, Richie gets to his feet, feels for his satchel and swings the strap over his head, then picks up his musket. His hand goes out to pull Elizabeth from the ground and she is silent too, although the pain in her ankle roars through her leg to her hip. She leans on him and they walk, down the track and towards the orange lamp light outside the Crown which has just flickered on in the mid distance. She is unsteady, moving in hops almost, unable to put any weight on her ankle. Richie turns his head to look at the darkness behind them, there's the sound of a horse's hooves stopping a few hundred yards away and Richie tries to quicken the pace, but by the weight she puts on him, it's clear that Elizabeth cannot move as fast as they need to. In the afternoon, Richie had time to get her onto his back, shuffle the weight around and take the going slow but now, in the grey dark of the summer night, he cannot. His heart begins in his chest as he hears the snort of the horse behind them, far enough away for the time being. Richie turns to her, puts his arm around her waist so he can hoist her up, but in the darkness, she cannot read his intentions. As he pulls her towards him, he feels her lips on his and there, in the new black of the summer evening, with the glow of the Crown half a mile up a mud track and a horseman following, they kiss. Her hand moves to the back of his head and grips his hair, she can feel his heartbeat and his chest shiver as their lips meet. He pulls her up to him and carries her in both arms, and she grips his shoulders.

He jogs, Elizabeth in his arms, and somewhere in front is Bess with her nose to the ground. Richie can hardly feel the muscles in his thighs and his brain fogs in and out as he holds her.

He cannot keep this up for long.

As he runs, Richie's ears hear the noise of the world rushing toward him suddenly, the squawks from the crows in the tall trees behind the pub, the crunching of the grass under his feet, the hot breath of Elizabeth on his face, his right hand gripping the musket and his left holding her body close to his.

Richie shouldn't be here.

He should be in the Bay Horse with a cup full of Philipson's bitter ale and Jonny Low next to him, the sound of a fiddle playing in the back room and the easy noise of conversation and laughter.

The orange light of the Crown is closer, and he leans back so that he does not drop her. His teeth bar in effort. There is only so much the mind can command the body to do. Behind them in the darkness, the rider has heard the movement and the snorts of the horse are nearer than they should be, the hoof beats in the soft mud are close together as it picks up speed.

"Nearly there," whispers Elizabeth into his face and Richie struggles on, but he is fading fast. The wound under his arm where he was stabbed is leaking once more from the effort, and his chest is wheezing, his muscles are losing energy and his mind is beginning to blur. The orange light from the lamp of the Crown is a few yards away.

Elizabeth feels his legs go under him, and he lets out a low groan. The musket clatters to the floor. He stops and Elizabeth tumbles out of his arms, rolling onto the hard mud of Hull Road. She lifts her head and stands as best she can. Cantering down the main street, and moving towards Beverley is the noise of another horse, separate from the dark rider behind them. It could be anyone, a courier bringing a letter from Bridlington or Scarborough, a soldier returning home from his time away, a lover visiting a lady he knows in one of the big old houses within the walls of Beverley. The light from the pub lamp barely reaches them, but Elizabeth can see the musket that Richie has dropped by his side. He is on one knee, his face bleak and pale with fatigue. She picks up the musket and, unsteady on her one good foot, shoulders the stock, cocks the action and her finger reaches for the trigger. As the horseman approaches, she fires into the air.

A single musket shot rattles into the night.

Several things happen at once.

The landlord of the Crown, a Scotsman, looks up from the newspaper he is reading while leaning on the bar. His eyesight is not what it once was at long distance. He puts down his drink and makes his way to the window, the one where the lamp hangs outside. He sees a very tall man clamber atop a mottled white cob with ease, sees him pull a lass up behind him, then sees them both canter off towards Beverley way. The landlord will testify that the man was a rider of some skill, although his eyesight is not what it once was.

The horse rider moving along Hull Road towards Beverley, feels his steed rear up at the sound of the musket shot, and he pitches backward, slipping from the saddle and crashing into the road below. Later, he will swear that a musket ball flew past his ear and that he is lucky to have his skull in one piece, although this is not true.

At the noise, the dark rider who has tracked Richie and Elizabeth, digs his heels into his mount and begins to canter towards the orange lamp light of the Crown, hooves spray mud behind them in the darkness and the rider lifts his body from the saddle and grips with his knees to gain speed. He must get to these two before they reach Beverley.

Elizabeth grabs the reins of the horse, pulls the big head of the mottled cob towards her and uses it to lean on.

"Get up," she whispers and Richie rises from his knee. As if he has been riding all his life, he lifts his right foot and slots it into the stirrup, holds the saddle and hauls himself up, swinging his leg over as he sits down. He holds his hand out, Elizabeth grabs it, and he pulls her up with the last of his strength. She uses his shoulder to clamber behind and her bum finds the back of the saddle. Richie is fading in front of her and she must get them moving as quickly as she can. Elizabeth puts her arms around his waist to grab the reins, gives them a flick, digs in her heels and the frightened horse begins with a start down the road towards the bridge over the River Hull and towards Beverley.

"Stay with me, Richie," she whispers.

She cannot even see over his big shoulder.

You shouldn't really ride a horse fast in the dark. Especially a horse you've never ridden on before, even though they have pretty good eyesight. Elizabeth is not the most skilled rider but she knows how to use her legs to signal, to keep the reins tight enough for the animal to respond. She can't really see where she is going but most horses aren't stupid, they don't run into things even if they're told. Richie grips the saddle with his knuckles white and his legs tense. The horse powers on as Elizabeth digs in her heels, the hooves thunder over the wooden bridge to the lights of Beverley some two miles ahead.

They are followed. Whoever it is will be faster than they are, given there is only one rider on their horse, and it will not take them long to catch up. There is only one way to go, should Elizabeth stray off the path the horse will almost certainly fall on some hole or divert. The only choice is to keep on and hope that the rider behind will give up once they reach the lights and houses of Beverley.

"You have to relax, Richie," she yells. The big lad in front is tense in anticipation and fatigue. The summer wind is in his hair and he realises that he's left the musket back at the pub where Elizabeth dropped it. He tugs the pistol out of his belt and swallows down his fear, holds the saddle with one hand and glances back into the darkness under his shoulder. There's nothing in the night behind them that he can see, he smells the blood coming out of him and the blue coat he stole from Mr Woodhatch all those nights ago is wet with it. He feels far away as he turns to look over the horse's head in front.

This is what dying must feel like. He is sorry to go, in a way, in another, glad of it. His body is weary, his muscles lack the strength to keep him upright and Richie feels himself tipping forward. Nana will be okay without him. He has done a great duty in rescuing Elizabeth and he is certain that her father will help the old woman out, even Miss Charlotte wouldn't be cruel enough to just kick her into the street. Jonny Low will be angry that he has to finish the hay baling on his own, but there'll be a drink at Richie's funeral for him, he'll be glad of that. Meg over in Etton will mourn him, aye, but not the way in which he died – at a highwayman's knife, that's Richie Jackson, died fighting three robbers in the woods, rescued a lass, he did. He can see Philipson from the pub telling the story to strangers in the winter in front of a roaring fire, how Richie Jackson used to drink in here, pointing to the corner where he and Jonny Low would play cards. There's a bellowing in Richie's ear.

"Don't you bloody die on me, Richie Jackson." It's the high voice of Elizabeth shouting up at him. The lad's senses rush back, he feels the night air on his sweating face, feels his hand limp around the handle of his pistol below and the muscles in the horse as it powers forward towards lights and a house ahead.

Looming out of the darkness behind, with his nose and face covered by a scarf, atop a black horse bigger than the mottled cob Elizabeth steers, is the man who has followed them from the clearing where Richie killed the highwaymen. He is intent, but he needs the lad alive and so, the blackwood pistol in the holster on his chest will remain there. His horse is much faster and its large hooves thud in four beats on the dirt road as it approaches and draws level with Elizabeth. She looks at him, only the pink of his eyes and forehead visible in the darkness. Richie sees him too, focuses on the figure in the darkness matching their speed, he lifts his sagging head and levels the pistol under his arm. There's something familiar about the dark man

"Slow down," commands the rider.

Richie pulls the trigger. Sparks and smoke roar into the warm night and the bullet erupts from the barrel towards the figure as the horse he rides pulls up and he falls back behind them. Richie cannot know if he has hit him.

The lane changes below them, as the horse finds firmer ground and there are lights suddenly. They have passed the moor lands to the east of Beverley and are on Hull Bridge Road proper where the ground is better kept. Elizabeth does not stop, nor does she look behind.

Richie feels himself falling forward as he drifts in and out of consciousness, he is, in one minute at home in bed with Nana cooking up something on the fire, the next he is in church listening to Reverend Page's earnest and clear voice of a Sunday morning, then he is deep in the forest of Dalton Park with Bess next to him as they hunt, and then, just as quickly, he is riding double with Elizabeth, turning at Mill Lane. They power down the path, past the creaking sails of a windmill and the houses, built close together and high. Elizabeth knows these streets, but she does not stop, a couple of lads scatter as she rides through them.

"We're nearly there, Richie," she calls and tries to keep the lad from falling. The light of the Angel pub looms in front of them and she banks right as the horse hits the cobble stones, slowing her steed up so not to slip, and she holds onto Richie so he can't slide off.

Her father's house is on Toll Gavel, not twenty yards away. She turns left up Walkergate and to her father's courtyard and livery, where, mercifully, the black wooden gates are still open. She bellows as they enter the yard:

"Lieutenant Pike!" and then, "Father!" Her voice rages out across the dark summer streets as she pulls up the horse and swings her legs over the side, half falling to the ground as Richie's body pitches onto her. She struggles to catch him and there are tears in her eyes as she does, her broken ankle buckling. She yells for her father again and falls to her knees with Richie's body on her lap and her hands sticky with his blood on his smooth face. She weeps. He cannot die, this brave lad, he cannot die in her arms when she has just found him, when she has only now just seen him and felt him and kissed his lips.

"Don't you bloody die on me, Richie Jackson," she hisses again. "Not now, not after all this." There's the clatter of hooves next to her and Elizabeth's heart drops as she looks up. The bullet must have missed him. At the gates, on the same black horse, is the rider that tracked them from Leconfield all afternoon and chased them from Tickton too. The blackwood pistol he carries is levelled down at her, the scarf is across his face, and his jet-black hair peeps out from under his hat.

· "Step away from him, Miss," he whispers. The voice is husky. Like he holds his blackwood pistol, this man is rock steady. "I'll not ask again," he adds. He swings his leg off the horse and steps down in a fluid movement.

"You'll have to shoot me," she says.

"I don't think he would want that, Miss, do you? After all his efforts this day to secure your freedom."

"I'm afraid, Sir, you will have to shoot me to get him." This, Elizabeth means, and her voice breaks as she speaks. She feels a hand on her shoulder and glances behind her, there's the muzzle of a blunderbuss that comes from the darkness and her father, Lieutenant Pike steps forward carrying it.

"You get back on your horse and out of my yard, robber," he says. The man in black does not alter his position, his blue eyes look over the old man.

"I mean to take this boy, and if I have to shed blood then I will." The Lieutenant considers this. It has been a difficult time, he has been robbed twice, lost his daughter and then got her back. He is not about to lose her.

"Get him quickly then, robber," he spits. The man in black nods. The Lieutenant pulls his daughter up by her arm and she rips herself from his grip in anger.

"He's not to take him, father," she yells and from the darkness behind her, two of Lieutenant Pike's men step out and take her by her arms, dragging her from Richie's body. She hits hysteria like her father has never seen before, her arms flailing and her legs kicking as the men take her backwards. Her chest screams. Lieutenant Pike watches the man in black pick Richie up by his arm and hoist him onto his shoulder. Elizabeth thrashes as they drag her back to the house, her distress is unpleasant. The man in black sets Richie's body on his horse in front of the saddle, and mounts.

"Get out my yard, robber," whispers Lieutenant Pike over his blunderbuss. There's no need to respond. The man gets back on his horse, grabs the reins and turns, with a touch of his heels the animal bursts into action and into the night, the hooves clattering on the cobbles as he moves.

Elizabeth's screams ring out over the houses and into the night across Beverley, and the robber rides with Richie's limp body over the front of his horse.

CHAPTER SIXTEEN

He is gone.

There's no chest to breathe in and no legs to run.

Richie has no stomach with which to worry, but he does worry. What's Nana going to eat? Where's Bess? Is Elizabeth safe? What of Stephen Middleton and the betrayal? Will Miss Charlotte kick Nana out into the street?

His eyes flicker open.

There's a palm on his chest with light but educated pressure and his eyes adjust. He takes a breath, one great gulp and his dry mouth opens, his nostrils flare. His heart quickens as he replays the last events of his memory, before he fired at the man in black, before clambering on the horse, before the musket shot – the kiss he and Elizabeth shared.

"Bess," he whispers.

"She's here," comes the answer. It's a woman's voice, familiar somehow, angry and yet relieved as he feels the hand that was on his chest move to his face. His eyes focus and he sees Meg above him. She has her blonde hair scraped back into a ponytail with the sleeves rolled up to her elbows like she always does.

"You big dumb bastard," she says, and Meg doesn't swear. "What were you thinking?" Richie can't understand the question. His brain ticks like a clock broken, like a drip upside down:

"I need to see her," he whispers. He hears a chair scrape on the floor and a grunt and then, in Meg's arms above him is Bess, with her long, thin tail beating quick, her eyes wide because she is uncomfortable being carried. "She followed you back."

"Where am I?" he asks.

"In Etton. You've lost a lot of blood. Someone knifed you, it's not a big wound, but I've stitched it up and cleaned it. You'll live. Just what on earth have you been doing? You look like you've been dragged through a bush."

"There was a robbery, Meg. I was in the carriage when it happened and they took the girl. I got her back." Richie grins as he looks up and he tries to sit, Meg helps him and he swings his legs over the side of the bed in the little cottage. He's still wearing his new boots and Bess fusses at his legs, his hands go to her face. Meg stands and walks to the table. Everything is in one room here, it's all she needs.

"Any lower and that knife would have done some real damage to you, Richie. There's no knowing if it'll fester either. You'll just have to wait to see. That dog shouldn't be in here, but if I put her outside, she'll make a right carry on." Meg tries not to sound too much like Nana. "You're quite the hero, Richie," she says as she turns. There's sarcasm on her voice. "Tongues are wagging about what happened. You rescued Elizabeth Pike."

"I did," the smile falls from his face and he holds out his two big hands as he looks at them. He frowns. He remembers. "How did I get here? Is Elizabeth safe?"

"You got her back to Beverley, Richie, to her father's house. Someone brought you back here." Her face is serious.

"Who?"

"A friend."

"Which friend?" he asks. Meg looks nervous. It's not like her to not know what to say.

"Are you going to tell me who it was?" he asks. Meg picks up a pestle and begins to grind something in her mortar.

"You have to look after yourself, Richie. Your Nana needs you. What would happen to her if anything happened to you?" This is a classic stalling tactic that Meg learned from Nana herself, she does not want to sound like the old woman, but sometimes it's the easiest thing to do. Richie gets to his feet slowly. He knows Nana's tricks too.

"Who was it that brought me back here, Meg?" His voice is cold. He has an idea who it might be. The door to the cottage opens and a man walks in, he has jet-black hair, blue eyes above a light beard and a handkerchief tied around his neck. He's shorter than Richie but not by much. He smiles and shows his white teeth.

This is the man he once called father, the one he sometimes still does. It's John the Pearlman, the one who ran off many years ago. Despite his wound, Richie launches himself forward, pulls his fist behind his head and punches him across the jaw. It catches the Pearlman off guard and he smashes into the table where Meg is working sending tin plates and her pestle and mortar crashing to the floor. Richie follows up, but Meg roars out at him.

"Not in my bloody house, Richard Jackson." She lifted this line direct from Nana. He stops and there's rage in his eyes. The Pearlman gets to his feet and his hand goes to his face.

"That's a solid right hand you've got there, Richie. You delivered if from your hip, just like I showed you."

"Did you know he was here?" asks Richie to Meg.

"It was him that brought you," she yells, "and if he'd not, you'd be dead." The Pearlman smiles at Richie.

"You've grown up good, Richie lad."

"I'm not your lad," he says.

"You are with a punch like that."

"What are you doing back here? We thought you'd gone for good."

"When I heard there'd been a robbery at Leconfield and they'd taken Elizabeth Pike, I heard your name. I tracked the men you'd finished off, tracked you to Tickton. I'd have helped you get that lass home if you'd have let me."

"You chased us."

"Didn't I teach you to think first before you run or swing your fists?"

"You weren't around to teach me anything." Richie wants the words to hurt. "Why in God's name did you cover your face last night?"

"I'm not supposed to be here, Richie. A life I had before I came to North Burton caught up with me and I had to disappear. I couldn't have people who wanted me dead know I had a family. I couldn't bring that to your Nana's door."

"Why didn't anyone tell me?"

"You know that little lads aren't good at keeping their mouths shut, Richie. It was easier if you thought I'd run off."

"It wasn't easier for me," says Richie. His face is flush with anger and his fists are clenched at his side. "Did you know about this?" he calls to Meg. She nods under a frown. "And Nana, did she know about it as well?"

"They both knew, Richie." The Pearlman's voice is earnest. "It's my fault. If you have to hate someone, hate me."

"I already do." Richie does not mean this, but he is not in control of what he says. It will take time to unpick his emotions, but what he feels right now, is rage against people who lied to him. "Where did you go?"

"Burton Agnes, to the North of Driffield. I work a livery yard in a coach house there. They call me Ploughman, Len Ploughman."

"Have you been back here? Have you been back here since?" The Pearlman glances at Meg and she returns his gaze. There's a spark in their eyes.

"A few times, Richie, but I couldn't risk staying. I shouldn't be here now." Richie is still angry.

"When were you going to see me? When was anyone going to tell me?"

"I was going to find you, Richie, when you were eighteen. I left things for Nana to give you, those boots and a hat."

"I've lost the hat already. Who are you running from?"

"There's a man in Beverley, Richie, who we served with when we marched in France, Carlos and I and Dandy Jim too. He knows me from back then and I robbed him when we got home, I robbed him of everything he had and he swore he'd kill me if he ever found me. Imagine my surprise when I saw him one afternoon up at the Pennyman House. He's a ruthless and slippery bastard, Richie and I know he'll hold a grudge, I should have killed him when I had the chance." The Pearlman takes a deep breath now he has delivered this information, he looks down at his feet and then back to Richie. "I missed you, Richie lad. I know it will take time. You'll visit me when you get your head right, won't you, up at the Blue Bell Inn, Burton Agnes?"

Richie's chin quivers. His eyes well with tears. It was never his fault then, that this man left. He feels frozen to the spot. The Pearlman examines his lad with fresh blue eyes.

"I'm sorry I hit you," says Richie.

"I should have seen it coming. I'll be on my way." He turns to the door and puts his hand on the wood, looks back at Richie with a frown. "You're a grand lad, Richie, everything I hoped you'd be. Everything we hoped you'd be, Nana and Meg here too." Before the emotion can get to him, he opens the door and steps out of the little cottage.

"The man who wants to kill you," calls Richie, "who is he?" The Pearlman stops.

"If you know, Richie, it won't make anything easier."

"I need to know."

"It's information that won't help you."

Richie knows a slippery bastard, one who has already crossed him and tricked him and lied to him.

"It's Stephen Middleton, isn't it? There isn't another as you describe."

"Aye," answers the Pearlman. "It's the magistrate, although he wasn't that when I knew him, and if he finds out you're my lad, he'll have your throat cut, no mistake." Richie follows the man outside and watches him untie the reins of a black horse from the fence.

"What did you do to him?" asks Richie.

"I robbed him," answer the Pearlman.

"That's not it," says Richie. "There's more." The man

holds the saddle and gets up onto his horse.

"I robbed him and his father, Richie and I humiliated him. That's all it is. I'm not proud of it. When you're ready, find me, The Blue Bell Inn at Burton Agnes north of Driffield." He pulls one of the reins and the horse turns towards the road, he looks down on Richie. This is the East Riding of Yorkshire, not a place for emotion or drama or feelings, just levelheaded reason, jobs that are to be done and decisions that are to be made.

"I'm grateful you brought me back," says Richie.

"I've not stopped being your father, not ever, lad." Richie nods. The Pearlman speaks his mind freely.

Richie watches him ride off, past the pond and up the hill He doesn't know what to think.

Richie sits down in front of Meg at the table. She's boiled water on her little fire and made a brew of something or other that she wants Richie to drink. It's brown and smells. Bess is across his knee and it's not the most comfortable position but she's happy enough, with her head on his lap and her legs dangling off. Meg has an embarrassed air to her and they have not spoken about the obvious – that a man who was meant to have run away some eight years previous, is back. Perhaps he has been back many times. Richie is not afraid to get to the truth, perhaps because it's not his truth.

"All that shite about love," he says. His words are not bitter, they have humour in them also. "Love destroys, you told me. Love destroys when you've had that man back here every weekend." She returns from the fire and sits down.

"Don't mock me," she answers. "He never visited."

"You could have told me."

"I was going to, Richie, but the longer time got in the way, the harder it was, especially when you were so certain what was true."

"Do you still love him?" There's pain in the woman's eyes.

"Aye. So, you see, Richie Jackson who knows everything because he is seventeen, love really does destroy, whatever way you look at it."

"Why not just pack up now, go off to Burton Agnes and join him at the bar of the Blue Bell?"

"It's not as simple as that, people here need me, they need my skills."

There's a knock on the door and then the handle turns. It would be polite to wait but this is Meg's house and there are plenty who treat it like their own. An older woman with blonde hair and a white maid's cap over it pops her head around the door. This is Mrs Allen the sexton's wife. She grins as she enters.

"He's awake then," she begins and she trots in. There is very little that happens in the East Riding that Mrs Allen does not know about and she is eager to share what she's heard with Richie and Meg, and of course, Mrs Allen knows who the man in black was riding up the hill, but there are certain bits of gossip that she keeps quietly to herself, especially for Meg.

"Have you heard?" she asks, knowing that they cannot have heard because she has only just heard herself from the barrow lad at the Light Dragoon Pub, who was told it by a coachman from Beverley, who heard it repeated by a lady through a window in Toll Gavel. Richie shakes his head.

"It's about you, Richie."

"What about me?"

"Is it true you killed three robbers in a fight and rescued Elizabeth Pike? There's talk that you stole a horse and rode her all the way back into Beverley." Richie's face is pale. The rumour mill has begun, in earnest.

"One of them is dead for sure," he answers. Mrs Allen examines him. Her expression is serious.

"You're a hero, Richie," she says. "We knew you were a good lad before, but this, why, you'll have every lass in the East Riding after you."

"I don't feel like a hero, Mrs Allen." Now the woman turns to Meg to explain more of the story.

"It was out at Leconfield, six of them, robbers the lot fell out of the night onto the carriage, and there was Richie, Lieutenant Pike and his daughter Elizabeth. They shot one of the horses and cracked Richie here on the head and they were off with Elizabeth, to ransom her just like what happened with that lass from South Cave." Mrs Allen is enjoying herself. "And Richie here, when he comes round from the thump on his head goes right after the highwaymen, finds them in a wood, shoots one and clubs another." The story is fairly close to the truth so far. Mrs Allen leans her face towards Meg as she gets to the best part. "But there's one highwayman that Richie doesn't want to meet, a real roadman, one of the best there is, Dick Turpin himself is there too with the robbers and he's too much for Richie. That's who stabbed you, Richie, isn't it? And he let you go too because he's never seen a lad so brave and with as big a heart."

"Who's Dick Turpin?" asks Meg. Mrs Allen's eyes go wide, as if she has not heard of the sun or the moon before.

"The Gentleman of the road, Dick Turpin, why he's famous from London to Glasgow. Always dressed in the finest clothes and with a dandy hat and a blue frock coat, with his horse Black Bess. He's a people's robber, gives what he robs to those that need it. And to think you met him Richie and fought with him too." Mrs Allen had never heard of Dick Turpin until this morning, and nobody had, not anyone, until Elizabeth Pike told the story in detail to her father while she knew the chambermaid was listening at the door. Elizabeth told it also to the livery yard lad and to both her neighbours too and to anyone who visits. She is a good storyteller. Richie looks paler yet.

"You'll be famous, Richie. What was he like, Dick Turpin?" Mrs Allen is so enthusiastic, she wishes she could tell the lad's story for him. Richie is confused for a moment. He is not sure whether to play along, Meg has always said that the truth was the best option, but this is pure fantasy. He did fight robbers and he did shoot Mr Woodhatch in the neck and shoulder, it did happen, but there was no famous highwayman named Dick Turpin who dressed in the finest of clothes. Who would know to call him that? It's Richie's mother's name, the one who died while she bore him. He suddenly understands when he thinks back to the way Elizabeth teased him about being a robber. It could only be her who has spread such rumours.

"I'd rather not say at this time, Mrs Allen. It was a right scrap." This is the truth. The woman nods at hearing this crumb of information. "When the time's right, I'll tell you all of it," he says to her.

"You'll be a hero," she says. "And you're to tell me first."

"Richie's still recovering, Mrs Allen," says Meg. "He needs a day of rest or more."

"Of course," she answers. "I'm off up to Grey's farm and I'll tell them all there. If there's any cream, I'll bring it back here." The old woman comes over to Richie and fusses his hair in admiration, scratches Bess on her head too before she leaves. When the door closes, Meg looks over the table at Richie with his light moustache and messy brown hair.

"Who's Dick Turpin, Richie?" she asks.

"I don't know, Meg. I honestly don't know." There is something more, however, if Elizabeth Pike is willing to spread rumours, then she must have conveniently forgotten that it was Richie that robbed her carriage first. He grins. He won't be hanged after all, not yet anyway.

CHAPTER SEVENTEEN

It's a summer morning. He's walking back over the hill towards North Burton.

Richie has been two days with Meg. It's tiring in her cottage. There were many visitors, an old woman with a pain in her stomach, a black gelding with a nasty gash along its side that Meg sewed up, a woman pregnant with a red face, a well-to-do lady from Market Weighton on a trap with a white horse to pick up tonics. Meg has all of it under control and Richie watched her calm sense of duty. Those that can pay do, those that can't promise there will be something for Meg's trouble. There was always a comment about Richie also, if they come inside. Is this Richie Jackson? He's taller than I thought. They say he killed four men with his bare hands. I thought he'd be wider. He doesn't look old enough – are you sure you're the constable of the peace at North Burton?

It's much quieter if Richie gets back to North Burton where he and Bess belong. It's not far from Etton. Two miles at most. There's a big hill with a mill at the top to catch the wind, and it feels good to stretch his legs. The pain under his arm is better now, Meg has fed him well, a lot of the payment she gets for her favours is in food, a side of pork or a stack of carrots.

There's a lot to think about too.

Richie needs to find answers. Why did Stephen Middleton send him to the carriage and did he know it would be robbed? He must have, for Elizabeth and Richie saw him at the clearing with the highwaymen. What stories has Elizabeth been telling? Where is his new hat and the musket he was given? He has the pistol but without the satchel and the bullets therein, it's nothing more than a heavy lump of wood. There will be questions too for Richie to answer. Nana will be furious with him. Jonny Low will be angry too, he will have had to work the fields on his own with the big cart horse, Patrick, at a busy time of year.

They are nearing the top of the hill and Richie looks across at the white mill half a mile in the distance, the sails move slowly in the breeze. He turns and feels the wind on his light brown hair, smells the fresh summer wind, the smoke from the chimneys at Etton below, the cut hay in the fields around him. He doesn't want to go back down to North Burton, somehow. Richie has tasted freedom and adventure.

He's robbed a carriage.

He's kissed a girl.

Richie puts this thought out of his brain for even the idea of it weakens him and makes his head spin.

There's a figure moving towards them in the summer breeze, stooped and with a stick, limping. Richie can't understand why he did not notice this man dressed in a grey cloak previous, and for a fleeting moment he remembers that Nana once told him that there are ghosts out on summer days too. He and Bess continue on till they get nearer the man and Richie can see that his face is old and wrinkled, he has scruffy white hair, and his cloak is tatty like his clothes and sandals.

"Well met," he calls to Richie as he approaches. Richie would tip his hat if he were wearing one. The floppy one he used to wear has been lost – just like the one gifted to him by John the Pearlman. Instead, he just nods and smiles. "By, you're a big one," says the old man. This is a common reaction to Richie. Anything out of the ordinary is mentioned, specifically a trait that is positive such as strength, handsomeness or height, other features such as a big nose or ugly eyes are mentioned, but not out loud and not to individuals. Richie responds in a friendly way, it's the most natural thing for him.

"Morning, granddad," he says, although this man is not his granddad. The old man stops and looks down on Bess the dog and then up to Richie.

"You seem like a good lad, have you got a coin for an old

man down on his luck?" By default, Richie does not ever have any money so it's easy for him to shake his head. The old man's shoulders drop and his face looks weary. It's well-rehearsed of course.

"Do you not want to buy yourself a bit of luck from an old man, lad? You know alms to the poor brings fortune. Is there not some lass that you think of, that a bit of luck might guide your way?" Again, Richie shakes his head.

"I'm a poor working lad," says Richie. The Granddad points at the pistol tucked into his belt.

"Poor working lads don't carry guns, not in the East Riding. That's why I stopped you, and look at that dog, why, she'd be worth a guinea of any man's money."

"Alas, Granddad, I have nothing to give. I'm just a lad making my way in the world. The dog was a gift, as was this pistol, I've no bullets or black powder." Richie believes this to be true.

"I've been walking for days," says the old man. "There was no help at that church back there, or the pub neither." He nods in the direction he has just come from and the way Richie is going, the village of North Burton.

"They don't like strangers, granddad, that's what people round here are like. It's not you."

"Aye well," says the man. "That's no comfort to an old man with a grumbling belly. "Are you sure you've got nowt?" Richie thinks for a moment. He does have something. He reaches into the pocket of his pants and deep therein touches the leather pouch of money that he pinched from Lieutenant Pike, gave back to Elizabeth and then she passed to him. He's quite forgotten about this money and forgotten too that he robbed it to pay Miss Charlotte Pennyman. Without taking it out of his pocket, he opens the string bag and reaches a thumb and finger inside and collects a coin. The old granddad cocks his head as he considers the lad in front of him with the summer sun catching the golden bits of his hair, perhaps he sees something that other's do not. Perhaps he knows that Richie has a pouch full of shillings and guineas in his pocket, or that he shot a man a few days previous and bashed in the head of another. Perhaps he knows that Richie has been a highwayman. There's serenity as the granddad gazes at the lad.

"What have you got for me son?" he asks. Richie takes the coin out of his pocket, a guinea, a good bit of money – you could rent a room for a week in a house for that in York, or buy a cart full of hay to bed a horse down for the winter. He holds it out for the man to take from his palm. It's not Richie's money anyway. Although Richie hasn't counted it, it feels like there may be more guineas in that pouch.

"I was given it," says Richie. He thinks back to the words Mrs Allen told him at Etton a few days previous. He might as well get some advantage out of his gift to this old man. "A gentleman named Dick Turpin passed it me, out of charity." The granddad does not take the money right away.

"Dick Turpin, you say? Did he now?" he asks.

"Aye, but with a caution. He told me that should I come by another who needs the coin greater than I, it ought to be passed on." The old man collects the money, slowly from the lad's big palm.

"Your friend Dick Turpin is a blessed man. Well met, young lad. Is it luck you'll be needing or advice?"

"Something else," says Richie. "If you're to chance on Mr Turpin in the future or those that know him, see that he's treated favorably, will you?" The old man grins.

"I'll pass that name forward, lad, to those that I meet. And I've a word of advice for you as well" Richie raises his eyebrows.

"No need, granddad," he cuts in. The old man smiles.

"Right you are." He puts the coin into his pocket and with the same slight limp makes his way off down towards Etton.

When Richie gets to the top of the hill he turns to see if he can see the old man, but he's gone. Nana says you get ghosts on summer days, just the same as you get them in the dead of night.

Richie's not sure he believes her.

Nana's in a bit of a mood. She's managed to get herself outside of the cottage, someone has moved her chair into the street for her and she's enjoying the midday sun. She watches Richie return, as he walks down the main street of North Burton and past the old Thorne Farm with his big smile. As soon as he is in earshot, she begins:

"It's alright for you," she calls at Richie. "You can just swan off anywhere you want without a care in the world. You've been gone three days." He's heard this one before but gets the feeling that it's a brief introduction to a full-scale performance from Nana. "I've had that Philipson from across the road looking after me, Richie and his sister, who's not all there. When poor Jonny Low heard that you'd not come back home and he had to do the baling all by himself, why, the air was blue with his swearing and cursing and I can't say I blame him. You've got responsibilities here, Richie. Do you understand?" Richie offers a weak defence:

"I got stabbed by a robber, Nana." She pats the information away with one of her flabby hands.

"I once got my leg near cut off when a bull went for me, I've had needles through my hands, hot coals dropped on my legs, and much worse." There's a grain of truth in these facts, but only a grain. "It never stopped me from doing what's right." Nana is glad he is home. This is why she goes on and on. "I've heard all sorts of rumours, that you'd shot a man, that you'd rescued some bloody rich girl from Beverley, and that you'd been run through by a highwayman with a sword, right through your stomach." She looks upset. It's a good rant.

"He caught me under my arm, Nana, it was just a scratch really. Meg sent word from Etton I was okay."

"It's a good job she did, Richie. You've changed, I say,

you've changed, you were once a good lad, you thought about others and you did what was asked of you. Now, look at you, with a pistol tucked in your belt and new boots. You don't understand what it's like to be old, Richie, it's my legs, I can't walk anywhere and I can't sleep and at my age, it's not right." Her face reddens and her nose flares. It's time for her finale. Two midday drinkers from the Bay Horse opposite have come out to watch the show and Nana bursts into tears, big ones as she bends over in her chair. Richie moves in and puts his long arms around her, whispers into her ear next to the headscarf:

"I'm here now lass." He rubs her shoulders and she blubs into his shirt.

"You're not to leave again like that, Richie," she splutters. "I was worried sick."

The drinkers move back into the pub now Nana has stopped shouting, but she continues to cry for a good few minutes more before she gets control of herself. Richie sits on the step of the cottage as she calms down. She sniffs and blows her nose on a hanky; Bess goes to sit next to her and rests her body next to Nana's legs with her head in her lap.

"There's another package for you," says Nana. "Bigger than the last one too, but it's not drink." Nana knows this because she opened it. "It was delivered by one of that Lieutenant Pike's lads from Beverley the day before yesterday. They brought your big musket back too and that satchel."

Inside the cottage against the wall is his satchel and musket, the one he used to shoot Mr Woodhatch in the throat. Next to it is a big package wrapped in brown paper, part has been torn where Nana looked inside already. Richie carefully peels back the paper, and there, cleaned bright, is his tricorn hat. On top there's an envelope with a wax seal on the backside and squiggles on the front that Richie cannot read. His heart drops. He picks it up and puts the envelope to his nose to sniff and it's her, all over it, perfume like he imagines wild orchids would smell like. She has written something to him here that he cannot read. It's frustrating.

Outside Richie pauses to look at Nana with Bess's head on her knee. He thinks to ask her to read the letter but he already knows the answer, she'll tell him to read it herself because she can't. He walks across the dirt road to the Bay Horse and goes through the green wooden door. Jonny Low may be here and if he is, Richie will take an earful. He looks across the bar and it's deserted. From up the steps to the cellar, Philipson approaches, he's wearing an apron and long gloves.

"I need you to read something for me, Philipson."

"Not now," he says. "I'm mashing a brew." This means he's making beer. This is an important part of Philipson's business. "Would you lend me your arms, Richard Jackson?" he asks. Richie nods. He follows Philipson outside and to a flatbed carriage which has two long bags of grain on the back and no horse. Philipson picks up one and Richie the other and the two men go back through the pub.

"The grain has been milled already," calls Philipson as he struggles down the steps to the cellar. "It makes it plenty easier." Richie follows him down the wooden steps and bangs his head on the low ceiling. Brewing is a complex business for those who do not understand it, and as well as being a fine publican, Philipson knows this art too. In the cellar there's a big fire under the brew kettle and wort pumps made from wood, these feed into a big mash tub below. Richie goes after him and they help each other to rip open the cloth sacks and pour the grain into the water. Philipson is sweating.

"I've something I need you to read, Philipson," repeats Richie. The landlord wipes his gloves on his apron and takes them off.

"Let's have it then," he says. "Put these gloves on, grab that big ladle there on the wall and stir this in."

"I don't need the gloves," says Richie.

"You do, I don't want any bits of muck from your hands falling in there, do I, it'll sour the brew."

"What is it you want me to read, lad?"

"It's delicate," says Richie.

"I've not got time for delicate, Richie Jackson. I have to get this mash brew and cooled and, in this heat, I'll be bloody lucky if I do. There's about a week's worth of beer left in the barrels over there, so if there's nowt to replace it, folk will go thirsty, so you see, I don't have time for any fannying around. Either you want me to read it now, which I shall, or you can piss off." Despite his flappable nature, there's a sense of no nonsense to Philipson which Richie likes.

"And you'll not tell anyone?"

"It's as it was before, lad. If it concerns me and mine, I shall surely tell." Richie is okay with this. The correspondence is from Elizabeth. He takes the letter from inside his shirt and passes it to the landlord, then pulls on the gloves and reaches for the wooden ladle. Philipson inspects the envelope for a few moments, noting the handwriting and smelling the perfume.

"Is this a love letter?" he asks.

"No," says Richie.

"It smells like one."

"How would you know, you're not even married?"

"I still know what a love letter is. That's what this is."

"Do you want me to stir?" asks Richie.

"Do you want me to read?" asks Philipson as he holds up the letter. Richie begins to stir with a frown of worry. He does not want anyone to know what is in the letter, especially if it concerns what happened with Elizabeth and he. What if she mentions that Dick Turpin she made up? He has no real choice. There's nobody as trustworthy as Philipson who can read in the whole of North Burton. The landlord carefully opens the seal and pulls out the letter, there's a big grin on his face. He opens up the paper therein.

"Dearest Richie," he begins. Richie cuts in.

"You don't have to read it in a stupid voice."

"That's my normal voice," grins Philipson, "and if you want me to read it, I'll read it the way I see fit." He clears his throat.

"Dearest Richie, my father and I are most grateful for your assistance on the evening of the 7th of August 1722 when our carriage was robbed by the highwayman, Dick Turpin, and his men. You displayed bravery and courage that cannot go unrecognized. We have returned your effects, your musket, satchel and hat which were collected at Tickton. The investigation into the identity of the robbers is ongoing, and my father, Lieutenant Pike, would like to invite you to convene at our residence at Toll Gavel, Beverley at your earliest convenience where you may be able to furnish us with further information to help conclude our enquiries. Best wishes, Elizabeth Pike."

Richie continues to stir the mixture and the smell of grain in the hot water is sweet in his nostrils. It was not a love letter in Richie's opinion.

"Who's Dick Turpin?" asks Philipson.

"He's a highwayman. Have you heard of him?"

"I think so. I heard it was him that robbed you, Richie and that it was him that stabbed you too." Richie looks uneasy. He's not a good liar like Nana.

"Something like that," he answers. Philipson frowns at the lad stirring the grain.

"Don't get mixed up with those sorts of people, Richie, if you can help it."

"I won't," says Richie. "What did it mean, the letter? I got the part about finding my hat but not the rest."

"She wants you to visit her father, as soon as you can." The lad looks uneasy. "Sounds to me like you'll be getting some sort of reward."

Richie takes a deep, worried breath.

CHAPTER EIGHTEEN

It's just past five and the summer sun is still strong on Richie's back. It hasn't taken him too long to walk over the fields from North Burton to Beverley. He's followed tracks that have grown steadily more used, and now he is in front of the North Bar, the old walled gate that stands at the edge of the town and in times gone by, has defended it. The streets here are well used with smooth and flat cobbles that make pulling a cart easier. Even though Richie is not from Beverley, he holds his breath as he walks under the dark red bricks, it's a tradition here not to breathe the air as you walk under. It's meant to be unlucky and while Richie doesn't need any Beverley luck, he doesn't want to make trouble if it's not necessary.

The streets are not so busy, but there are people here that you seldom see in North Burton, even though it's only a few miles away. There are ladies in huge dresses that balloon from their hips, unsuitable for fields or muddy paths, children with brilliant white socks, coachmen in black suits with sleek top hats. Richie is a stranger here. With his musket on his back, his tricorn hat, the thin hunting dog Bess next to him and his brown satchel banging at his side, he is not dressed for polite society. Even his height marks him out. Outside St Mary's Church, a poodle strains on its lead to bark at Bess, but she does not even look in the little dog's direction. The man holding the poodle, with a powdered wig and white face sneers at these two foreign creatures in his ordered town. Neither does Richie look at him.

He passes through the big marketplace that is all but deserted apart from a group of three lads rolling a metal hoop from a carriage wheel. Even they look like they've had a wash. He passes Porter's gun shop on the right-hand side and goes down Toll Gavel, past the chemist shops and the confectioner, past a group of workers thick with coal dust from the tanneries at the south of the city where they stoke the fires. He feels nervous and Bess keeps close. There's something about the noise of the town that doesn't sit right, with the shouts from a few streets away and the cackle of laughter from an unseen drunk, there's the mixture of the sweet smell of pies cooking, perfume, sweat, coal, spices, the tanneries, beer and a hundred other things Richie does not know or understand. Bess keeps her ears down as they walk along the wide and open main street.

Halfway down, at the big red door to Lieutenant Pike's house, Richie takes hold of the silver fox door knocker, picks it up and bangs it twice. He stands back and his heart thumps. He doesn't remember the last time he was here, but he was, round the back. In his pocket he has the pouch of money that he robbed from Lieutenant Pike, he is not sure what he will have to do with it.

The door opens and a woman with a sour face looks out. She cocks her head.

"Richie Jackson," he says.

"Beggars round the back," she answers and slams the door. This is how Richie expects to be treated. He and Bess walk to the fork in the road, and he moves down Walkergate to the back of the big house where there is a yard and a small livery. He remembers the gates were open last him he was here, just as they are now. Richie wants to put his hand on the pistol at his waist for comfort, but here in town this would look like a threat. Instead, he walks to the edge of the yard and looks down the path along three good sized stables to a bright red door. Richie walks to it and knocks, again. This time he takes off his tricorn hat. It opens, and there in a dark green dress with her shoulders bare and her hair pinned up is the clear white smile of Elizabeth. Richie feels his stomach turn as he sees her.

"Richie," she beams. "Please come in. We've just finished dinner, we're in the dining room. Come through." He looks down at Bess in apology.

"I'll leave her out here," he says and Bess stares up with her big, sad eyes.

He follows Elizabeth's perfume and they go through a corridor, past the smells of a kitchen where Richie can see two women dressed in white, busy with pans and billows of steam. They go through another door and into a small dining room. It has nothing of the grandeur of the Pennyman House, but it speaks of moderate wealth. Lieutenant Pike gets up from the dining table and walks over to shake Richie's hand. He wears a wig and a frilly shirt that peeps through his cuffs, unsuitable for any actual job but excellent for the kind of polite society within which he dwells.

"I'm glad you came," he says. "I must say we're in slightly different circumstances to last time we met, Sir, although you are dressed very much the same." It's a lighthearted dig, but very much a dig all the same. "Elizabeth," he explains, "Mr Jackson and I will retire to my study to conclude the business we have?"

She appears let down.

"I thought Richie could take some tea with us, here, and you may discuss whatever business you like." Her face sours. Her father did not teach her to be a wallflower.

"I'll send Mr Jackson down when we have had our discussion." His voice is flat like an order.

Richie follows him up some stairs and into a room with a desk in front of a window. He goes to sit behind it and bids Richie to settle in one of the two plush chairs opposite. On the table there is an inkwell, paperweights and letters, books and a newspaper with an empty glass of wine.

"I'd rather stand," says Richie. He knows that his trousers are dirty and he does not want to ruin the seats with them.

"Very well," says Lieutenant Pike. The old man is silent for a moment as he creaks back on his expensive chair and considers Richie. "I have a few questions for you, Mr Jackson, about the evening in question. Are you of a mind to answer these?"

"Aye," says Richie. He thinks about the leather pouch of money in his pocket as he looks down on the Lieutenant.

"Who taught you to shoot?"

"My father."

"Was he a soldier?

"Aye, he was off with the Duke's forces at Blenheim, so he says."

"Where is he now?"

"Long gone, Sir. Eight years since. Whoring and whatever."

"My daughter tells me that you displayed exceptional courage and bravery in protecting her. If it were not for you, then she may not be sitting downstairs now. I cannot explain to you, in terms that you may understand, just how important she is to me. She is worth more than this house and all the horses I have, all the wealth of the East Riding and of the whole world to me." He pulls open a draw in the right side of the table and from within, using his fingers like a stork catching a fish, draws out a tower of coins. He sets this opposite Richie.

"Twelve crowns. All yours. What do you say?" Richie has a lot more than this in the leather pouch.

"I say thank you, Sir," he answers but does not grab for them. The Lieutenant reaches inside his draw and pulls out another tower of coins, roughly the same height and he places this down next to the first.

"Another twelve crowns. I'll explain. Since my daughter's return she has become a little infatuated with you. She speaks of nothing else, pesters me to ride out to North Burton, urges me to write more correspondence. It seems her normal faculty for reason has been displaced." This is not really true. Elizabeth is not some silly girl who giggles when a handsome man speaks, and she is not infatuated with Richard Jackson, however, Lieutenant Pike knows his daughter and he knows the time she spent with this tall lad Richie has impacted upon her, as much by what she has said by what she has not.

"I'll be clear with you," continues Lieutenant Pike, "there can be nothing between you two. She is a woman of means and of education. She will marry one, when she is ready, but it will be a man of substance, and not a thug from North Burton. I'm not saying this because I want to disrespect you, Richie Jackson, I owe you her life, but I expect you to understand, that any feeling you may have for her, would never be felt back, and it would be impossible for you to be together, as impossible in fact, as a fish to fly high through the air. Do you understand?"

Richie nods. It does not sink in quickly. The Lieutenant reaches to his drawer once more and pulls out another stack of coins which he places next to the other two.

"Twelve more crowns. My daughter said she did not know who the man was who carried you away from here when you were injured but, it's my belief that he was a highwayman too. I think it was the man who robbed my carriage first. Tell me who he was and the last twelve crowns are yours as well."

Richie blinks.

"I don't know who he was, Sir. He took me out to Etton to the healing woman there."

"This I know, but why would he help? Is he known to you in some way, Mr Jackson?" Richie is not good at lying unless it's cards and in cards you don't say anything, you just don't let your face do the telling. He thinks upon his oversized feet.

"I believe he thought he could fetch a price for me, Sir?"

"Ransom you? You're a strapping farm hand, not exactly anything delicate."

"I know, Sir, but the healing lass out at Etton, she's like my mother. He must have known me, and about her. I don't know what happened, but she paid him off in herbs and the bottles of tonics that she makes."

Lieutenant Pike looks at Richie as if he does not believe him and puts his finger to his lips in thought. He remains still for a good thirty seconds, and Richie stares him dead in the eye.

"Take the money, lad," he says. "I can tell when a man lies. It's all in the eyes. I've heard of that woman out at Etton too, she's got a reputation for her skills. Do you know what she paid for your safekeeping?"

"She didn't tell me."

"Would it have been a lot?"

"A lot of effort to make them, aye."

"How much would cover it?" This is becoming ridiculous. There are more than a few guineas on the table there.

"I think I can make it up to my Meg with some of this money, Sir." Lieutenant Pike nods as if Richie has been fair and doesn't have a pouch rammed with guineas in his pocket already.

"You're a fine man, Richie Jackson and all that money on the table there is yours, but I'd counsel you to remember what I said about my daughter. Do you remember?"

"Aye."

"Would you tell it back to me then, just so as I know you've retained the facts." Richie has not had the time to consider what Lieutenant Pike has explained to him, even though he knows the words. He repeats:

"I'm not to think there can be anything between us." There's a bad taste to his mouth as he says this.

"Mark those words you have spoken well. If she is to make contact with you, ignore her and if it persists, contact me. I can't impress upon you, Mr Jackson how much she means to me and how impressionable she is. She's like her mother was, sees magic when there's nothing but horseshit." Richie frowns. The Lieutenant has both praised and insulted him, paid him and made a mockery of his bravery. If he were a rich man, Richie would refuse the money, but as it is, he sees how much he can do for the people he loves with it. He and Jonny Low could buy a horse, they could go to Market Weighton for a drink at harvest time, they could get a pig at Christmas, Nana could have some new shoes and a new shawl. He unclips his satchel and sweeps all three piles into it. The coins scatter between the contents inside. Richie fastens it shut and stands back.

"One more thing, Mr Jackson, when you go back downstairs, she will ask you if you want some tea. I would like you to make a pale excuse, something that indicates you are not interested in either the tea or her, something as watery as looking through the windows of a shop or staring at the sky or watching grass grow. Let her know that you do not value her company. I promise, it will be a service to her."

Richie should be happy as he walks down the little staircase and past the door to the dining room, he has a satchel full of crowns and is free as a bird for robbing the carriage, not under any scrutiny at all for killing two men either. At the doorway, with her smile wide and honest stands Elizabeth, she's put on more perfume in expectation and her eyes twinkle. Richie has kissed those lips, his stomach gurgles at the sight of her, electricity fires through his legs and up his back.

"I have poured some tea for us, Richie Jackson and have some pork pie that was left over from dinner. I wonder if you would like to take some rest, it's the least we can do for the trouble you went to." It's a well-rehearsed speech. Richie stops and looks down on her as if he is going to cry.

"I'm afraid I have to go for a walk," he says, a weak excuse without thought, as Lieutenant Pike asked. She looks up at him with her hazel eyes.

"Is that so? The pork pie is fresh, and I can have some of father's ale brought through if that is more to your taste."

"I have to walk with Bess," he repeats. It's one thing to lie to a man for money or to save your own skin, but it is quite another thing to lie when you feel as Richie does as he looks at Elizabeth. Lieutenant Pike cuts in from behind.

"The lad's busy," he says. "Let him be, Elizabeth." She steps back a little stunned. The stern-faced woman appears at Richie's side and beckons him, he follows her down the corridor to the back door which she opens for him. Richie turns and waves goodbye to Lieutenant Pike, there is a weak smile for Elizabeth.

He doesn't feel real as he walks past the three stables and into Walkergate past the open gates of the Pike residence. He stops and turns to look back when he is in the street. At a window on the first floor, he sees her looking through the little squares of glass at him from above. She won't be able to see his expression from this far away, his face has no emotion at all.

It's dark when he gets home to North Burton. There's been no moon to light his way back from Beverley along the Malton Road and as they walked down the tracks over the fields. The darkness does not bother Richie or Bess. They know the way so well that they could do it asleep. All is quiet as they pass St Michael's and the wrought iron gate to the Pennyman House is locked shut. When Richie gets to the Bay Horse opposite Nana's cottage, it is after ten and the lights are out inside the pub. Richie's mood is dark. Unlike when he stood and spoke to Lieutenant Pike, now he understands that he was paid off, like a hired worker or a servant, as if he were someone who had clipped one of the man's horses, when instead, he'd risked his life to save Pike's daughter. Richie needs a drink and even if Philipson is closed, he's going to get him to unlock the doors and pour him a glug of something expensive, now he has the money.

He and Bess walk around to the back of the Bay Horse in the darkness and his new boots crunch on the ground, his hat covers his eyes. Richie's mouth is a low snarl when he thinks about the money he's been paid, money that prevents him from speaking to Elizabeth again. He stops in the darkness suddenly and presses his back up against the wall, he has heard voices.

The backdoor of the brewery opens and yellow lamp light spills into the night, then, stumbling backwards, comes the figure of Philipson, as if he has been shoved outside. Richie watches from some distance. Following after him is the silhouette of a stocky man with no neck and a square head, he moves on Philipson, grabs him by his collars and picks him up. The stocky man shakes Philipson a few times before he drags him back up, spins him, and slams the landlord against the outside wall of the pub. Philipson lets out a sigh. He's not a small man so to toss him around like this, the stocky gentleman must be a big bugger. Richie edges along the back of the Bay Horse in the darkness, reaches down and tugs up the handkerchief that is round his neck so that it covers his nose and mouth, he pulls the pistol from his pants and holds it up. Richie can hear the stocky man talking to Philipson as he holds him, with the light from the open brewery door outlining their faces. The man is bald, and huge, the back of his head bulges with a big layer of fat, his shirt is stretched tight over massive shoulders. His voice is just a whisper:

"You can't run, Philipson. You and your halfwit sister, you can't run from what you've done. We'd find you if you went halfway around the world." Philipson's face looks back up at his attacker.

"I've paid. I've paid over and over. She did wrong and we made it right. You people can't keep coming back for me."

"Your kind make me sick," whispers the stocky man. "Ungodly you are, you'll go straight to hell. Now, I have asked nicely. If you don't have the money for me next time I come a calling, something is going to break. It might be bottles or it might be one of your legs, depending on how much you have."

There's the sound of clicking as Richie pulls back the

action on his pistol, so that the flintlock is ready, he has moved much closer to these two. The stocky man turns his head and the barrel of the gun looms at him from the darkness, he can just make out the hat and how tall the man who holds it seems to be.

"Who in God's name are you?" he whispers.

"Turpin," comes the answer.

"There's no one here to rob," he spits. "The landlord says he has no money."

"My pistol does not point at him, friend." Richie feels his throat whisper as he says these words, like they come from someone else entirely. The stocky man lets his hands fall from Philipson's collar as he turns. "I didn't ask you to move, friend," says Richie. "Turn as you were." The stocky man does so.

"I've no money, you bloody fool. Try to rob me and you'll be on the wrong end of a barrel yourself." The stocky man has a gutter mouth, used to getting what he wants by foul means and Richie can smell his rotten breath from where he stands.

"I couldn't help but hear," says Richie. "How much does this landlord here owe?"

"What's it got to do with you?" comes the answer. It's a struggle working with some people.

"I'm happy to blow a bullet through your head, friend, but I'd rather not waste the powder. I've robbed a good few this last week, perhaps you've heard." The stocky man has heard. "It was the intention for myself and my associates," continues Richie, "to stop here in this quiet inn for drinks, however, upon arriving I find the landlord is not able to serve those drinks. So, I'll ask you again, how much does he owe you?"

The stocky man scoffs.

"Five guineas." It's a large sum. A ridiculous amount. You could buy a fine horse for this much, a wedding dress or a cart, passage on a ship to the Indies even. Richie reaches for the pouch deep in the pocket of his pants.

"Step back into the light, friend," he whispers. "Not too quickly now, the trigger here is sensitive, and a sudden movement could put a hole in your chest." The man steps backwards and Richie's gun follows him into the glow from the open door to the brewery. "Landlord, take hold of this money pouch," says Richie as he tosses him the leather purse. The coins clink as Philipson catches it. The pistol is level and rock solid, the handkerchief is tight over his face as he looks down from his six-foot four height.

"How much is a bottle of your finest brandy, Landlord?" He whispers. Philipson steps to the side of the tall dark man with the gun, who he does not realise is Richie Jackson from across the road.

"A shilling at tops," he answers.

"I'll take five guineas worth of that brandy, then, Mr Landlord. Count out the money from my purse now. If you would." Richie does not move the gun. He hears Philipson clinking away with the money in the pouch as he fishes out the coins. Richie has seen that there are many more than five guinea coins in there already and, when he has taken his money, the landlord passes the pouch back. He lowers his gun, and the three men stand a few yards apart from each other. Philipson breaks the silence.

"Will you require lodgings, Mr Turpin?" he asks.

"Five guineas of brandy, landlord, that'll be it." It's with some trepidation that Philipson steps forward towards the man who only five minutes earlier had him up against the wall by the scruff of his neck. He holds out the coins in his palm.

"Here it is," he says. "It's all there, five guineas." The stocky man collects the money from Philipson.

"This is honest business," says the man, as if to absolve himself. "Philipson owes this money fair and square, as reparations." Richie is motionless, his face covered by the darkness of his tricorn hat.

"Of course," adds Richie, in his low voice. "That's the

business completed then. You'll be on your way."

"Aye," says the stocky man. He deposits the handful of coins into his shirt and steps backwards, keeping his eyes on the two men as he does so. They watch him as he unties his horse and then mounts up.

"You'll not be back in North Burton again," says Richie.

"Not I," answers the stocky man.

"That is good news, friend. I can't promise to be this friendly if I ever see you again." The man digs his heels into the horse, and it clatters off into the darkness. They hear the thud of the hooves as it moves off up the street on the road to Market Weighton.

Richie follows Philipson into the yellow light of the brewery through the open door. The landlord is not himself at all, he dabs at his face with a handkerchief.

"If you come through to the bar, Mr Turpin, I'll bring your brandy," he says to the figure behind him. "When do you expect your associates to arrive?" He's been taken in by it all.

Richie lets Bess come in behind him, closes the door, then pulls down the handkerchief from his face. Philipson turns and sees Richie's wide smile, illuminated by the lamp from the low rafter. It takes him a minute to realise who he's looking at and he steps forward towards the lad with a confused frown.

"Richie?" he asks.

"Aye."

"Richie Jackson?" It's taking Philipson some moments to understand who he is talking to. He has questions before relief can set in.

"Where did you get five guineas, Richie?"

"Dick Turpin pinched it."

"He gave it to you, did he?

"Aye," says Richie. Philipson is confused still. He feels he has to explain to the lad.

"It was my Mary's debt that she ran up, they were reparations for what she did, and I have to stand by her. There was a man up at Driffield, tried to have her and she wouldn't have it, so she smashed a bottle in his face, and the scar was terrible. There's no one else to help her but me. You could have done a lot with that money, Richie. You could have set yourself up somewhere with something, bought a horse and a cart too. What would you want to waste it on me for?"

"It's what we do around here, Philipson," says Richie. These are Nana's words. "We look after each other." Philipson's face takes on a kind of strange grin in the yellow light from the lamp.

It's the first time Richie has ever seen him smile.

"I'll get you that brandy," he adds.

CHAPTER NINETEEN

Richie opens one eye and hears Nana shouting from down below, they are long bellows of his name and then thudding as she bangs her walking stick against the walls. Bess stirs next to him. She gets up and walks to the edge of the raised platform, then barks for Richie to carry her down. He must have brought her up with him last night when he came up to bed. His head hurts a little. Last night Philipson poured him a pint of brandy, they ate pickled eggs with pepper, and talked of things that Philipson had never talked of before. Richie feels groggy as he swings his legs over the ladder and picks Bess up under one of his arms. Sat in her chair by the fire that is not lit, Nana shouts up at him, but his thick head deflects most of the tough words.

"It's just after sunrise, Richie," she goes on, "you've to be out in the field as soon as now, I'll not have no one thinking that a Jackson is a lay about and drunk, even though you bloody are." In a few careful steps on the ladder, Richie is on the floor and he sets Bess down. The dog goes to the back door of the cottage and he opens it up for her to go out. He buttons up the top of the pants that he did not take off the night before, stands in front of Nana and does his wide and true smile.

"I've got something for you, lass," he says. Nana is not a lass by any means, but Richie calls her this because she likes it. She looks up at him with a frown as he goes to his satchel against the wall, opens it up and pulls out one of the crowns that he was given by Lieutenant Pike the night before. He tosses it onto Nana's lap. "There's more where that came from as well," he says. Nana picks it up in her fat fingers and holds it to her face.

"Where did you get this?" she asks, her voice suddenly without anger.

"It's payment for getting that Pike lass back. The lieutenant gave it me himself, and more too." Nana eyes him with distrust.

"I don't like it, Richie. A lad should earn brass by hard work and the sweat on his brow or else he should nick it fair and square. Gifts and such, why it's not right, you'd best get shot of this as soon as you can. It'll have bad luck all over it."

"You keep that one then," he says. Nana has already put it down the side of her chair.

"And that poor Jonny Low, why he's worked his fingers off in the fields while you've been gone another bloody day. It's not what we're about, Richie... you'll be at it today and you'll put your back into it too, or you'll get a ruddy clip round the ear." This is Nana's way of worrying and the words do not mean anything other than the noise that they make in the cool of the summer morning, like birdsong. Richie has known her for longer than anyone else. He squats down next to her and takes her hand in his as he looks in her eyes, he could listen to the rambling abuse all day but with this, he can cut straight to her.

"What is it lass?" he asks. Nana's eyes water and the voice changes, the soft inside of the woman he knows bleeds through, the one who held him as a child and taught him right from wrong, the one who stopped him from being buried alive with his mother.

"I'm worried for you, Richie. Do you know what you're getting into?"

"I think so," he says. He will take the money he has, this day, up to Charlotte Pennyman up at the house and give it to her, as the rent she asked for. Nana will be safe. The woman grips his big hand in hers.

"I don't understand it, Richie. There's guns in my house, people don't talk to each other like they used to, there's an ill wind blowing and it's not for me I worry, it's for you. A fine boy like you should be with a lass, not chasing after highwaymen. I knew we shouldn't have let that man in, I knew all them years ago that we shouldn't have let that Pearlman into this house. All the money I've got in my chair, and some silver, and a little cross I found, and a ring too, it's not for me, I want it so that, if we ever fall on hard times, we'll have something to see us through." She is fretful. "I don't know how long I've got left." Richie squeezes her hand tighter.

"Time's passed for you looking after me, lass," he says. "Now it's my turn to look after you and Meg too if I can. It's the way of things, like night following day."

"Aye, Richie lad, but if there are no new young ones, then there'll be no more days at all."

"What do you want from me, Nana?"

"Take a wife," she whispers. "These walls need noise and shouting, children crying and pots clanging, that's the only reason they're still standing." Richie blinks and he thinks of Elizabeth, with her smile and her high cheeks and her ginger hair and the sun behind her. Nana looks into his eyes and sees her there too. "There's someone, Richie, I feel her. You've just to ask and if she says no, you'll move on."

"It's not as easy as that, Nana."

"Of course it is, there's nothing more simple. A boy loves a girl and she loves him back. It's like the birds in the trees."

"Not if they're different kinds of birds."

"You're talking nonsense, Richie," she says. "Who is she?"

"Nobody you'd know, lass."

"You might think you've got all the time in the world, but you haven't, there'll be another lad willing to court whoever she is if you can't. I haven't got the time either, Richie, I'm an old woman."

There's a thump on the door. Richie stands, goes to the front of the house, and opens up. There's a man in a tall, black felt top hat with dark sideburns and a stern face. He's unfamiliar.

"Richie Jackson," he says as if he already knows who he's speaking to, "the magistrate has asked for your attendance at

the quarter session. You're to grab your effects forthwith."
Richie frowns in confusion and the man in the top hat sees
this. "Get your musket, there's a coach behind the pub."

Richie walks around the corner of the Bay Horse and there
is a large coach parked there with four horses up front. The
man with the top hat who knocked at Richie's door finishes
his brandy and sets the glass on the tray that Philipson holds
next to him.

"Fine morning, Richie," he says in lieu of hello.

"Aye." Richie is wearing that long blue coat that has seen
better days, has his musket in one hand and the pistol is tucked
into his belt with the satchel over his shoulder. His eyes are
bloodshot. He doesn't know this man, but he seems official.

"You're coming with me to Bridlington, lad. There's a
session of the court the morrow and there'll be a man hanged.
You'll need to testify." Richie looks pale. It all sounds
complex.

"Who's the man?" he asks. The coachman taps on the side
of the carriage and an ugly face looks out. It's the highwayman,
the one that got away, Mr Rail.

"Do you know him, Richie?"

"I do," he answers.

"Good. We've got him in irons in there. If you know him,
it saves you the trouble of having to lie that you did. He's one
of the robbers we've been having so much trouble with. No
doubt he was one of the ones who robbed the carriage at
Leconfield."

"He was," says Richie.

"Excellent. We'll get him to Bridlington and hang him in
the afternoon." The coachman's familiarity is off putting,
especially as Richie has never met him.

"Why not Beverley?"

"Parish lines, Richie. He's to be punished in the place he
did the crime. You'll ride up top." Richie examines the large

carriage, it's sturdy and well made. There's space for perhaps six inside and another four up behind the driver. Richie looks at the shifty eyes of Mr Rail through the open window, his hair lank with a big bulbous nose and a half-snarled smile. It doesn't look like a face that is going to hang tomorrow to Richie. There's another body behind Mr Rail, a small and thin faced woman with tight curly hair and big eyes. She looks like she's still a child.

"What's she done?" asks Richie.

"Nicking swans to eat," answers the coachman. Richie doesn't want to go, not with this coachman and not with these two either.

"I have matters to attend to here, Sir," says Richie. "I'm a working lad."

"That may be, however, as constable of the peace, you have certain duties to attend to. This is one of them. I've orders from the magistrate, Stephen Middleton."

"There's only one man, you can manage it on your own."

"Like I said, Richie, we need you to testify so we can hang him. That's how it works." The coachman steps forward so he can talk to Richie out of earshot of Philipson and the man inside the carriage. His blue eyes sparkle in the morning sun.

"I know you don't like leaving, Richie, but this will put an end to all the madness. We can't have men like him running around the East Riding. Then there's this bloody fool, some Dick Turpin, robbing folk on the highways as well. It'll just be a day, lad, you'll be back in the Bay Horse before the sun goes down tomorrow night." Richie gets the feeling that if he gets on the coach, he will never come back at all.

"What if I say no?" he asks. The coachman's face darkens.

"You wouldn't do that."

"People need me here," he whispers. "My Nana needs me."

"Perhaps you should think of this, as a duty to your Nana then. I mean, you do want to keep her safe, don't you?" The question is heavy with threat but light enough to be reasonable.

"Aye."

"Any of these men, could be along the road, they could knock upon your Nana's door, they could rob her of what little she has and leave her worse for it. An old woman like that might not survive." Richie stares blank into the tall coachman's eyes, at the smooth well-shaven face and the dark hair in a knot at the back of his head under his tall felt hat. Richie does a grimace, the one that means begrudging resignation and he looks down at Bess with her ears down.

"How do you know me?" he asks. The man smiles.

"The North Burton lad who fights highwaymen? There's talk of you in the alehouses in Beverley. It's a good job you're on our side." The coachman walks over to the carriage and mounts the steps to the high seat, he grabs the whip as he sits down.

"Step up on board, Richie. You and that dog there can sit up here next to me."

It's a long way further than Richie has ever been before. He once went to a fair in North Frodingham when he was younger and he's been a time to Hornsea, to look at the wide ocean, and it frightened him at how huge and flat it was. The carriage travels out to Leconfield and onto places that Richie has heard of but never visited, Watton, Hutton Cranswick and Driffield. Then they roll further on the huge, creaky wooden wheels, out into the rolling hills of the East Riding past villages like Nafferton and Mill Pond that are new and foreign to Richie's ears, and he knows he is very far away from home as he hugs Bess sat next to him on the leather seats of the open carriage. It is a marvel that in this day and age they can travel such a distance and with such ease in less than a few hours too.

They take the north road around the top of Bridlington

and the coachman, who has still not given his name, says they are going to Flamborough Head on the cliffs to the east of the fishing town. Richie has not thought to ask why.

The coachman is friendly to a point but details that Richie asks about, he pats away with his hand in his black leather gloves. Unlike those men in pubs that Richie knows so well, the driver will not talk about his family or his past. They speak of Bess and how well she can catch rabbits and her lineage, the coachman thinks she's French. It's been about four hours and it's just noon. They have stopped a few times to stretch their legs and to let Mr Rail from inside the carriage relieve himself. As before, Richie does not think he looks much like a man who is to be hanged that very day. The woman is slight, thin and frightened, unlike the man she goes behind a fence to wee, and the coachman watches her to make sure she doesn't run off. Her eyes are big, round, and worried and her smooth face, unlike Mr Rail's, seems genuinely scared.

The landscape around them has changed. The big iron and wood wheels have taken them out of the flatlands where the fields stretch for miles and the horizon is a thin line. Now they climb a gentle hill upwards, with the North Sea on the right of them and the summer wind in Richie's light brown hair. They have come through the village of Flamborough and are heading towards the coast. The carriage crests over the hill and Richie looks down at the ocean, wide and endless under a vivid blue sky. Bess looks across at the waves far out to sea and the breeze makes her blink.

The coachman pulls up the horses, cranks the brake handle on the side of the carriage and they stop. Below them is North Landing, it's a patch of beach between cliffs on either side with a rowboat far below where figures like ants are unloading boxes. The coachman turns to Richie.

"We're here," he says to the lad next to him.

"I thought we were going to the quarter sessions at the courthouse?"

"We will, first we're here. There's someone who has asked to see you as well, lad." The coachman nods and in front, there is a figure on a horse overlooking the sea from the great cliff.

Richie takes Bess in both arms as he walks down the steps of the carriage. He reaches back up and collects his musket, then he and the dog walk the hundred yards on the soft grass to the man getting off his horse in front of them.

It's Stephen Middleton. Richie stops when he is a few yards away.

"My thanks for coming, Richie," says the magistrate. He is dressed in black as always but has his blond hair in a knot at the back of his head. Richie nods. There's something not quite right here with the blank coachman, Mr Rail in chains in the carriage and being here on the coast when they are supposed to be at a courthouse. Mr Middleton looks out over the North Sea with his sharp blue eyes.

"Have you been here before, Richie?" he asks.

"No, Sir," he answers.

"It's a natural harbor down there, built by God himself, can you see, out in the water, far away?" he points. Richie looks down over the white cliffs and his stomach rumbles at the sight, in the mid distance he can see the many white sails of a lugger ship, her sharp bow pointed forwards. "She's anchored there while the cobble lads bring in the supplies." Stephen Middleton turns to the lad with a half-smile of admiration.

"I was told about a trial, Mr Middleton."

"Would you walk with me a little, Richie?" asks Stephen Middleton by way of avoiding the lad's question. "There's a path that overlooks the cliffs and it's a powerful fine view." Richie nods. He follows Stephen Middleton across the green heather, puts his hand to his hat to stop the wind from blowing it off and looks down to see Bess with her ears flat to her head. Richie glances to the carriage he is walking away from, the coachman stands with his back against the mahogany of the door and inside the window, he can see the face of the lass who he has been told was going to be hanged for stealing swans. She is pale even from this far away. They walk along the cliff side and out of sight of the coach until Stephen Middleton stops near the edge. From here, there is a solid viewpoint of the coast on all sides, to the right, North Landing and the huge lugger boat anchored out to sea, to the left, the white chalk cliffs of the East Riding of Yorkshire. Gulls bank in the midday blue sky overhead, and the wind gusts in from the North Sea, more refreshing than cold on such a fine summer noon.

"I'm afraid that there is no trial, Richie, not today anyway. I've brought you here for another reason. There are a number of things that need setting straight between us." Richie swallows and his palm is suddenly clammy on the musket that he grips in his right hand. "Foolishly, I asked you to be the constable for North Burton, not because I thought you were up to the job but because I wanted you out the way. I can't have lads upsetting the natural order that is in place for the good of everyone. When you stopped those highwaymen all those months ago out at Dalton Park, you rather set my plans back." Richie feels his heart beating in his chest, there is not the rush of adrenaline of a brawl here, but something is out of place. "I asked you to meet the coach at Leconfield because I knew it was to be robbed, and with it, you could come to some sort of accident."

"How did you know?" asks Richie.

"I gave the order for it to be robbed. Continue to listen before you ask any more questions, Richie lad, your value today lies in how well you can listen and understand. My men did not arrange a good enough accident for you, it seems, and indeed, you rescued the Pike lass who was my target, or rather her father was. I underestimated you. Just who was it taught you to shoot?"

"My father?"

"The soldier who came back from the wars in Europe?"

"Aye." Stephen Middleton examines Richie's smooth face and his frown of worry. "I don't understand, you're the magistrate. Why would you give the order to have a carriage robbed?"

"Let me explain. The lugger out there is unloading brandy which the lads will bring up here to the carriage. The coachman will take it down to Beverley and sell it for a tidy profit. There's nothing in it for me, understand, just as long as I know what's going on. That, simply, is it, Richie. There are bad men and women all over this world, and good men such as you and I cannot stop them doing bad things, if we know the shape of their deeds we may contain them. Miss Charlotte Pennyman is a drunk and an evil woman, as you will no doubt know. She is in league with a group out of Kingston Upon Hull, they call themselves the Society for the Reformation of Manners and pretend that they give solace to drunks and the poor, but, Richie, men like Lieutenant Pike and his proud daughter are members of an order that seek to shift power in this great country. They are the same cloth that started the civil war against the king some seventy years ago, and they would start another today if they could. They want to rip the order that we know and understand. Did Elizabeth explain to you, what she and her father want to see?" Richie's mouth is dry.

"She told me she wanted to feed the poor."

Stephen Middleton scoffs.

"What she really means is cut the throats of every lord and lady in England, toss the way of life we know to the wind, let the unwashed in the cities feed like rats on their dead bodies. If that happens, our England, and our East Riding will be ruined in a generation. It's this order I defend and it's why, Lieutenant Pike and his daughter Elizabeth, Charlotte Pennyman too, need to be stopped. I had hoped to reason with the man by taking his daughter, but you stopped that, now he's strengthened himself with his comrades, the time for games is lost. There are men upon the road who I no longer control, like this Dick Turpin fool."

"Why is this important to me?" asks Richie, although he knows he is not supposed to ask any questions.

"Your bravery, Richie, is of value to me. I need men like you on the road, to oversee those of little character, to make sure they do as I ask. I am only sorry I did not bring you into my confidence previous. Join me, lad, and you'll not work the fields again, your Nana will have a servant girl to wash her feet and your dog will sleep next to a warm fire in the winter." Stephen Middleton cocks his head. "This very night, at North Burton, Lieutenant Pike and Elizabeth will attend a dinner at the Pennyman House. From the fields behind, my lads will fall upon the estate and there'll be a robbery. There will be shots fired too and, when the dust thins, Lieutenant Pike and his high cheeked daughter will be dead. Miss Charlotte Pennyman will have watched the whole affair. Grisly though it sounds, this is what we need to do to defend against these people, Richie. Do you understand?"

The tall lad nods, but he doesn't understand at all. The talk of kings and civil war and of an order, this is not what he fixates on when he glares at Stephen Middleton. He thinks of Elizabeth. He cannot quite understand what he hears.

"Was it your lads that took the girl from South Cave too?" Stephen Middleton's eyes look out across the chalk cliffs and out to the North Sea, then back again to Richie.

"We all do things that we don't want to do. Her father was a dangerous man, and he is not dangerous anymore. She was a fine lass." There's a light grin on Stephen Middleton's lips. Richie's face darkens. "Don't look at me like that, Richie. You're a country lad, you know that you can't keep all the puppies in a litter, you have to drown a few so that all of them can survive. Bad things have to be done on the farm so there's enough food for everyone." Richie's hand goes to the pistol in his belt, but he does not draw it. A smile flickers across

Stephen Middleton's face. "Oh Richie," he says. "Have a little class. This isn't some brawl in a country pub. You can't flash your eyes and touch your gun to make this go away. I'm one step ahead of you already. Men with my breeding occupy their superior positions because of such intelligence. I added something extra for this. I've asked the boys attending the robbery tonight to make another visit, down the street to the cottage opposite the pub. You've no idea what men like that can do to an old woman. I'm sure she'll pull through, your old Nana's a tough old bird, but they'll test her sure enough." Stephen Middleton walks a few steps closer to Richie, so he stands in front of him looking up. "You'll be my lad, and if not, on my say so, they'll return to North Burton, and they'll kill her."

Richie takes a deep breath.

He smells the sea air in his nostrils, feels the soft ground below his feet and the steel of the musket in his left hand. This is not right. Killing Elizabeth and Lieutenant Pike is not right however Stephen Middleton is able to frame it. As Richie stares down into the man's eyes, he knows that he cannot follow him, here, under the deep blue East Riding sky, he will have to make a stand. Middleton has the confidence of the rich about him, with the knowledge that whatever mistake he makes, he will always be better than kindhearted sheep brained boys like Richie here. Arrogance and wealth are why he's free to allow lads to smuggle brandy over from Holland, why he can turn a blind eye to illegal dealings in the city council and why he ordered the kidnap of that lass from South Cave and watched as she was raped. This is Stephen Middleton's world, just like it was his father's.

Richie tugs the pistol free of his belt, and his big thumb cocks the flintlock as he does. He aims the barrel at Stephen Middleton's stomach. The blonde man with blue eyes in front wears a smooth and serious expression across his face.

"Are you going to kill me, Richie lad?" he asks. He looks

up into his face, sees the light moustache and the nostrils flared in earnest. It's like breaking in a young horse. "If you should choose to pull that trigger, your Nana will die. The blood will be on your hands. You won't walk away either. The coachman is a fine soldier, with much experience in Ireland against the poor folk there." Stephen Middleton is honest for a moment. "You might think my kind hate you, Richie, the working poor, but we don't. I'm offering you a chance to step up."

Stephen Middleton is not a fool, he knows how far he can push people of a certain type, but he has got this one wrong. Any other poor lad might not do what Richie is about to do.

He squeezes the trigger, and the hammer of the pistol sparks the black powder in the pan, there's the flash of smoke as the lead bullet fires down the barrel and into Stephen Middleton's stomach. It's not the best shot. It should have blown him a good few yards. The man with blonde hair steps back as his hand goes to the wound on his belly, it looks like the ball passed right through, it might not be so bad after all.

"You could have done better than that, lad," he says as he looks up with a grin.

Richie steps forward and shoves Stephen Middleton backward, just hard enough for the man to lose his footing. His eyes widen as his foot slips and then, like one of the seagulls wheeling in the clear blue sky, Stephen Middleton falls backwards over the side of the chalk cliff with his mouth open wide and silent in terror.

Richie looks down at Bess and she stares up at him as if he's done a good job. They don't hear a splash, but that coachman will have heard the shot.

Richie slips the pistol back into his belt and moves off the path to the right, keeping low. He drops behind a ridge and the heather prickles his chest as he lays on his front with the musket pointing forth. Richie looks down the barrel. Sure enough, there is the coach driver, running over the cliff edge path with his pistol drawn and the felt black hat rolling off his head as he jogs. Both he and Middleton have misjudged this lad. Neither were they aware of who has trained him, or who he has become. Richie narrows his eyes down the sights as he aims at the coachman whose name he still does not know; he waits till the tall man is just near enough and then squeezes the trigger. The musket ball blows a hole through his ribs and his insides splatter from his back out into the blue midday sea air. He takes a few more steps before he crashes to the ground.

Richie walks through the smoke of the gunshot, his satchel across one shoulder, pistol tucked in his belt and the tricorn hat resting on the back of his head. He's already reloading the musket as he approaches the carriage. There's the face of the thin woman inside still. Her expression is as pale as it was a few minutes before. As Richie gets closer, she points with her thumb behind her, Richie looks and raises the barrel of the musket. Fat Mr Rails stands there, at the back of the carriage without any irons, looking like he is about to cry with the gun trained on him. Richie cocks the musket.

"Run," he calls. Mr Rail turns and begins off, on his big legs, across the heather and down to North Landing beach below.

Richie steps forward and opens the carriage door.

"Can you walk?" he asks the thin woman inside. She nods. Richie steps back and the lass climbs out and then stands looking up at him with her big eyes. He's killed two men this day and there's no getting out if it either. There's a witness also in the fat Mr Rail. He opens his satchel, reaches inside and takes out one of the crowns that Lieutenant Pike gave him the day before. He passes it to the lass, and she takes it quick enough.

"Are you Dick Turpin?" she asks.

He might as well be.

"Aye. How did you know?"

"The bird scar," she says as she points to his chest. The

collar of Richie's shirt is open and, on his breast, is the red swallow mark that the railing from the fire made on his skin all those years ago in North Burton. "That's how," she adds. "Anyone knows Mr Turpin has a bird scar on his chest. Where's the magistrate?"

"I shot him in the stomach and pushed him off the cliff." She nods.

"That's what Dick Turpin would do. Are you setting me free?"

"Aye. No need to steal anymore swans," he says. She smiles and many of the front teeth are black and others on the turn to being rotten.

"I'll not forget this," she says. "I was to be on that ship."

"I thought you were up for trial."

"That coachman gave me a choice, favours on the lugger out there or a year in jail. I'd rather have taken my chances on my back."

"What's your name, lass?"

"Kat."

"Well met, Kat."

"Am I to tell that I was saved by Dick Turpin and that he gave me a coin as well?" Her big, clever eyes examine the man looking down on her.

"Aye, if you want. I enjoyed giving you the coin. It was the best part of the day." This is the truth. Kat looks off down to the calm beach far below them, she sees the figure of Mr Rail approaching the other men unloading the cobble on the shore. Mr Rail's arms are waving. He'll be telling them what happened.

"I owe you. There's a pub at Scarborough, the Golden Ball. It's where I go sometimes. It's full of the wrong sorts, like me and you." Richie nods. He's not the wrong sort at all.

"Good luck," he says.

"Best of luck to you as well, Mr Turpin. Well met."

CHAPTER TWENTY

Richie has done a fair bit of running in his life and not just because he doesn't ride. He likes the feeling of his feet pounding on the ground and Bess next to him, with his chest open as he takes in the fresh air, the sweat on his brow and the wide sky above.

He's been running twenty minutes and at this rate, it will take him all day to get back to North Burton. Stephen Middleton said his men would be at the house that evening and Richie thinks this will be when it is dark. His legs are already tired and his stomach growls. He looks down at Bess beside him and then up to the road ahead. Richie has ditched the blue coat but not the musket, he carries this in his left hand as he runs. The ramrod under the barrel clacks. If he's to make it there before it's dark he cannot stop, whatever his legs may feel like and whatever his stomach tells him. There are lives at stake, Stephen Middleton told him the Pikes would be killed.

He thinks about Elizabeth and the time they spent by the river, her hand on his chest and her pretty freckled face. He sees her straight white teeth and ginger hair falling over her hazel eyes, smells her perfume too. Then there's Nana, and Richie does not like to think of what he will do to anyone who tries to hurt her, for the old woman will not back down from a fight. In her chair, stuffed down the side is a knife she uses to cut up anything she eats, and she will use it, if she has to. This is what Richie fears, if she wounds an attacker, they will do worse to her. He jogs on.

Richie is not taking the coastal path, he's cut round the north of Bridlington and will hold the Driffield road inland. Neither does he know if he is followed or if word of what happened to the magistrate, Stephen Middleton and his coachman, has reached the ears of anyone noteworthy. Either way, there is no path out of this now for Richie. Whatever he says, whatever truth he tells, he is a murderer and if they catch him, not all the goodwill in the world will keep him from the gallows. As long as he makes it to North Burton, it doesn't matter. They can do what they like to him if he can make sure Elizabeth Pike and Nana are safe.

There's another reason Richie has taken the road around the north of Bridlington and towards Driffield, there's a place on the way, he's sure of it, a place called Burton Agnes and a pub called the Blue Bell there. The man who runs the livery yard is someone he knows.

It's been nearly an hour and the sun is up. Richie is sweating hard and Bess next to him has her long tongue lolling out her mouth as she pants. They're not sprinting, that would tire them too quickly, this is the slow thudding pace that will deliver them as close to North Burton as possible. After the wide-open fields to either side, the road narrows and snakes between tall hedges. Here, Richie passes folk on the road, a lady and her tiny daughter both with matching bonnets, their faces hard for a stranger and his dog at a light jog. There's an old man leading a donkey with a straw bale tied to the beast's back and a shout from his elderly chest as Richie passes him, some joke or something. You don't often see a tall lad with a musket running down the lane towards Burton Agnes. Whitewashed houses appear at either side as Richie and Bess run, there's a low barn on the top of the hill to the right, and to the left are run down hovels with their rooves patched up with thatch and there, opposite a great lane leading up a hill is the coaching inn, the Blue Bell.

Before the main entrance to the pub, there's a yard where the coaches can turn in and let their well-heeled travellers get out while their horses go off to the livery behind. There's a side door and a young lad of perhaps five sits on a bench whitling a stick. He looks up as Richie approaches and then gets to his feet with surprised eyes, he sees the gun, the big boots and the height of the man approaching and is quite frozen to the spot.

"Lad," calls Richie. "I'm looking for a man named Len Ploughman." The boy does nothing but point to the smell of the livery yard and, in a few steps, Richie is behind the pub looking at a bare-chested man washing down a horse with a rag and a bucket of water. He turns and there is the face of John the Pearlman with his skin looking more creased than it ever has.

"By God," he whispers. "Richie?"

"I'm in trouble," he says over his heavy breath. "And because of me, so is Nana"

The Pearlman has taken a big black shire horse and they are three miles out of Burton Agnes. He rides in front and Richie sits behind him on a beast that is not known for its speed. They move at a trot, but it is at least faster than the slow thudding jog that Richie could muster from Flamborough Head around the top of Bridlington.

The Pearlman is too used to a crisis to be worried by one. He made Richie stand in the shade of a stable and tipped half a bucket of water on his head and the rest on the dog to cool them down, then, he readied the big black shire, steady and as calm as you like, and with not a single word to the little stable lad who watched him. He collected his pistol and cloak from somewhere behind the stables, clambered up into the sleek black saddle and pulled Richie up behind him.

The road is clear in the afternoon and the Pearlman keeps the shire to a trot so it's as fresh as it can be. They will travel much faster and further if they maintain a steady pace. The dark-haired man up front has not asked Richie a single thing about what sort of trouble he is in. Bess keeps the pace beside them. He only knows that they are bound for North Burton and that they should get there by nightfall at the latest, and that Richie has done something. The tall lad who sits behind breaks the silence first.

"Will they be okay with you taking the horse?" he asks.

"No, not at all," he replies over his shoulder. "This is the landlord's pride and joy, but I figured it was the only horse big enough to take the two of us." Richie is expecting the Pearlman to comment on the fact that he can't ride, but this is not his style at all. Nana would blame Richie, she'd blame him for not being able to ride and for whatever he'd done. Because the Pearlman does not ask anything, Richie feels guilty.

"Will you lose your job?" he asks.

"I hope so," he replies. "It's time I moved on anyway. Now you've come of age, and everything."

At Nafferton, the Pearlman, heads south so they will miss the market town of Driffield. He will ride across the fields. People know the Pearlman there as Len Ploughman and that he plays cards and has a past. The feeling of guilt rises in Richie.

"I shot him in the stomach," he says. "Then I shoved him off Flamborough Cliffs."

"Who?"

"The magistrate, Stephen Middleton." The Pearlman looks over his shoulder at the big lad. It's unusual for him to have to look up at anyone.

"Stephen Middleton," he repeats.

"Aye," says Richie. The Pearlman beams.

"You don't do things by halves do you, lad? How much did you get?" The Pearlman does not assign any blame, a life spent with those who do wrong has taught him not to.

"Nothing. I got nothing from it. I shot his coachman as well. Middleton said he sent men to hurt Nana, and Miss Charlotte Pennyman too, and Lieutenant Pike and his daughter, tonight at the Pennyman House." The Pearlman continues to ride. The highwayman in him is proud of the lad. "Will I go to hell?" he asks.

"For killing Stephen Middleton? He was a crook if ever there was one, Richie, we all knew it. Who do you think supplied all the rum in Beverley?" Richie has not heard people speak ill of Stephen Middleton before.

"He said he'd kill Nana."

"A lot of people have said that."

"I think he really meant it. I think if we don't get to North Burton, his men will. It's because of me, of what I've done, and not just because I shot him through his stomach." It's hard to talk properly when they are not facing each other and riding too, but there's a fatalistic sense in the lad's voice. "I'll swing for it," he adds.

"I shot men too, Richie, and they never got me." He looks over his shoulder at the lad once more. Now he knows the shape of what's happened, he digs his heels lightly against the sides of the beast below them and it speeds up. "Is anyone following?"

"I don't think so," he answers.

"Hold on."

The Pearlman clicks his tongue and the great black shire horse under them responds, the huge hooves leave round holes in the soft grass as they cut across the plain south of Driffield with the vivid blue sky above them. Richie holds onto the Pearlman's back as they go, and he worries for the future. He worries that they will not get there in time to stop Stephen Middleton's men from carrying out his orders. He worries about what will happen to Nana when they catch him, and what Meg will think and who will help Jonny Low do the rest of the baling and who will look after Bess. He wonders who will marry Elizabeth and who will kiss her. With the wind rushing into his light brown hair, Richie does not care who she kisses as long as she lives to do so.

There are lanes and paths that are seldom used out here in the wilds of the East Riding. Nana says there are villages that are there one afternoon and not the next, great towers you can only see on windy days, and huge mouths in the ground that open in winter and can swallow you up whole so you'll never be found again.

The Pearlman pulls the great shire horse up beside the wood at Bealey's Beck and gets off. Bess appears at the side, and she goes down the little bank where she laps at the cool water. They are just south of Etton, not ten minutes ride from North Burton and the sky has taken on an orange hue. Richie slips off the back of the animal and his legs hurt, the Pearlman leads the horse down to the beck also so it can take a drink. They have not spoken much, these two, since they picked up the pace a few hours south of Driffield. Richie takes off his musket and begins to load it. The big shire horse laps up the water with its huge tongue.

"They won't attack until dark," says Richie.

"How do you know?"

"Well, that's what I think they'll do. They'll come from the north that's for sure. The same as they did last time, the back of the house. They might be in the woods there right now." Richie looks pale and his eyes are red. The Pearlman wanders up to him and takes a waterskin from the side bag of the horse.

"You know, once we've done this, there'll be no going back to the way things were before," the man who Richie called his father is earnest.

"It's already too late for me to go back," says Richie, "and you don't have to do anything. I only asked you to help me get here. I've shot men before; I can do it again. You can go back to your life in the livery yard of the Blue Bell." The Pearlman hands him the waterskin. Richie has thought about what he might say to this man, how he hated him and loved him in equal measure. Now he stands in front of him, he does not know what to say, so much has happened to Richie, it is, as if he is a different person to the child who looked up to the Pearlman with his dark hair and blue eyes.

"I want to help you," he says. "I've been laying silent for too long. Len Ploughman is kind of an arse anyway, he doesn't cheat at cards, only drinks on a Saturday night. You can rely on him. That's not the man I once was, Richie. Until I met

Meg and You, and Nana, I was a rogue, a loveable one, at times, but a rogue all the same."

"What will I do if I survive, Pearlman?" It's the first time Richie has called him by this name and not John. "Where will I go, how will I live?"

"Well, you have everything you need. A brave heart, smart wits, a musket and pistol, a satchel full of bullets and a friend too." He nods at the dog. "You know, Richie, there are three in a gang of robbers, do you know that?"

Richie nods.

"Aye, the heart, the head and the eyes."

"You remembered?"

"You taught me."

"We three of us could be a set of robbers. You, Bess and I. Three brothers, even though Bess is a girl." Richie does his wide grin. "You know, Richie lad, I've heard stories already in the Blue Bell back there, whispers on the lips of rich men and those that know, the talk is that there is a roadman already here who has some of the quality needed to be a highwayman. Have you heard of him? Turpin, they call him."

"My mother's name," says Richie. The Pearlman does not seem to connect the clues, he continues:

"The rumour is that he's six foot five. That's a bit taller than you even, and that he carries a mahogany pistol and that his hat is made by Atkinson's of York. He has a black stallion named Bess and he's as calm and as smooth as the mist over the moors on a moonlit night."

The Pearlman stops himself, cocks his head and looks at the lad in front of him, slightly taller than six foot four in his boots and with the expensive hat, crafted by expert milliners out in York. Bess sits herself down in the long cool grass next to him, she's been running all day.

"Is it you?" he asks.

"Not by design," Richie answers. The Pearlman beams with his white smile and his eyes twinkle. It makes Richie's heart jump in happiness.

"I heard you robbed a carriage at Leconfield. Is that so?"

"Aye?"

"With who?"

"Just Bess and I." The Pearlman grins.

"What did you do with the money?"

"I gave it to the new landlord at the Bay Horse to pay off a debt he had." The Pearlman considers this.

"You gave it away?" he repeats.

"Aye, a lot of it."

"Why would you do that?"

"It wasn't my money, and why would I need it? I've got everything I need. It's the least I could do for that Philipson anyway, he's helped me before."

"Do you know," asks the Pearlman, "that it takes some men a lifetime to understand that way of thinking? But you, a farm lad from North Burton, you seem to get it perfectly. It took me many years to come around to the fact that none of the money was mine and I didn't need it either. I never wanted you to be a robber, Richie, but I never wanted you to be a wretch either. If this business at the Pennyman House is done clean, then you and I, with this big black shire horse and that hunting dog, we'll take off north. The land is wild up in Northumberland. We'll be free."

"What about Nana?" The Pearlman has not thought it through. He doesn't need to.

"The village will look after her, Richie. That's what country folk do. We could do some real damage, lad. We could rob the stagecoaches between Newcastle and York, spend the winter in Scarborough on the drink. There's space for men such as us. You'll not believe the feeling, to rob a rich man of the money he and his family have already robbed and then pass it back to those who need it. There's a pub on the docks there called the Golden Ball and full of rum lads it is."

"I'm not sure," says Richie. There's fear in his eyes, not for what could happen to him, but for what he'd miss, the card games with Jonny Low, Nana shouting at him, the church at Christmas, the Pennyman barn dance in October... Elizabeth.

"Like you said yourself, Richie, there's no going back if they think you murdered Stephen Middleton. He was a rich man, and powerful too and his friends will want to see justice done for him."

"You said he was a crooked man."

"Aye, but so are most of the rich folk in Beverley town. You know that." Richie nods. He sits down on the grass next to Bess and takes a slug on the waterskin, rests his back on the fence post that doesn't have a fence anymore. He's tired and lost.

"Now don't go looking like that, Richie lad," says the Pearlman. "You've got opportunity in front of you. Once you turn up to the Pennyman House and we see off Stephen Middleton's robbers, you'll be free. You won't have to stay at Nana's house or work the fields, you won't have to drink in that pub anymore. Do you remember when you were a little lad? We used to talk about pirates on great galleons in the sunlit oceans, robbers with golden teeth in the warm forests of Europe, adventure, and as I recall, lad, you could tell a fine tale before you'd even lived. Now it's your chance to live, you follow this beck here, this trickle of water and it leads to the River Hull and you follow that, and you're onto the Humber and then The North Water, and then the whole world. You could go anywhere, you could be anyone." The lad looks up at the Pearlman and there's some of the wild in him, behind his eyes, just enough so he can see the wonder of the dream that the Pearlman weaves with his clever words but there's sadness as well. "And if you need home, why, there'll be Bess right next to you."

"There's someone else," says Richie. "It wouldn't be so bad if there wasn't. I could leave North Burton and never come back so long as Nana is kept well, but there's another."

"A girl?"

"Aye."

"Who?"

"Lieutenant Pike's daughter, Elizabeth. The one I brought back from those robbers." There's no judgement from the Pearlman at this sentence.

"Do you love her?"

"I've kissed her," he adds, as if that means he does.

The Pearlman walks to the saddle bag of the big shire and pulls open the flap. He draws out one of his black pistols and checks the barrel.

"We best get ready then, Richie lad," he says.

"There something that Meg said, back in Etton. I wanted to ask you." The Pearlman frowns in readiness for a question he may not be able to answer.

"Go on."

"Meg said that …" he struggles with the unreasonable nature of talking about something that is not real. Meg has told him that love is dangerous, and that it destroys, and he wants to know if this is true. "Did you love her?" he asks, just as easy as that. It's not the kind of question people round here ask. The Pearlman is not afraid of his feelings like most men are.

"If there is such a thing, aye, I felt it for her, I still do."

"How does it feel?"

"It's not good, Richie. It leaves you weak."

"That's what she said. She told me it destroys everything."

"She's not often wrong, is your Meg, Richie." The Pearlman searches himself as he takes out his other dark pistol from the saddle bag. "Love makes you vulnerable and that can destroy you, aye, but there's strength in it too. I could never have changed if it weren't for Meg. I'd be hanged by now, if it weren't for her, and for you." They have never spoken this way. "I missed you all these years, Richie and I never forgot. I just wish I could have told you." They are moving into subjects that should only be discussed when drunk or at funerals, weddings or christenings. Each man is uneasy. "Whatever Meg says, Richie, don't be afraid of how you feel." The lad is hot and young and he cannot help himself.

"I love you," he says and there are tears in his eyes. The Pearlman puts his hands over his face and winces as he feels emotion come over him also, as he hears these true words.

"You're not even my lad," he whispers. Richie stands up and the two men embrace, the Pearlman small against his son. Of course, Richie is not his son, but there is nobody in all of the world who could be his father, except this man.

This is how night becomes day.

Everything impossible can be true.

CHAPTER TWENTY-ONE

It's dusk in North Burton.

The carriage that Richie robbed and then was robbed again the other evening is now the right way up on four fixed wheels. The horses have been unhooked from the carriage and it looks strangely injured there, in front of the Pennyman House, with the breeching bars on the ground. Richie and The Pearlman climbed over the estate walls half a mile away and stayed low in the bushes as they moved round to the front of the house. Now, they are crouched against two trees out front with their faces covered and tricorn hats tight over their eyes. The noise of the starlings in the trees above is good cover but there's nobody around at the front of the property, and this is unusual. The Pennymans don't have many servants, but they have enough to make it feel like someone lives in the property. The two men have waited a good five minutes watching the front door and the sides for movement but there has been nothing. Bess sits close to Richie, he's told her to be as quiet as she can, unless she sees something to chase, she'll not make a sound. The tall lad looks off down the drive to the gates that are, unusually, open. About this time of the evening, Miss Charlotte's coachman will be out to lock them up. So far there's no sign of him. It's too quiet for a working house. Richie pulls down his mask to get a clear breath.

"There's something wrong. What if we're too late?" The Pearlman shrugs and Richie can only see his playful blue eyes. "Shall I go to the door?" The man nods and Richie pauses. They have no idea what is about to happen. Richie's stomach is churning, and his palms are wet with sweat. The Pearlman was always like this, even when he was meant to be Richie's stepfather, John, he didn't ever tell the lad what to do. It was Richie's decision to get it right or wrong, unlike with Nana when whatever he did would be the wrong thing to do. Richie looks at the man again, the Pearlman has been a soldier and highwayman, served in the Duke of Marlborough's forces in Europe, fought men in pubs, slashed others with knives, been shot a good few times as well, but, this is going to be Richie's game. The Pearlman leans close to the lad:

"You be the heart, Richie; I'll be head and Bess here can be our eyes. We're a gang remember, we work from each other. Your blood's up, where you lead, we two will follow." Richie steadies himself and returns the scarf over his face and nose.

"Trust yourself," says the Pearlman. He's the worst and the best kind of teacher, rather than tell you, he lets you work out how to do it for yourself. Richie gives him another look in disbelief, for if he gets this wrong, they could die this night, or be caught and then hanged; it's not some sort of game. The Pearlman's eyes twinkle in the half-darkness because, this is a game.

Richie looks to the door of the Pennyman House and the silence of the great building as the darkness begins to creep upon the summer evening around them. He draws his pistol and sneaks forward through the bushes to the deserted carriage that stands in front of the house, skirts around the front and there, above the three steps, the great door to the manor is ajar, just by a few inches. Richie presses on, still crouching towards it, and he peeps through. He can hear voices from the study off the hall and there is the faint yellow glow of a lamp. The voices are deep and there's a laugh, rough and cruel like you might hear in an alehouse.

They are too late.

Stephen Middleton's men are already here.

Richie feels the blood rush to his face and hands, and before he can look back to see if the Pearlman follows, he pushes open the door with his shoulder and goes inside towards the noise and light. The voices are closer, coarse and heavy, and coming from the study off the hall where Richie went to talk to Miss Charlotte Pennyman some time back. The dark wood door is open wide and in the half light, Richie moves on silent feet. He can see inside. There are three figures standing, dressed in black and facing away from the door, robbers at that, the middle has a saber strapped to his belt. In front of them and sitting down at the study table are the three, Miss Charlotte Pennyman, Lieutenant Pike and his daughter. Richie sees a flash of Elizabeth's ginger hair pinned up and her hazel eyes are round with fear, on her cheek there is a red scuff, as if she has been struck or pushed against something. Seeing her like this has a profound effect on Richie, electricity shoots through him and his muscles spasm as he gets to his feet and powers forward into the study before him. This is why Richie is the heart today, he's full of fire and bluster, rage and under that, fear, he is not in control of himself. Soldiers of more measured sensibilities and experience would have planned their attack, but the Pearlman knows as he creeps through the open door after the lad, that anything can happen once men start shooting whether you have thought it through for an hour or a few seconds. Richie has the stomach and the passion for a fight and sometimes this is all you need.

Richie rushes into the study behind the three men holding his musket in his big hands by the barrel, he clobbers the man on the left in his head with the stock. It's like cutting down hay and the robber crumples to the ground as Richie turns to face the middle one.

The speed of it all has caught them off guard.

This lad has a nasty, snarling face and goes for the sword at his waist, but there's a loud crack from the doorway where the Pearlman crouches pointing his ebony pistol. The head follows the heart and keeps it safe. The heavy lead bullet hits the man under his arm and gets most of the way through his body, splintering ribs and a lung so that he collapses onto the table beside. Richie grabs his musket in two hands as he steps to the man on the right who is already bringing up a pistol. He clatters the weapon out of the robber's hands and, with the musket held horizontal, shoves him back and pins him against one of the bookcases by his neck. The robber's head slams against the wooden frame and his fingers claw at the mask that covers Richie's face in desperation, scratching at his cheek and pulling the cloth off his nose and mouth. Richie bars his teeth, pulls the musket back and slams him into the wood once more so the robber collapses. The Pearlman enters the room through the pistol smoke and there, sat behind the table like they are about to have dinner are the three of them. Miss Charlotte, Lieutenant Pike and his daughter Elizabeth. They have varying looks of shock and horror across their faces. Not so Elizabeth, she wears a thrilled smile. From Behind them Bess barks as she too enters the study. The eyes. Richie turns and despite the scratches across his face and his legs shivering with adrenaline, he beams down on Elizabeth with a sense of wonder.

"I knew you'd come, Richie," she says.

"Are you the Jackson lad?" says Miss Charlotte. She is trying to match what she sees in front of her with what she knows.

"There are more of them," calls the Pearlman as he pulls the man he shot onto the floor. He leans over and grabs the other edge to pull the big study table onto its side, it will give them some cover. Elizabeth rises and helps him push it over. There are shouts from the hall outside the study door and the Pearlman fires a shot from his other pistol into the darkness before he jumps behind the table. Richie follows with Bess soon after. Miss Charlotte falls to her knees, turns and puts her back to the underside of the table. There's a bit more scrabbling as Lieutenant Pike joins her and then, they are all in place.

From left to right. The Pearlman, loading his ebony pistol with his calm fingers, his heart beating in his chest, and his eyes sparkling for the thrill of it. Miss Pennyman sits with her hands together and her thin lips red, she needs a drink. Next,

Lieutenant Pike, someone has struck him across the face and there's a bruise, he frowns, he's been robbed too many times of late. Elizabeth sits next, her ginger hair is pinned up, she too has been hit by one of the robbers, but the mark is faint on her cheek, she looks to her right and gives a beaming, toothy smile amid the acrid smell of black powder. Bess is next, with Richie's arm around her. The lad smiles at Elizabeth as she grins back at him. It isn't the right place for this kind of thing, but he can't help it, and neither can she.

A shot rings out from the hall and hits the table, splintering the wood at the top and ricocheting off and through one of the little panes of glass in the window above them. The Pearlman leans forward and looks down the line of faces behind the upturned table to his lad.

"Are you ready, Richie?" he yells.

This is how you fight, like you dance, putting one foot in the place where it feels like it should go. Richie does not know what he is supposed to be ready to do. He yells:

"Aye." The Pearlman swings around the side of the upturned table and shoots into the smoke, then returns to where he sat. Richie turns and rises to his knees, brings his musket to his shoulder, sees the movement of something in the hall and pulls the trigger. There's the boom as it recoils, and he sits back down. His eyes sting from the smoke and he's not sure if he hit anything or not, he draws his pistol from his belt. On the opposite side, the Pearlman loads his weapon once more. In the hall outside there seems to be quiet and they wait there, behind the well-made study table with the smoke settling. Lieutenant Pike turns his head in the direction of the Pearlman,

"You'll all be hanged for this," he whispers.

"You'd be already dead, Sir, if it were not for my friend and I. We're not here to rob you."

"You'll be hanged anyway," says Miss Charlotte from next to him. "Not that Richie Jackson, mind, he's got Pennyman blood in his veins." The Pearlman is glad that she does not recognise him, why would she, with the scarf over his face and the fact that he left North Burton some eight years since?

"Just wait," calls out the Pearlman. He turns his head to listen out into the house around them. Richie feels a hand on his arm and looks down to see that Elizabeth is holding him just above his wrist with her slender and smooth fingers. He can feel her squeeze his skin, it makes him tingle.

"Miss Charlotte!" there's a woman's voice coming from the hallway. "Miss Charlotte," she calls again. Richie knows the throaty shout. It's Mrs Heather the cook from the kitchen. "The one that was left, Miss Charlotte, he's ridden off over the back fields."

"Stay where you are," whispers the Pearlman as he edges round the corner of the fallen table with one of his pistols in front of him. The smoke is clearing. Richie moves out of his position also, with his own pistol held out. He can see the fat figure of Mrs Heather walking into the study, and at once, there is something not quite right about the way she stands and holds her hands out in front of her. Richie sees the barrel of the pistol come out from under her arm. One of the robbers is behind her and has, no doubt, put her up to this. He hears the dull boom as the flint strikes the stone. The old woman gives a shriek as the gun fires, but Richie is already moving towards her as whoever behind pushes the woman forward, he side steps, smells more smoke and narrows his eyes at the figure dashing to the side of the study. Richie doesn't have time to think, he brings the pistol up level and pulls the trigger. Mrs Heather shrieks again as Richie's gun roars out in the dim light, and there's a half slap, half thud as the bullet hits the robber. He hears a groan. Richie moves forward and laid with his arms out, is the robber who had hidden behind the cook, his chest is wide open from the shot and he is trying to breathe through lungs that have been splattered across the leather book spines behind him.

"He was going to shoot me if I didn't do as he asked," yells Mrs Heather into the summer darkness. "Oh Miss Charlotte. Where are you, Miss Charlotte?" There's the scraping of a chair and Miss Charlotte's harsh voice cuts through the room that has seen so much violence in such a short time:

"Pull yourself together Mrs Heather," she snaps. "Get to the kitchen and light a lamp. Bring my brandy while you're at it." Richie stumbles to the table on its side and he feels Bess under his hands, he sees the Pearlman getting to his feet next in the dim light coming in from the window. He goes to help the man.

"Were you hit?" he whispers.

"He clipped a wing, lad, that's all." The Pearlman gets to his feet and reaches to pick up his pistol. "It's time we were gone," he says.

Mrs Heather returns with the lamp bright, and suddenly the darkness outside is pitch black and the chaos of the study vivid and clear. There's a man slumped at the bottom of one bookcase and another with his lungs blasted through at the opposite side.

"Is that all there were, Mrs Heather?" ask Miss Charlotte.

"Yes, mam. It's been a right affair. The coachman's been battered black and blue and I've sent for help down at the village. I'm shaking so much I can hardly walk, Miss."

"What of Mr Pennyman, my father?" she asks.

"If nobody's moved him, Miss, he will be in bed where we left him earlier."

"Quick as you can with that brandy then, Mrs Heather, we don't need to hear you blathering on and on." The big woman sets the bottle down on a shelf next to Miss Charlotte. Lieutenant Pike makes his way to the front of the fallen table and addresses Richie

"Richie Jackson. You have my thanks again this day." The tall lad nods. Now the situation is calm, he does not want to look at Elizabeth at all, even though she stands behind her father staring at him with her pale hazel eyes. There is something more in Lieutenant Pike's demeanor, he's not at all a fool. He can see that the Pearlman is the one who came after Richie the night the boy rescued his daughter, the one who laid him over a horse and rode him away. He realised the minute he saw the man holding the dark pistol.

"It was you two that robbed us first, on that night near Leconfield. Now I see you dressed as you are, Richie Jackson, I know it was you that stuck a pistol in my daughter's face. It was you that took my money. Then, you had the audacity to stand in my house in Beverley and take more." Pike is not angry. Not yet. He is stating the affairs as he sees them.

The Pearlman puts himself between these two.

"If it wasn't for us, Sir, you'd be dead." He does not like having to say this again.

"I have expressed my gratitude already but I don't imagine, Sir, that you two came here to save us. Perhaps you saw another chance to make a profit."

"Did these men who attacked you, did they steal anything from you?" asks the Pearlman.

"They would have done," answers Lieutenant Pike.

"They were under orders to shoot you two, you and your daughter," it's Richie, he has returned his pistol to his belt and carries the musket in his right hand. He looks pale.

"Why would that be so, Richie?"

"He wants you and the Reformation of Manners Society stopped and crushed. It was his men who took Elizabeth, he was to use her as a bargaining piece to make you give up. I saw him with my own eyes that day, so did your daughter." This has already been explained to Lieutenant Pike and he did not quite believe it. Now he knows it is true.

"How did you come upon this information, Richie?" asks the Lieutenant.

"Mr Middleton told me so himself." There's the clink of a bottle on a glass. The thin figure of Miss Charlotte has poured herself a large measure of the brown apple brandy. She takes a gulp and turns to face her guests, both the invited and the uninvited.

"Was I to be killed as well?" she asks Richie.

"I don't believe so, Miss Charlotte. He said he had a special interest in you."

"I bet he does," she snarls. "Do you know where our magistrate is now? He was meant to be here this night. I have the letter stating his appointment." Richie swallows down his fear.

"I shot him, out at Flamborough Head. I shot him in his stomach and shoved his body off the cliff." Elizabeth puts her hand to her mouth in shock. "He's dead." Miss Charlotte scoffs at this and then catches Richie's eyes. She's seen Richie at work, like a whirlwind, fearless and powerful. Her face is serious.

"If he's dead, then so is my debt," murmurs Miss Charlotte. "I wonder if you remember what we discussed a few weeks back, Richie, about birth?"

"I do," he says.

"Do you remember what I told you? That my father used your mother for a whore, and let her die on the cowshed floor?" It is unnecessary cruel language.

"I told you then it was a lie," he replies.

"Here it is, proof, Richie. Look at what you have done?" She presents the bodies in the study around her with one of her thin hands, in the other sways the glass of apple brandy. "You are a man of quality, as my father was, a Pennyman, through and through, albeit a bastard one. Thank you, brother for saving me this day and, if it's true that you killed Stephen Middleton, you've written off the debt that this house owed to him as well." Richie's hand moves to the pistol on his belt and lightly touches the handle. As he does, Miss Charlottes face loses all emotion.

"You would be doing me a favour, Richie, if you did pull

out that pistol and shoot me too." There is no joke in her voice. Her eyes are hollow.

"I'm no Pennyman," he says. "Not ever. A Pennyman would never risk anything for another. You know that already and that's why you know I'm not part of you."

"I'll turn your Nana out into the street," she whispers.

"The people of this village won't let you," he answers. The Pearlman moves behind Richie.

"We have to go," he says. "There's no time for this."

"Your colleague is correct," says Lieutenant Pike, "if you have killed Stephen Middleton, the magistrate, then it will be murder. Regardless of how bad a man he may have been, it will be murder just the same."

From outside the front of the house, in the darkness of the road opposite the church, there comes the blast of a high-pitched whistle. Lieutenant Pike knows the sound well enough; it is the call of a Captain bringing the men under his command to a halt.

"It will be the militia from Beverley town," says Lieutenant Pike and Richie looks to the Pearlman in fear. "You need to leave here now, the both of you. If they've learned of the murder, they will stop at nothing to find whoever did it." The Pearlman puts his hand on Richie's shoulder to pull him back out of the room and into the hall. Now that he knows he must go, he looks at Elizabeth and she rushes to him, past her father and the two embrace, Richie's battered hands around her shoulders as he holds her tight and smells the perfume in her hair. Her fingers dig into him and her mouth finds his ear.

"At dawn tomorrow," she whispers, "I will be at your secret place, the old oak at Dalton Park. I'll get away." Her father pulls her back by her shoulder and opposite, the Pearlman peels Richie's arm off.

"We have to go now," he commands. "There's no time for this." Richie half stumbles as he and the Pearlman leave the study and go through the door the hall. At a run in the darkness, Richie leads them down the corridor to the kitchen and the backdoor of the house. They can already hear footsteps and men entering the front door behind. In a few moments, Richie and the Pearlman are out into the night.

The door of Nana's cottage is not locked. Richie opens the latch and walks inside. There she is, sat in her chair like always, with a light blanket across her knee.

"What the bloody hell time do you call this, Richie Jackson?" she begins. She has been waiting for him and has stored up the insults. She is angry. There's an urgency as he steps inside.

"You have to leave the cottage, Nana," he says. His words are hot and quick.

"Whatever's going on?" asks the woman. "If I don't get you out this house, Nana, you'll be shot or worse." This gets the old woman going.

"I've got my knife here Richie, anyone that comes not welcome through that door will get a taste of it."

"There's no time, Nana," he yells. Richie goes behind the old woman in the darkness, and he takes hold of the top of the chair and drags it, with Nana still sat inside. "Hold tight," he commands as he drags her to the door, then with two bumps down the steps they are out into the street. The Pearlman stands looking up the hill, there are lights outside the Pennyman House opposite the church, more than he can count. There must be fifty men. Richie drags the old woman across the dirt street and to the door of the pub, he tries the latch but it's locked so he bangs on the wood in the night, glancing up the hill to the lights as well.

"What have you done?" whispers Nana below.

"I killed someone," he answers.

"Did he deserve it?" she asks.

"Aye," comes the reply.

The door to the Bay Horse opens and Philipson looks out

into the darkness. He has a white night hat on his head.

"What's all this?" he asks. Richie barges past him and drags Nana, still on her chair, up the steps and into the pub.

"Do you remember when you said you owed me, Philipson?" he asks.

"I do, but what are you doing?"

"Look after my Nana this night, while this all blows over. I'll drag her down to the cellar."

"Hang on," says Philipson. "I never agreed to take care of your Nana, I've got mouths to feed of my own, and think of how much beer she'll pinch." Richie does not stop, he pulls the old woman back, behind the bar where there is a trap door. He flings it open to reveal shallow wooden steps and pulls her down to the cool air inside. Richie has made up his mind on how to protect her.

"You can't just leave me here, Richie," she bleats as she bumps down the stairs.

"It's either that or get shot, lass. If they've a mind to, they'll do worse. They're looking for me."

"And where are you going?"

"Away."

"When will you be back."

"I don't know."

"You don't know. All the bloody men in my life are the same. They all bloody leave, one after another like rats running off a ship that's sinking." Richie does not have time for this. He moves his face so it is close to Nanas in the pitch black of the pub cellar.

"I love you, my Nana and I'll be back for you, just as soon as I can." She grabs his arm though she can't see his face.

"You're a good lad, Richie, just remember that, whatever you've got yourself mixed up with, you'll aways be a good lad." He kisses her on her forehead. He closes the heavy trapdoor above and slips past Philipson into the night outside.

CHAPTER TWENTY-TWO

They jog up behind North Burton in the darkness. The grass along the path is wet with dew and the Pearlman slips a few times as he follows Richie. He seems out of breath. Bess keeps a steady pace beside. The night sky is clear but there is no moon, they follow a way they both know, over the hill at the back of North Burton and through the fields that Richie has spent his life working in.

Richie's heart is beating heavy in his chest. In the darkness he gets flashes of the violence from the Pennyman Estate, how the first robber's head rocked as he clobbered it with the handle of his musket, how one of them looked up at him with his chest blown open. Richie feels ill. Behind him, in the darkness, the Pearlman slips in the wet dew again and gives a grunt as he goes down, Richie looks back to see the man on his knees, breathing hard, he goes in with sarcasm.

"Are you tired already, old fella?" he whispers. He sees the flash of the Pearlman's smile in the darkness as he tries to get to his feet. There's something wrong.

"The years are getting to me, lad. I need your help to stand." Richie furrows his brow and goes to the man, as he reaches round his side to pull him up, he can see that the Pearlman is sweating heavily and there's the iron smell of blood. Even in the dark, Richie can see his pants and shirt are wet. The man feels cold.

"You told me the shot clipped you only," says Richie.

"It seems I was wrong. I've shrugged off worse," he says. He knows he is lying. Richie tries to help him up but the Pearlman's legs do not have the power to get him more than a few steps. They struggle on three yards more to the top of the gentle hill.

"I'll get you to Meg," says Richie. "She'll fix you up just like she fixed me. I can carry you."

"That's the first place they will go, Richie. It means Meg

will be in trouble too." His voice is weary. "You'll have to set me down lad. I can't go on."

"We'll go further, to York if we have to or south to Kingston upon Hull, I have money to pay for the treatment you'll need."

"Listen to me, Richie. Set me down here, next to this fence. I need to rest a moment." With effort, Richie helps the man to sit down with his back on one of the posts and his legs out in front of him. Dawn is coming up on the horizon. Richie sits down next to him and Bess snuggles under the Pearlman's arm. It's calm.

"Would you get my pistol for me, Richie lad?" asks the Pearlman, the man's arms are not able to move although one of his guns is tucked into his belt.

"What for?"

"I need to hold it in my hands."

"Why?"

"It's the old way, Richie. Would you help me?" He feels under the Pearlman's coat to the blackwood pistol and draws it out, then fits the handle into the man's cold palm, there's a sigh of gratitude, and the Pearlman holds it flat to his leg with the barrel pointing down to his foot. Richie sits back.

"We have to get going soon," he whispers. "They'll be after us."

"Aye," says the Pearlman, "just let me catch my breath. You know they'll not come till after the sun rises. They'll be at the Pennyman House planning where to search, some of them will be looking for a scrap as well, like a fox hunt. Miss Charlotte Pennyman will be handing out drinks to the captain."

"We saved their lives."

"Doing the right thing isn't always the right thing to do."

"You need a drink," says Richie.

"No. Save it."

"Well, you're going to get off your arse. What do you

propose that we do, shoot it out with them here?" Richie's attempt to fall to sarcasm does not work. This is too serious. "Why do you need your gun?"

"That's how you die, Richie. That's the old ways. You die at war and not with a rope around your neck."

"You're not going to die." The Pearlman looks into Bess's face. She leans on him, just as she does with those she likes.

"She's a fine dog, Richie. You're lucky to have her."

"You can't die on me here. We're going to be hunted across the East Riding by God knows how many men."

"You are," says the Pearlman and there is a spark of humour in his voice. "Not me."

"I won't let you die here,"

"Listen to me, lad," and the Pearlman's voice suddenly has iron to it. "I'll not get up again, but you will. That's how it works, Richie. It's the circle, if you remember, I can't believe I've lasted this long without it being my turn to go back to where I came from."

"We were together, the three of us."

"Aye, and it was a good fight. As good as I've ever had and you, by God you're a force to be reckoned with, Richie lad. Good and tall and brave and with a big strong heart."

Tears begin in Richie's eyes.

"I've just found you again," he says.

"Now listen, Richie. I've had a long life and I should have been shot and killed many times before. When I was just a bit older than you, I was in war in Europe, you can't imagine what battles there were, the smoke and the noise and the blood. I've robbed a good few men and taken the lives of those who have stood to defend it too, I'm not proud of that. It wasn't until I came here that I found peace. It's been the best part of my life to see you grow up to be the lad you are."

"I murdered a man."

"You murdered a very bad man. You murdered a man than nobody would dare to touch and you, Richie Jackson of North

Burton, just a poor lad with a big smile. You've upset the balance here in this land. There'll be folk who hear the news of Stephen Middleton tomorrow and they'll cheer like it's Christmas. You'll be a hero, and I can promise you, that name you have, Turpin, it's already known. You present yourself in the right way, and anyone in the East Riding villages will help you, especially when you're willing to donate money that never was yours to start with." The Pearlman wears a grin with his head back on the fence post. "By God I wish I were coming with you, Richie lad. Maybe I will. I sometimes hear the lads I lost in years past, or I see them in the faces of strangers, they come to my dreams or I hear them shouting on the wind. Not forgotten and not gone."

"You'll come with me, Pearlman," whispers Richie.

"Aye, take one of my pistols as your own. Leave me the other."

Richie pauses, he listens to the summer night around them, far away there's the call of a dog fox over the fields, the light breeze rustles the uncut hay in front and behind, the smell from the woods at the bottom of the hill is sweet.

"Are you there?" he asks. He listens again, there's the first few tweets of waking birds and the slow in and out of Bess breathing on the Pearlman's chest.

He's gone.

Perhaps because nobody can see him, Richie weeps into his hands, like he has never done, his chest cannot keep up with the sobbing and so Bess gets up and comes to him in the light starting from the horizon.

Take one of the pistols the Pearlman had said. Richie reaches under the dead man's jacket and removes the second black gun that sits in a holster. He wipes away his tears and stands to his full height looking down on the Pearlman resting against the fence post with his eyes closed.

That was the man he once said he would kill.

Richie bends down and picks up a handful of brown earth

from the ground, he tosses the dirt over the man's body.

"Goodbye Father," he says.

He runs with the morning rising behind him and tears in his eyes again. There is someone he is to meet at dawn. She whispered in his ear.

Elizabeth.

It is perhaps two miles to Dalton Park. Richie cannot feel his legs as he runs. He cannot feel his heart beating in his chest or his stomach churning in his guts. It's as if he is not there at all.

Whatever happens today, Richie will not be going back to North Burton. There will be no ale or cards with Jonny Low, no poaching with Bess, no songs round the fire at Christmas, no Easter celebration behind the church, there will be none of this at all, ever again. He will have to go North.

What will become of the Pearlman's body when they find it? Who'll pay for the funeral? Of course, Meg and Nana will not be able to say they know who he is. Miss Charlotte will turn his Nana out onto the street for Philipson will not be able to keep her. Who will help Jonny Low in the fields? Who will sort the drunks from Walkington at the Bay Horse without Richie's big fists? The dawn is coming over the horizon as dim light bleeds into the sky behind, the noise of the birds is loud with the roar of the chorus around him, proclaiming the new day as they do always.

There are so many questions.

Will Elizabeth be there? He told her about the place, the big old oak in Dalton Park. He told her that was his secret hideaway, even though she thought he should have a cottage on the cliffs.

Richie climbs over the fence and crosses the dirt track that leads north to Dalton and slips into the forest. He knows this place. He's been there a thousand times before. Richie darts down a little path between the hedges and then quickly, he and Bess are moving through the trees, into the undergrowth. Where there seems nowhere to go, he dips his head under a fallen branch or forces through the bushes. It does not take him long to reach his destination, but he is not foolish enough to run out into the space under the great branches, instead Richie exercises the caution of a poacher who knows it's not wise to rush in. He's not always a hothead. There's an uprooted tree thirty or so yards away from the oak, the roots stick out into the forest and mushrooms grow along the inside of the moist rotten parts, milking bonnets and pig ears, things Richie would normally collect. Not so today. He clambers inside the roots and sits, hidden in the darkness of them. He draws the Pearlman's pistol and loads it from the black powder at his belt and a bullet from his satchel. His hands shake as he does. Bess joins him and she looks up with her big and sad eyes. He puts his fingers to his lips so she knows to be quiet, but there is no need, Bess will not make a fuss unless she has too. He pulls back the action on the pistol and holds it in both hands in front of his face. They will wait.

Bars of sunlight break through the horizon above the forest and, as Richie settles in stillness, so the birdsong gets louder as they chirp and call to each other. He will already be too late. How will she have got away from her father, or the soldiers? It will not take men on horseback long to find him. He prays that Nana will be safe and that Meg will be safe too and in the chirping of the forest Richie curses himself for the passion that made him kill a man. What kind of fool was he to think he could make a difference? He should have joined Stephen Middleton and let Elizabeth and her father die, he should have taken the bribes and free drinks and he could have lived a life of ease. The Pearlman would still be alive. His life would be easier. He curses himself too for doing what is right, even when it is the worst choice for him.

A twig breaks somewhere behind. It's out of place in the

forest at dawn.

There's someone here.

He hears her voice and his heart stops. It's faint at first and perhaps a few hundred yards away through the thick trees, but the noise of her calling gets closer. She is shouting his name in the summer morning. Richie puts one hand on Bess to steady her, for she knows this voice already, and will go to it if he allows her. He shakes his head. Not yet.

"Richie," she calls into the trees around her. She is not yelling, that would be too rude for a woman like her. Richie wishes he could stand up and look at her over the broken roots and growing mushrooms. He wishes he could see her face, even if he did not go to her, but he dare not give himself away.

"Richie," she calls now she is nearer the tree. "Is this the place?" Her voice sounds weak. "I'm here. I have a horse at the edge of the forest, we can go, you and I, together."

He should not have come. He feels his eyes hot with silent tears once more, and his hand begins to shake holding the gun, his teeth bar in his head - for Richie will not go to her. He has already lost so much and this path he is on now, this way, it's not a road she can join him on, whether he goes to the gallows or to freedom. She can have another life with a man who will love her and trust her. Not Richie Jackson of North Burton who is too poor to afford new shoes and cannot read and write. He closes his eyes tight shut and shakes as he fights his feelings, for even just to see her once more would be enough. Her sweet voice calls to him in the morning of the forest.

"Richie, they know who you are. The soldiers know that it's you who has the Turpin name. They know that you got it from your father, the man you rode with and the one who rescued you."

Richie's eyes open in the half darkness.

This is not the truth and Elizabeth knows it. She knows where the name is from, that the Turpin woman, his mother, bore him on the cowshed floor on the Pennyman Estate before she died. Richie blinks.

"Where's Bess your horse?" she calls out into the forest. "Richie, where's Black Bess?" At the call of her name, the dog pulls but Richie has hold of her to stop her from running. It's Elizabeth who made and spread the stories of Dick Turpin. It's she who knows this is not true and there's purpose to her lies.

She is saving him.

Just like he saved her.

There are others with Elizabeth. Soldiers. Another voice breaks into the clearing, sharp and loud. A man.

"You're wasting your breath, lass, he's not here."

"He'll have gone south," she calls. "He told me about his uncle in Kingston upon Hull, he will have gone there and will try to board a ship, probably." Elizabeth's words are loud enough to carry across the forest. Warning him where not to go.

Richie listens to the voices as they leave Dalton Park, not so quiet as when they came, now they don't think they have a highwayman to be silent to catch.

He holds onto Bess until he can hear them no more.

Elizabeth saved him, she saved him just like he saved her.

It's what people who love each other do.

It's late afternoon when Richie breaks from the cover of Dalton Park forest. He goes a way he has never been before, north and into the rolling hills of the Wolds towards Malton. He wears the black tricorn hat low over his eyes and carries his musket over one shoulder and the satchel over the other. There's a solid black pistol tucked into his belt and beside him, Bess keeps the pace. His eyes are keen and bright in the afternoon sunshine, ready and alert.

"It won't be so bad, Bess," he whispers.

And yet, every part of him breaks with every step.

It's late October. There's still some heat in the last of the evening sun but it's colder than it has been. Jonny Low is in the front meadow with Patrick, and he has baled nearly all the hay himself. A single rider approaches from the bottom of the hill with a cape billowing out behind in the orange sunlight. The horse is going at quite a rate. Jonny looks around as if there may be some other that this rider is heading for, but it is just he and the great shire horse. He swallows and suddenly, he thinks of Richie Jackson. He never had him pinned as a murderer or a highwayman. They didn't catch him even though they tried. Jonny heard he went south to Hull and caught a ship to Holland. Nana in the pub says he's dead for sure.

He can see the rider now, dressed in black and without a hat, small and with curly dark hair and the face covered in a black scarf. The horse comes to a standstill a few yards away and Jonny can see the expensive leather gloves, the smooth black tack on the animal and the shiny boots. Here is someone who has something. The figure pulls down the scarf from her face and Jonny can see that it is a lass. She does not get off the horse but looks down on the farm lad. He does know her, but she is Kat from the Golden Ball up at Scarborough.

"Can I help?" asks Jonny Low.

"Are you Mr Low of North Burton and is this Patrick?" The lass has a couple of rotten front teeth.

"Aye," he answers. She fishes in her jacket pocket and pulls out a single coin, a guinea. This, she tosses down and Jonny catches it in one hand.

"Regards from Mr Turpin and the Golden Ball," she says. She turns the horse and flicks the reins. Jonny watches her ride away down the meadow faster than she rode up.

Nana is not so much of a pain as Philipson would have thought. She's a good storyteller and has a quick wit that can stop drunks from causing a fuss. She drinks more than she earns, but she knows how to clean and, as long as she is allowed to moan, she will wash cups and plates. The old woman can walk much more than she says she can as well. She can knead bread, and she has taken a liking to Mary his sister. Nana is happy to boss the lass around and Mary is proud to be bossed by someone who seems like they care. It has even made Philipson's life a little bit easier although he would never admit this.

It's late October. Nana sits in the window of the pub before teatime and Philipson stands and reads his correspondence on the bar. There is nobody here on a Wednesday. A figure dressed in black walks into the front room of the Bay Horse pub. She wears expensive looking leather gloves and has shiny boots as she presents herself at the bar with a smile. A couple of her front teeth are black. She takes a shiny guinea coin out of her pocket and places this on the counter in front of her.

"Can I help?" asks Philipson. The woman nods down at the coin waiting on the wood.

"Courtesy of Mr Turpin," she says. On the way out she catches Nana's eye and smiles.

The old woman grins back.

It's Wednesday market in Beverley, late October and fairly busy but nearing the end of the day. Those that have sold most of what they came with are packing up their stalls. There are shouts from barrow lads hawking the last of their roasted chestnuts and the barking of a dog on a lead. Elizabeth is dressed in a brown shawl with a polite straw hat pinned to the back of her ginger hair.

She is thinner than she was. Lieutenant Pike says she needs sea air in her lungs. She stands at the bread stall and looks down the rows of loaves left, some of these will be from yesterday, and she has to pick the best one without fingering them too much. Hooked in her elbow is a wicker basket with vegetables she has bought and flowers from another stall. A figure knocks into her and she turns. It's a woman dressed in black with a wide smile that shows a few blackened teeth. This is not a chance encounter; the woman looks at her too intently.

"Elizabeth?" she asks.

"Who is asking?" The woman produces a coin in her black leather gloves and drops this into her basket. It lands heads up.

"A gift," she whispers, "regards, from Mr Turpin."

"Where is he?" asks Elizabeth as she glances down on the guinea coin in her basket. When she looks up, the woman with the black teeth is gone.

#

Printed in Great Britain
by Amazon

10454574R00149